The Painted Lady

Amanda Moncrefe

Linda,
Thank you so much for
Reading and Reviewing my book!
I hope you enjoy!
Mandy
xx

The Painted Lady

Copyright © 2015 Amanda Moncrefe

Published by Amanda Moncrefe

ISBN-13: 978-0692514245

Dedication

This book is dedicated to the Triple A's in my life.

Quote

You don't have to know how to sing; it's feeling as though you want to that makes the day happy and successful.
-Monica Crane

Table of Contents

Acknowledgements

There are so many people to thank, but first and foremost, I must thank my family for being the supportive structure in creating Jaymes and Asha's story. A huge "thank you" goes out to those amazing women of the Mocha Girls Read Book Club! To Terri, Holley, and Jackie--you guys are my ride or die! I love you! Thank you for being my rock when I was still floundering around like paper in the wind.

I will always strive to have my characters receive everything their hearts truly desired. After all, love is a powerful thing and can heal any wound this world can throw its way.

Peace and Blessings!

Mandy

Prologue

Spring 1990

"There's a letter on the kitchen counter for you." My mom called to me from her bedroom as I walked through the front door of our small two-bedroom apartment. My son Austin was on my right hip, and I held his diaper bag on my other side. Sighing wearily as I closed the door behind me; I'd just picked Austin up from his sitter after finishing the last final exam at my high school. Those tests were a bitch to get through and I was glad they were finally over. Being a teenage mom was no joke, but I still tried my best to keep my grades up while also taking care of my son. I knew that if Austin and I were to have any chance at a future, I couldn't end up as a high school dropout.

"What sort of letter?" I asked disinterestedly. I walked into the living room area, placed Austin in his playpen, and sat his bag on the floor. As soon as he was put down, Austin immediately began tugging at the stuffed lion I'd gotten him for Christmas a few months prior. He was letting his best friend know how his day went with a series of "ga, ga" noises. I walked into the kitchen and opened the refrigerator door looking for something to drink.

"I don't know. I've been waiting until you came home to see. Hurry up and open it so we can see what it says," Momma said as she walked in and took a seat at the kitchen table. There were vegetables and a cutting knife already laying there where she apparently was preparing for dinner. "It's from Natchez State."

That got my attention. "Natchez State?" I asked, closing the frig. "Why would they be sending me a letter?" I then saw the letter on the counter and picked it up. My fingers tore through the seal as I looked at her questionably.

"Maybe it's because a friend of mine works in the admissions office. Maybe it's because I let her know that you hadn't applied to go there. Maybe it's because when I found out you hadn't applied, I went ahead and sent your information to her. Maybe it's because this may be a chance of a lifetime," Momma said evasively.

"Momma," I said exasperatedly. "You know I want to go to the University of Illinois because it's closer to home. I still want to be able to take care of Austin. He's too young for me to be gone for long periods of time like that. I don't want him to not know who I am whenever I come home."

"That won't happen," Momma said confidently, brushing my concerns aside. "Open the letter."

Sighing, I pulled the letter out and began to read aloud.

Dear Ms. Asha St. Claire,

Congratulations! It is with great pleasure to inform you that you have been selected as a "Dean's List" scholar at Natchez State University for the upcoming 1990-1991 calendar year. This distinction comes as a result of your exceptional high school academic performance, college entrance test scores, and recommendations. This full academic scholarship will cover full room and board, tuition costs, and will grant a yearly book stipend of $500...

Momma cut my reading off as she screamed, clapping her hands loudly. "YES, YES, YES!" she cried over and over.

I heard a faint humming in my ears as I looked at Austin. I didn't want to leave him here in Chicago while I went to school all the way in Mississippi. I looked back at my mom, my eyes betraying both my shock and anxiety.

"Momma, MOMMA!" I yelled, trying to interrupt her happy dance in the middle of the kitchen floor. Austin had ditched his conversation with his friend and began to clap his hands excitedly along with her.

"I don't want to go to Natchez State." I tried to state calmly after finally getting her attention.

Momma stopped her dancing and turned to look at me. "You will go to that school."

"Mom, I want to stay here so I can raise my son."

"I will take care of Austin while you're gone. You will take that scholarship and that is the end of the conversation." Momma sat back down at the kitchen table, picked up the cutting knife, and began to chop vegetables as if I hadn't said a word.

"Momma, please," I pleaded, a familiar feeling of desperation starting to creep up. "Please let me go to the University of Illinois. I can get a job to help with the costs. It doesn't even have to be the U of I. I could go to an inner city college where it's even cheaper. Please, I don't want to leave him that long." Tears began to well in my eyes as a feeling of hopelessness washed through me. "He's my son and my responsibility. I want to take care of him. I want to try…."

"I said that's it!" Momma said, pointing her knife in my direction. "You. Are. Going!" Her voice held that tone that meant it didn't really matter what I thought. Or what I wanted. Or how I felt. Or anything at all. I closed my mouth and dropped my head in defeat.

The phone rang on the wall next to Momma. She put her knife down on the table and answered the call.

"Hey Caroline! Yes, she got her letter. Uh huh…we are absolutely THRILLED with the offer. Of course we're taking it! I know, I know…." Momma's words began to fade in the background as I felt my heart begin to bleed at the thought of going away.

I walked over to Austin and picked him up. I then walked down the hall to my bedroom and closed the door behind me. I laid Austin on the bed and walked over to the CD player on my dresser. I found the track I needed and pushed play; letting the melancholy sounds of Stevie Wonder's "I'd Never Dreamed You'd Leave in Summer," permeate through me. I then climbed in bed next to Austin, hugging him close to me as he patted my cheeks with the palms of his little hands. I finally let my tears fall as I began to sing.

Chapter One

Crabology
Freshman Year

Asha

"Figures this is what I get…" I muttered to myself as I clumsily hobbled into the half-filled auditorium, feeling a little nervous and a whole lot of pissed off. It was a hot, steamy Monday morning in August, and this place reeked of sweaty armpits and dirty gym socks.

It is too early in the morning for anybody to be this funky, I thought to myself.

My ankle was killing me. Coming into the doors of the new administration building earlier, while also struggling to carry two textbooks and a crutch, left me feeling like I was an act in a three-ring circus. I poorly juggled everything with one hand and prayed nothing hit the floor so I wouldn't embarrass myself as I hobbled my way to my classroom.

What have I gotten myself into? I asked myself for the hundredth time. I found an empty seat near the back of the room and quickly limped over to slide into it, placing my books on the desktop. I let my thoughts drift as I struggled to remember why I came here in the first place.

Winning a full scholarship to Natchez State University (NSU) my senior year of high school had, at the time, seemed like a blessing to my mother. However, it was slowly becoming a nightmare to me. The small country span of land the university sat on was strategically placed 40 miles north from any normal, 21st century civilization in a little town called Lorman, Mississippi. Lorman was also surrounded by thick dogwood and magnolia trees with several winding side roads; better known as the Natchez Trace. Many an unsuspecting vehicle had been known to be hit and ultimately destroyed by unseen deer, wild boar, or other large game wandering freely across its tree-shadowed path. The two-lane highway leading toward the University from the main expressway was also littered with small trailers and country shacks. This town didn't even have a McDonald's within walking distance.

How was I supposed to eat a decent meal?

Being from Chicago and not having had an opportunity to do the normal "college road trip" that other high school kids had, I had to rely on the mailed brochure the recruiter sent me over the summer to prepare for the upcoming school year. I knew I would have to take a 14-hour train ride from Chicago to Jackson, Mississippi. Once I got to Jackson, I'd then have to hitch a ride with my 74-year-old, nearly senile great uncle to drive the remaining 45 minutes to school because my mom's car was not the most reliable of vehicles.

I remembered finally being able to drum up some excitement when I first read about the University's rich history, as I thought about my own growth potential. Founded in 1782, NSU was known as one of Mississippi's oldest state-supported institutions for higher learning. My mother actually completed one year of college here before she ended up pregnant with me.

She'd always raved about NSU's academic successes and personal growth opportunities. The brochure also described lavish and spacious dorm rooms, beautiful classroom settings, a decadent cafeteria with the finest cuisine, and a student lounge that housed the latest video and sporting table games available.

No one bothered to tell me before I boarded the train that I would need linen for my bed, food in my room to kill my hunger pains during those times the cafeteria was "conveniently" closed at 3 o'clock in the afternoon, and a nice supply of personal products like tampons, deodorant and washing detergent because the local grocery store was over 10 miles away.

Did I forget to mention I didn't have a car?

When I arrived in Jackson last Friday, my uncle met me at the station and drove me to campus. After arriving at my dorm and taking a really good reality check of my surroundings —I hightailed it down seven flights of stairs (because of course, the elevator was jam packed with other educated freshmen bringing in their belongings like they knew to do) to try and catch my uncle before he drove off. I pleaded with him to take me to the store for supplies because I would not let him leave me high and dry like that. Unfortunately for me that high speed chase also ended with me stumbling over my own two feet by the time I reached the second floor; very conveniently twisting my left ankle. Now I was left hobbling around alone on campus with a swollen ankle and a foul mood. This was my first class on my first day of my new college life and it was just one more reason to regret coming here.

Someone tapping on a microphone on the front stage interrupted my thoughts as I looked toward the front of the room. A short older man appearing to be in his late 50s, with thinning hair and hard-rimmed black glasses that were too small for his chubby face, began to speak.

"Welcome to Freshman Orientation 101. My name is Dr. Kennedy. I will be your instructor during this course to assist you in overcoming the challenges many of you may face in transitioning to college life...."

I sighed as my thoughts started to drift again. I missed my Austin. I could still see his little smiling face grinning wildly and waving goodbye to me as I boarded Amtrak last week with my suitcase, $100 in my pocket, and a stomach full of knots. "Ba, ba! Ba, ba!" He'd said to me as I walked up the train steps, his way of saying goodbye to me.

He had no idea he wouldn't see me again for another four months. He would probably begin to learn a whole slew of new words and I wouldn't be there to witness any of it.

A sense of deep regret filled my thoughts. *God, did I make the right decision to leave my son and come all the way here for college?* My stomach churned a little when I thought about what Austin might be thinking about me. *Would he think I abandoned him? Would he wake in the middle of the night and cry for me, wondering why I wasn't there to comfort him? Would he think I didn't love him and didn't want to see him anymore when he woke from his naps and couldn't find me?* My eyes started to tear up as more painful thoughts plagued my mind.

"I know Crabology is a pain in the ass, but it shouldn't be all that bad."

My eyes immediately came in line with a pair of dark blue jean clad thighs that were wide and strong. The scent of Issey Miyake assaulted my nostrils and I immediately took a deep breath to take more of the scent in. My eyes slowly drifted up to take in a broad chest displaying a gold t-shirt with "NSU Ravens" across the front. He was also sporting the sexiest pair of muscle-toned biceps I had ever seen. Damn, was that a tattoo on his left arm? I felt my mouth begin to water.

My eyes continued to drift up to take in his cafe latte skin tone flavoring his strong neck. His shadow beard covered his jawline and also surrounded beautifully thick lips. I sighed wistfully. *What would it be like to run my tongue across those lips and feel that beard stubble tickle my thighs?*

Those lips tilted upward as he waited for me to finish my assessment of him. He had to be at least 6 feet, 7 or 8 inches tall, a giant of a man. God's Christmas package seemed to go on and on; and my eyes absolutely loved unwrapping His gift. My eyes continued to move over his face, finally taking notice of his eyes as I felt myself give an involuntary gasp. I'd never seen such a memorizing pair of blue-green eyes in my life. He also had the longest pair of lashes any top model in America would kill for. His short-cropped hair was covered with an Eagles' football cap that was turned backwards. This man was so beautiful he made all conscious thought instantly leave on a red eye straight to Vegas. The temperature in the room suddenly shot up a thousand degrees as I felt my panties grew painstakingly moist.

I shook my head slightly to clear my mind. *Not now...* I scolded myself. *That Adonis is not why you're here. Focus. Remember your plan—College, Degree, Job, Get your son back: nothing more, nothing less.*

"Mind if I sit here?" The Adonis smirked at me as he slid his body in the empty seat next to mine. "My name is Jaymes. What's yours?" his baritone of a voice whispered over to me.

"Asha," I replied meekly. I could feel my face heat up with embarrassment and turned my head to stare straight ahead. Did he catch my previous gawking episode? I did a quick side-glance at him and saw him give me a quick wink. Yep, he caught it. I felt my cheeks flame.

Suddenly I was irritated. Yea, he was good looking. OK fine, he was drop-dead gorgeous; but he didn't have to be so cocky about it. I'd been perfectly happy stewing in my own self-pity juices before he gallivanted himself in front of me, disturbing my train of thought. I'd been pissed, damn it, and I wanted to stay that way.

"What are you smiling at?" I frowned at him, taking in his humor at my expense.

"You. Before I sat down I could have sworn you'd just lost your best friend. Then you looked like you'd just rolled off the best piece of ass you've ever had. Finally, you looked like you were ready to commit murder—all in the span of 10 seconds. You could be your own one-woman show with all of the emotions playing out across your face." He leaned a little closer toward me. "I'd pay for that ticket," Jaymes replied slyly. He continued to grin at me.

I flushed. "Why were you watching me so hard?" I asked grumpily, feeling my defenses rise.

"I saw you struggle earlier to open the doors when you first walked in the building. I was going to offer my help, but the scowl on your face was screaming an emphatic 'no.' I then saw you were going in the same direction as me, so I followed you to make sure you didn't drop anything." He paused and looked at my crutches. "How did you hurt your ankle?" he asked sympathetically.

I sighed. "Being stupid—which is not unheard of for me," I responded.

Jaymes' smile dimmed and his eyes darkened just a bit, but he then quickly dismissed whatever thought he was entertaining.

"I'll ask again," he said. "How'd you hurt yourself?" His voice dropped a degree, sending a slight chill through my body, but not out of fear. I felt my shoulders drop some of its tenseness as my eyes drifted to the floor.

For some reason, I felt like I wanted to be completely truthful. I *needed* to be truthful. "Running after my uncle," I confessed. "I needed him to take me to Port Gibson to buy a few things and I ended up tripping down the stairs."

I paused. *Why was I telling him this?* I thought. I usually don't open up to people this quickly. I felt my face starting to close, but something he said earlier caught my attention.

"Why did you call this class 'Crabology'?" I asked curiously.

"Because that's what upper classmen call freshmen on this campus—crabs. Why they call them that I have no idea. I just figured it was better to embrace a depiction rather than let somebody else categorize you. One less way someone has control over you." He paused. "So where are you from?"

"Chicago," I answered. "I don't really know anyone here. My mom grew up in the south and went to this school for a little while. I found out about the school through her. Where are you from?"

"Philadelphia," he answered. "Don't worry. There are a lot of kids here from the Chicago area. Their parents did the same thing it sounds like your mom did—grew up here, moved north, and then sent their children back to the south to go to college. My roommate is from Chicago too," Jaymes said and chuckled lightly.

"Apparently kids that come from out-of-state get labeled with a nickname according to their hometown. Makes it easier for people to pick up where their accent is from. My roomie already labeled me with 'Delphi.'" He stared at me for a couple of beats. "I'll have to think of something cute for you to fit the cuteness you clearly already have."

Alrighty then…. "Why did you choose to come to NSU?" I asked, choosing to ignore his nickname comment. I couldn't decide if he was flirting or being nice—so I quickly opted for the nice route. That way hopefully my heart rate could try and slow down. Hopefully.

"Because I got a football scholarship here. My mother went to school here as well. When she graduated, she moved to Washington, D.C. where she eventually met my father. Later they moved to Philly

16

where they had me. Is that why you came here, because your mom sent you?"

"That and the fact that I won a scholarship here too," I answered.

"Oh really? What sport do you play?" he asked curiously. His eyes slid over me in a predatory manner, as if he could see straight through the tan and blue pinstriped sundress I wore.

I straightened my posture. "I don't play any sports. I like to run, but I'm not on the track team," I replied. I shifted in my seat. Damn, that beard and those eyes had me drooling.

"What was your scholarship in?" he asked.

"Academics, I won a full ride. That's the main reason why I came. I wanted to attend the University of Illinois, but they only gave me a partial scholarship and it wouldn't even cover half of the total costs." I didn't want to think about my lack of actual true choices right now.

"Well, I'm certainly glad you decided to come here." He smiled sincerely and I noticed the cutest dimple in his right cheek. *Get it together girl,* I told myself.

"I will now start roll call." Dr. Kennedy announced, disrupting our conversation. "If you don't hear your name called, it means you still have unfinished business with the financial aid office. If that's the case, I would suggest that you make your way there, handle your business expediently and return to class as soon as possible. This class will continue with or without you, and I can guarantee you cannot afford to miss even a moment's worth of instruction," he said with a patronizing air.

Dr. Kennedy then began reading off names from his printed class roster.

"Jaymes Allen," Dr. Kennedy called.

"Here," Jaymes answered.

Jaymes then looked over at me and gave me another wink. I shook my head and looked at the floor, trying to hide my smile. Damn that man was fine. I felt my breath becoming choppy and my palms starting to sweat. What was wrong with me? Jeez. You'd think I'd never seen a nice-looking guy before.

Dr. Kennedy continued with his roll call. "Asha St. Claire," he called. "I'm here," I replied.

Dr. Kennedy went through several more names before he folded his roster list. "That was it, people. Anyone whose name I did not call, please leave now and report to the Financial Aid office," he announced.

Several students got up and headed out of the door on a mission to prepare for battle. I'd heard financial aid workers couldn't care less about a student owing money; even balances as low as $100. They would not hesitate to kick a person out of school and contact security to toss their belongings out of their dorm room. From the school's point of view, there was always another student waiting in the wings to grab their dorm room that had their tuition costs already paid in full. Dorm space was prime real estate on this campus—especially if you came from out of state.

Dr. Kennedy then began to speak about the various clubs, organizations, and athletic programs around campus. He went in-depth about the school's study abroad program and the local internships that were available for those that were interested. He also spoke about the student local government and how it was structured.

"That's it for today everyone. I will see you on Wednesday," Dr. Kennedy said. The remaining students began shuffling for the door, but I remained sitting in my seat. I decided to wait until everyone left and then would try to make it to the student lounge to buy myself something to eat. The SUB, as I'd heard other kids call it, had better food to offer students than the cafeteria. Of course, you had to pay a nice premium for it, but it was worth it. I snuck another glimpse at Jaymes. *I also needed to take the extra time to get my hormones together,* I told myself sarcastically.

"Give me your books," Jaymes said. "I'll help you back to your room if that's where you're going."

"I was actually thinking about going to the SUB to get something to eat," I answered.

"Then I'll walk you there. I have to get ready to go to practice now and it's on the way. Coach has us on two a days and I'm finally just starting to get used to it," Jaymes said, shaking his head.

18

"Thanks," I said. "I appreciate the help." I handed him my books and slowly rose to my feet. My ankle was still throbbing, but without having to deal with the books, I could function and move around quite nicely with just my crutches.

"You sound like you don't like practice," I said reflectively, walking slowly alongside him. "I thought that was why you're here--the love of the game." We moved toward the door heading out towards the Yard, where the SUB was located.

"I never said I loved football; I said I got a scholarship to play. Football is just a means to an end, sweetie," Jaymes said. "What I actually want to do is go into Criminal Law. Eventually I want to go to law school and open my own practice."

"Really?" I asked, my curiosity peeked once more. "What made you choose that career?"

"I want to help people who can't help themselves. I like being needed..." he shrugged.

I frowned. "But how would you be able to tell the good people who really need help from those who are just trying to get over on somebody?" I asked. His comment surprised me. I thought for sure he would be one of those jocks who thought he was God's gift. Well, he WAS a gift to my immediate sight, but nevertheless...

"I'm a great judge of character," Jaymes said confidently.

I rolled my eyes at that comment. "Right. You mean to tell me that you can spot at first glance the difference between a person who is truly innocent from those that are seemingly innocent, but end up being so unmistakably guilty their own mother wouldn't defend them?"

"Yes," he said with a straight face.

I shook my head. "Ok, well good luck with that. In the meantime, I think I'll stick with my major. I like to help people, too. I think my decision would give me a broader opportunity and scope to do that."

"What are you majoring in?" Jaymes asked.

"Political Science," I replied. "It seems like a good area to go into."

Jaymes studied me for a minute. "I think you should rethink your major," he said.

I paused and turned to stare at him. "Why would you say that?" I asked defensively, staring up at him.

My major had been a choice I'd made toward the later part of the summer. I hadn't figured out quite yet what career I wanted long term. I just knew I needed to be grounded so Austin and I could have a chance at life. At first I didn't ever expect to go to college after I'd got pregnant with Austin when I was just 15 years old. Luckily my grades helped to open doors I'd otherwise thought were closed forever. Now that the opportunity was here, I felt a little better about my chances of having steady employment in the future. I chose Political Science as a major because a friend of mine in my senior class was going into that same field. I couldn't think of anything else at the time and had no idea what the next steps of my life's academic journey were. I was too busy trying to keep my grades up while taking care of Austin. But Jaymes didn't need to know all of that.

"Because you don't like to argue, you would prefer to let someone else make the decisions for you instead of you trying to defend yourself or your actions. You'd just rather serve instead of being the one constantly justifying why the service is necessary. Be careful with that, by the way. Having that type of personality is a magnet for all types of predators," Jaymes warned.

I continued to stare at him. What was he talking about? I've always made my own decisions, for the most part. Memories of previous conversations with my mother caused me to pause and a slight feeling of helplessness starting to spread. I shook it off and began walking again toward the SUB.

"You know me so well, don't you?" I huffed sarcastically. "I'll have you know I intend to one day go to law school, too. Just not in the criminal capacity. There are a lot of governmental agencies out there that could benefit from my services. "

Jaymes smiled and chuckled a little bit. "Okay, Asha. I would love to see that. Far be it for me to kill your dreams, especially for someone as obviously intelligent as you."

We reached the doors to the SUB and he opened the door for me to go in. I hopped my way over to an empty table a few feet from the door. Jaymes placed my books on the table and leaned toward me.

"What would you like?" he asked.

"I was going to get a slice of pizza and some fries. The cafe isn't open yet and I'm starving," I said. "Don't worry about it, I can get it. You've already helped me out by carrying my books for me. I can take it from here." I turned to make my way to the counter.

"Sit and rest yourself. I got it," Jaymes said in a no-nonsense tone, pointing to the chair. Obediently, I turned back around and obliged his directive. He walked toward the front counter to place my order, allowing me a great view of his ass. I sighed. *An ass that good has got to be criminal,* I thought to myself. He was definitely going into the right field.

Jaymes walked back to the table with my food and two bottles of water. He placed the food and a bottle of water on the table for me and opened one for himself. He drank it down quickly and glanced down at me.

"I gotta run. I know we'll be seeing each other around campus since the classes we need for our majors are in the same administration building." He paused and tilted his head as he looked at me. "I'm looking forward to it actually. See you around Asha." He grinned at me and walked out of the SUB.

As I watched him walk away, two things suddenly occurred to me. One, I was no longer upset at the thought of being abandoned here to die a slow and horrible death over a four year period. And two, my heart still hadn't slowed down; in fact, it sped up even faster at the thought of seeing him again.

I think I can do this college thing after all, I thought a little more confidently.

I sat at the table and quietly ate my lunch; content with watching the people that strolled into the lounge. A group of fraternity guys came in wearing blue and gold t-shirts with what looked like lions roaring on the front. They stopped in the middle of the lounge and began to perform what looked like a well-rehearsed step routine.

Southern colleges were infamous for having fraternities and sororities conduct spontaneous step show performances at any given time or place. This particular frat line moved gracefully, lifting their legs high and spinning around to a choreographed rhythm while chanting their patented phrases. They seemed to be able to jump what seemed a thousand feet in the air, all while singing, "We love, we love, we love, we love, we love our Nu Psi Phi!!!!"

"The Lions are strolling.," said the girl sitting at the table next to me. "I just love me some King Lions!" she said excitedly, drawing my attention away from the guys. She referred to the common nickname the fraternity men were associated with.

As I looked at her, I noticed something else, too. My table was sitting inconveniently in the direct path of where the strolling line of men would eventually end up. I felt my panic start to build because there was no way I'd be able to move my books, my food, and myself out of the way in time to avoid the sure collision I saw in my mind happening in less than 2.5 seconds.

"I'll help you with that." I heard a voice say behind me.

A pair of lean arms reached around me, grabbed my books and pushed my table back against the wall. I looked behind me as he pulled my chair with me still sitting out of the danger zone. Those arms were attached to a tall, lean body appearing to be about an even six feet. He had a clean-shaven face and a pretty mocha skin tone. He was handsome, but my heart didn't feel like it was speeding out of my chest like it did with Jaymes. There was a faint flutter--but nowhere near Jaymes' rampant stampede. I smiled shyly in his direction.

"Hello there," the guy offered. "My name is Ramon."

22

Chapter Two

American Government
Sophomore Year

Asha

"Come *ON* Asha, I'm trying to get to the Café before it closes!
Estoy muriendo de hambre and I can't be late first period again!" whined
Terri as she stormed out of our dorm room. Terri Cortes and I became
roommates my freshman year and we hit it off instantly, continuing that
bond into our now sophomore year. She was like the sister I never had.
Her bubbly personality was the boost of sunshine I needed to taper the
loneliness brought on by not knowing anyone on campus. She helped to
quickly transform what had started off as one of the worst experiences of
my life into the wild ride I was quickly labeling as my "awakening"
years.

Terri's hometown was Vicksburg, Mississippi, a town about 45
miles away from campus. Her long, dark brown hair hung down to her
waist and often tended to curl in the extreme Mississippi humidity. She
had a killer figure and could easily give Jennifer Lopez a run for her
money. When she got excited, she also tended to lapse into her native
Spanish tongue. On those occasions I would just stare at her until she
laughed uncontrollably and eventually flipped back to English, like she
hadn't just thrown me for a loop. She was also a member of one of the
largest sororities on campus. She was constantly surrounded by gorgeous
fraternity guys and was often, not unwillingly, dragging me with her to
campus events.

"I'm starving too! I'm coming, I'm coming!" I yelled after her.
Her constant Spanish cries of "I'm starving" was one phrase I had grown
accustomed to hearing. We both had 8 a.m. classes; but right now our

stomachs were taking precedent over the tardies that were sure to be marked for us.

I grabbed my purse and books, kissed the picture of Austin on my desk goodbye and headed out of the door. I caught up with Terri in the dorm's lobby after I got off the elevator and we headed out toward the YARD.

The YARD was a large area of parkland surrounded by the campus' dormitories and classroom buildings. It was also the place where any and all daily social events and drama occurred. You want to see a fraternity or sorority performing the latest step or stroll? Go to the YARD. You want to hear about the latest political news happening around the world? Go to the YARD. You want to hear the latest gossip and see who was out cheating while their significant other was in class? Go to the YARD. You want to see a fight between two females over some guy while that same guy was off to the side talking to a third chick? Well, you get my point.

Terri and I crossed the YARD and walked up to the Café. The Café's building had certainly seen better days, but the current state of its deterioration was not a concern at the moment. Our top priority was obtaining food.

We quickly sped through the glass doors of the one level brownstone and steered to the right. We then walked down the narrow hallway until we reached the food counters. Grabbing one of the green trays on the utensil bin along with forks and green plastic plates, we each proceeded to fill our plates with runny eggs, cold patty sausages, and stale toast. We slid into the nearest bench table we could find and began stuffing our mouths full of food.

Terri finished her meal before me, as usual. "See you girl! Gotta run!" she said and took off. Terri was a business marketing major and often complained about the long work assignments and projects her professors assigned to her. I couldn't relate because I'd found a great group of study-buddies over the course of my freshman year. On many occasions we would meet up at the campus library where we would tackle our major assignments together. Levi, Jackie, and of course, Delphi, were great partners to work and brainstorm with.

I glanced at my watch: 7:45 a.m. *I still have time to grab something else if I hurried,* I told myself. I was still kind of hungry.

"Don't even think about it," said a monotone voice behind me. "I saw you when you came in. That's all you need to eat for now."

I looked up. Ramon slid into the bench seat beside me. Ramon Towers and I started dating after that first meeting at the SUB last year. He was originally from New Orleans, and had the facial features and skin coloring passed down from his Creole ancestors. With his curly black hair, dark blue eyes that almost appeared black, and dimpled chin; he caused a lot of girls around campus to turn heads.

It seemed a lot of NSU's student body lineage was mixed with at least two or more heritages, including Delphi. Delphi's mom was African American, but he had a Caucasian father.

I sighed as an image of Delphi passed through my mind. While he and I were still close, Delphi still hadn't made any move toward trying to know one another outside of friendship. I didn't want to be that awkward, stalker girl begging for his attention like so many others on campus, so I kept up with pretenses and resided in the fact that at least we were friends. I still felt my heart pull every time he walked in a room, but I did my best to try and mask it.

I forced a smile at Ramon. Ramon had his good moments sometimes, too. Right now, though, I was trying really hard to remember them.

"I wasn't thinking about getting anything else," I lied. "I have to get ready to go to class. What's on your agenda today?"

"Me and some of the guys are working on this complex algorithm for Dr. Switcz," Ramon said. "If we solve it, we'll get 30 points extra credit on our final. I want to be the one to solve it…you know how competitive I am." He looked down at my plate and frowned. "I meant what I said, Asha. Don't get any more food. Your weight is just where I want it. I don't want your hips any wider."

I felt my face flush and my jaw tick as I glanced at the floor. I'd always been self-conscious about my looks; and hearing Ramon's criticisms always stirred my deepest insecurities. While I was definitely not what one would consider a large woman, I filled out my size nine jeans with little room to spare. My hips flared around my slim waist, but my thighs were nowhere near as toned as some of the other girls I'd seen walking around campus. My breasts were always hidden underneath a t-shirt or jersey. The common practice of wearing my shoulder length light brown hair in a ponytail underneath a Bulls' basketball cap was no exception today. My hazel eyes were my best feature, but were often hidden behind sunglasses so as to not draw too much attention to them. I hated people staring at me, regardless of the reason.

"Yes, I know," I said. "Good luck." I smiled forcefully again and gave him a quick kiss on the check as I rose to leave. "See you later on?" I asked.

"Sure," he responded. He walked me to the front of the Café. "I'm headed off to class." He moved forward to kiss me on my cheek when he suddenly froze. "Shit," he said. "On second thought, I've got time to walk you to your class if you'd like."

I glanced over my shoulder to see what had caused him to pause. Delphi was walking over toward us wearing a huge grin and the sexiest pair of basketball shorts I'd ever seen. They molded his obscenely large frame to perfection, outlining his sculpted calves and lean hips, while giving emphasis to what looked like a magnificent piece of manly machinery nestling between his thighs. And, of course, that beard…geez. The reoccurring vision of me running my tongue across his jaw to see how he tasted assaulted my line of thought. I felt my breath hitch and my heart pulled, again. However, with experienced practice of having done it again and again over the past year, I masked my excitement and sent a friendly smile his way.

"Hey Delphi! What's going on? On your way to class?" I asked.

"Yep. Hey beautiful," Delphi responded. He walked straight up to me, bent down and swooped me in his arms for an embrace, leaving

26

my feet dangling in the air. He always seemed to morph my mere 5-foot, 5-inch frame with his Andre the Giant height.

"It's great to see you." He smiled again, putting me back on the ground. I laughed at his antics. He's never once greeted me with a simple hello. After our initial meeting last year, he now always approached me with an enormous, over-the-top hug. He'd explained it was his way of killing off any negative vibes I might be having for the day--because a hug from Delphi naturally made everything better.

Ramon initially hated when Delphi hugged me. Not because he was jealous, he'd always clarify. It was because in his opinion, a person didn't need to be hugged on every possible occasion like that. It wasn't natural, he would argue. Then suddenly one day out of the blue, Ramon's whole attitude changed, like he didn't mind at all. Jackie hinted during a study session one day that she'd heard about an escalated confrontation involving Delphi, several players of the NSU football team, and Ramon behind a dorm building one afternoon. However, since neither one of them mentioned anything to me about it, I didn't push the issue. I did notice, however, that Delphi never hugged any of his other friends or dates, but I kept that observation to myself.

I heard a throat clear interrupting my thoughts and turned around to look at Ramon. My eyes scanned his face as he had his typical blank mask of indifference sketched across it, but I could tell Delphi's presence was agitating him.

"I'm good Ramon; you don't have to walk me to class. It's out of the way for you anyway. I'll just walk with Delphi. We're in the same class so it just makes sense," I responded. I turned and gave Ramon a quick peck. "I'll talk to you later."

Ramon nodded briskly at me, casting one final glare at Delphi before sauntering off. I looked back at Delphi as he watched Ramon walk away as well, but with a scowl etched across his beautiful features. When he looked back down at me, all traces of his former irritation disappeared and were replaced with a grin. I sighed. I stopped hoping long ago that they would get along, especially with what Jackie told me. Now I just tried my best to avoid any long interactions between the two.

"Let's go, little one," Delphi said. "We're going to be late." He grabbed my hand and pulled me toward our American government class in the new administration building.

We arrived to class just as Dr. Wilson was closing the door.

"Just in time again I see Ms. St. Claire, Mr. Allen," Dr. Wilson chided. Jaymes smirked while I lowered my head in embarrassment. Delphi still held my hand and pulled me down the row toward our seats. We'd been assigned seating arrangements earlier in the semester, like we were still in high school. Somehow I had gotten conveniently seated directly in front of Delphi.

Delphi released his grip on my hand and sat down behind me. I took my seat in front of him, trying to spell the feeling of loss taking his hand away had suddenly caused.

"Today we will be discussing the various practices of gerrymandering and how those efforts had lasting effects on election results over the past few decades..." Dr. Wilson began.

I sat back in my seat and started taking notes. About halfway through the period I felt something brush against my backside. I turned around to look at Delphi, and he looked innocently at me with a questioning expression. I looked over to my left and saw Levi sitting across from me, looking at me and rolling his eyes.

Levi Blackburn was my ride or die partner in crime. He soon became one of my closest friends since I arrived here last year. I could always find a frank and sincere answer with him whenever I needed a realistic viewpoint. Levi was originally from Pearl River, Mississippi, which was primarily a Choctaw Indian community. He was actually here on a band scholarship, although he could have easily won an academic award like me based on his ACT scores alone. He was part of the infamous "Sounds of Fire" NSU Marching band; and he often traveled with Delphi and the football team when they had away games. He was also an academic genius in the literal sense, but always tried to downplay his intellectual gifts by joking around and being silly. I learned a lot of self-disciplined study techniques from him over the past several months.

I looked toward the front of the classroom as Dr. Wilson continued with his lecture. Again, I felt something brush my ass and this time I held perfectly still to try and figure out what it was. There. It brushed me again. *What the hell was that...his knee?* I sat completely still so I could be certain. There was another brush. Yes, that was definitely his knee. I assumed his large body was too big to sit comfortably in those small desks and decided to help him out. Maybe he needed more legroom?

I scooted my seat up an inch or two to offer more space. I then heard the desk behind me move up as well. *Interesting...* I sat back again in my chair as I tried to continue listening to Dr. Wilson's lecture.

Once again his knee brushed more firmly against my ass. A spark of lighting flew up my spine and headed back down right to my crotch. My butt was such an erogenous zone for me. No one knew that, not even Ramon. I snorted softly. Ramon didn't try to please me sexually. He never really seemed interested if I got off. Sex had always been about his pleasure. He'd always expected I would make sure all his needs were met, emotionally and physically.

I sighed. Terri had never understood that concept when I finally broke down and shared with her one night after an unfulfilled romp in the hay with him. She was always confiding in me about the pleasures I was missing out by not seeking a fulfillment of my own. I'd always just been content with serving him, that is, up until this very moment. Suddenly I wanted. I desired. I craved. I craved...more.

Another brush against my ass--this time it was a lot more forceful. My breathing increased and I felt my breasts grow heavier. I hung my head low as if I were jotting down notes, all the while trying to reconcile these sudden feelings of lust that were overpowering me. I closed my eyes and counted to 10 to calm myself down.

Not happening. Delphi brushed his knee against my ass again, and this time I felt a soft whisper of something skim across the back of my neck. I kept my eyes closed so I wouldn't be able to see if anyone noticed how aroused I was becoming. I didn't want to try and explain why my nipples were hardening at the sound of Dr. Wilson's lecture concerning de facto segregation and its relationship to *Brown V. Board of Education.*

Something touched my neck again. I opened my eyes and snuck a peak at Levi. He looked at me, then nodded his head toward Delphi and continued taking notes. Suddenly I felt Delphi's body heat against my back as he leaned forward to whisper in my ear, "I love how you respond to me, little one."

I looked over my shoulder and caught Delphi's blue-green stare as he studied my face. I realized in that moment that he knew exactly what he was doing and what he was causing to stir in me. Biting my bottom lip, I faced forward again. I shifted in my seat, feeling the lining of the crotch of my jeans press against my pussy in an intoxicating manner. I placed my arms across my desk and leaned forward, in either an attempt to get away or to present a better position of my ass. I wasn't sure which at the moment.

Delphi leaned forward again and this time passed me a piece of paper he'd scribbled on. I carefully opened the note so as to not draw attention to myself. Looking down, I read the message and stifled a small moan.

"I smell your arousal, sweetie," the note read.

I quickly closed the note and folded my fingers together to both stop my hands from shaking and to prevent me from running them across my sensitized nipples. I glanced at the clock on the wall. Ten minutes left of class; ten minutes left to endure this petty torture. I turned my head to look at Levi again. He was watching me, too. He gave me a small smile, looked back at Delphi, nodded his head to him and gave him the thumbs up sign. Suddenly the heat I was feeling went artic cold. Did he and Delphi previously plot to drive me crazy during class today? I glared at Levi and his smile just got wider.

Feeling manipulated, I turned my attention back to Dr. Wilson. "I expect your research papers to be turned in no later than 12 noon next Friday. Those papers will be worth 50 percent of your final grade." He then continued to explain the steps that would be taken to finalize midterm examinations this semester.

"That's it for today ladies and gentlemen. Have a good day," Dr. Wilson said, dismissing the class. I stood up and rushed out of the classroom before Delphi or Levi could stop me. It was past time we all had a heart-to-heart discussion on manipulation; and I decided we needed to have that discussion right now..

I walked out of the NAB and waited on the front steps near the entrance, tapping my foot impatiently. As an afterthought, I folded my arms across my chest so my hardened nipples wouldn't be so obvious to my other classmates.

Delphi and Levi walked out smiling and laughing between themselves, causing my irritation to spike even further.

"I did NOT appreciate being made fun of in there, Levi!" I spat venomously as they finally approached me. It was easier to direct my anger towards Levi rather than to Delphi with his smirking face. I couldn't handle it if I saw in his eyes any hint that he was not as bothered as I was regarding the whole incident.

Levi looked at me with a surprised expression. "What are you talking about Asha?" he said with what looked like a sincere expression on his face. I wasn't buying it. "No one was making fun of you."

"Yes you were! I saw that look you gave me in class and then you gave Delphi a 'thumbs up' signal! I know you were talking about me! I don't like being made fun of!" I replied angrily.

Levi shook his head, his face becoming serious as he realized he'd upset me for real. "Asha, it's not what you think at all," he said. "We were just…"

"Hey guys!" Terri said walking up to us.

Levi continued as if she hadn't said a word. "Let's just say it was sort of a test that both of you passed." He then turned to Terri. "Terri," he acknowledged wryly.

"Levi," she answered just as nonchalantly.

I shook my head as his explanation fell on my deaf ears. "Whatever Levi. Terri, let's head back to the room." I turned to Delphi and just as I'd braved up enough to give him a few choice words as well, he leaned over, put his lips close enough to my neck so I could feel his warm breath against my flesh, and whispered. "I'll see you around Asha." With that he winked, turned and started walking towards the men's dormitories. I stared at his frame, trying to stop the hurricane of lust floundering inside of me. Licking my lips, I turned to Terri as she caught me watching him walk away. I felt my cheeks grow hot with embarrassment.

"Alrighty then girl." She smiled. "Let's go." She looked at Levi once more. "See you later, Levi," she said saucily with what sounded like extra emphasis on rolling the "L" in his name with her tongue.

Levi stared at her mouth, nodded his head and quickly turned to walk in the same direction as Delphi, his posture stiff and rigid. My eyebrows furrowed at his departure. What was up with that?

As Terri and I walked past the Café on our way back to our dorm room, I spotted Ramon leaning against the building's railing with a dark look on his face. When we approached him, he grabbed my arm and pulled me close enough so that only I could hear the next words that came out of his mouth.

"Let this be the last time we ever discuss this, Asha," he said between clenched teeth. "You belong to me, and only me. It would be safest for you and anyone else to always, always remember that."

I looked into his eyes and saw the seriousness there. A feeling of trepidation started at the base of my spine; but I quickly stopped its ascension. *Ramon would never physically hurt me,* I told myself. I tried to make light of the situation. "You know you're the only one for me." I smiled a little too brightly.

"Make sure you remember that," he said as his jaw tightened.

Terri stood a little distance away. I realized she was far enough to give the façade of privacy, but still close enough to listen in. She silently looked at me and slowly raised one perfectly arched eyebrow, tilting her head slightly.

I sighed, feeling embarrassed someone had witnessed the tenor of everyday conversation that occurred between Ramon and me.

"Let's go Terri," I said, completely pulling away from him. Now she would be one more person added to the list of people I felt I had to justify my relationship to. I straightened my back a little more as I walked beside her. I would show them, I thought as Terri and I continued across the YARD back to our room. I can handle this relationship. Damn it.

Chapter Three

Club Finesse

Delphi

"Your dad owns this spot?" I asked Levi as we pulled up outside a plain barn-like structure located off highway 20 outside of Jackson. A sign with the letters "FINESSE" lined the marquee across the building's archway.

"Yea, he told me to bring you to the club instead of the house when your 'hidden potential' finally starts to show," Levi said, using his fingers to imitate quotation marks. He reached over and opened the passenger door to my white two-door Monte Carlo. "And you definitely showed signs of true Master potential last week, my friend."

The episode with Asha during our American Government class had been an experiment of sorts for both Asha and me, as Levi called it. Levi wanted to see if I had the discipline it would take to fully commit as an apprentice under his father, Master B.

"Becoming a Master is not something you just sign up for," Master Blackburn had once explained to me after I went home with Levi one weekend. "You're either a natural born Dominant, or you aren't. There isn't any leeway between the two. You just don't wake up one morning and say, 'Hey, I think I'd like to become a Master.' Only fools believe they can turn it off and on like a light switch. In order to discover one's dormant Dominant strand, one also has to find their one true submissive. That sub will trigger that hidden instinctive and blatant need to protect, own, and cherish above all others."

I thought about those words a lot after that weekend last year. Whenever I reflected, my mind always circled back to Asha. God, I craved that girl with everything I had. And not just crave her; I NEEDED to devour her, dominate her, and see her willingly give me all her submission and trust. I wanted to wrap her up with a blanket of love and protection and never let go.

The need rose so heavy whenever I was around her that sometimes the sheer intenseness of it actually scared me. I licked my bottom lip as I exited my car. Just thinking about Asha on her knees, looking up at me with those Egyptian-like hazel eyes, full succulent lips, and flawless Milky Way skin tone immediately got my cock at attention.

Damn, I've wanted her from the first moment I saw her in Crabology.

Levi hinted to me before Dr. Wilson's class last week to try and get Asha riled up, just to see how she'd initially respond. He didn't mention exactly how to do it so I'd let my imagination fly. I knew he and Asha were close, so I'd assumed they had already discussed something I wasn't aware of.

I had no idea Levi was trying to see if Asha fit the bill for being a true submissive until he told me last night. Apparently, by his description, she definitely was. He said he already knew what I would do, but he needed to see if his suspicions were right about her.

I was just glad she went off on him instead of me.

He also pointed out I needed to ramp up my own control in order to give her exactly what she needed. Once I had ultimately gained her full and unconditional trust, she'd open up to me like a flower, nothing withheld. However she would never give me one hundred percent of herself if I didn't first demonstrate that I could be a safe place, a place where she could place her heart, soul, mind, and body. I couldn't rush her; otherwise she'd clam up even further into her shell. She was already so introverted and I didn't want to scare her off with how intense I wanted to get, so I had to take it slow.

I followed Levi up the stairs to the club's double door entryway with thoughts of Asha still on my mind.

She also has the heart of a true fighter, I thought to myself. That's what first attracted me--watching her fight against her small hurdles that first day. Anyone who really cared about her could see right through the masks and sarcasms she always tried to hide behind. Her true feelings were always written plainly in her facial expressions. No matter what jazziness spewed from her lips, her eyes never lied.

The possibility of one day finally being allowed to tame that fight is what calmed the beast inside me. It was that same beast that constantly roared and clawed my insides because she still dated Ramon. Everyone could plainly see she wasn't as into him as she wanted everyone to believe.

I felt myself grimace as thoughts about her significant other flashed through my mind. Ramon was an idiot to the ninth degree. I'd heard he constantly downgraded and belittled her at every given opportunity. Too bad he's never made the mistake of letting me hear him; I'd have to wax that ass for the slightest hint of transgression.

I've also witnessed for myself the amount of flirting and over the top touching he's done with other girls around the YARD whenever Asha wasn't around. Because of that, I had no qualms whatsoever about hugging her every time I saw her. He'd once tried to say something about it, but after me and a couple of teammates met with him and explicitly went into great detail about what might happen to him if he tried to keep me from her one night, I no longer had any issues with demonstrating my affection for her. She needs to know somebody cares about her.

The killer part was that I'd vowed to never disrespect her choice to date him. It was ultimately her decision; and calling her out on it would only make her defend the jackass even more. Besides, his time was almost up. Once I got a few pointers from Levi's dad, I'll help her see what a joke of a man he really was. After that, she and Austin could finally be mine.

My heart warmed at the thought of her little boy. Every time she let me speak with him some sort of paternal instinct took over me. In my mind I was already his father. And his mother was already mine. Those eyes would be mine. That smile would be mine. Those lips would be mine. Those lips….

I adjusted myself as I followed Levi through the door, my dick pulsing with every step. That girl's lips were made to suck me. *Me,* I thought. *Not that jackass.* I can just imagine what her tongue would feel like caressing my head, slowly licking my shaft...

"Hey Pop," Levi called toward the back office, disrupting my wayward thoughts. "We're here."

My eyes scanned the open recreational area of Finesse. Finesse was a BDSM (bondage/discipline/dominance/submission) club-mainly catering toward the Dominance/submission (D/s) aspect of the lifestyle. It was owned and operated by Master Bryce Blackburn, who took the seclusion and privacy of its members very seriously. The outside of the building resembled something like a warehouse. That's what he wanted people to think when they saw it, anyway. Inside however was a completely different story.

Upholstered love seats covered in what appeared to be a mixture of velvet and satin lined both sides of the lobby as you walked inside the entryway. The floor leading from the main lobby to the spacious recreation room was covered in rich, cocoa-colored hardwood. Three crystal chandeliers hung from the 20-foot ceiling. Winding stairs leading to the second floor toward the private rooms and dungeon area were to the right. A fully stocked bar lined the back of the room, and several small dinette sets were scattered throughout the now empty floor. The place was only empty because we drove here right after lunch—it was too early for the evening crowd.

Master B's office sat behind the bar, where he emerged as he heard his son call his name.

"Levi, Delphi, come on back and close the door behind you." Master B called. We obeyed and followed him into his office.

Master Bryce Blackburn seemed like an intimidating man to most people; but I considered him a great confidant and mentor. Standing a little over 6 feet, 3 inches in height, he presented an intimidating image of 100 percent full-blooded Choctaw Indian. He wore his long silky black hair pulled in a ponytail at the base of his neck, and his eyes seemed to pierce right through you with his intense black-eyed stare. He was an attractive man with sharp cheekbones and an even sharper IQ, just like his son.

I could also tell he was lonely since his wife died a few years ago from cancer. Master B would get this far away look on his face he often tried to hide when he thought Levi wasn't looking. I'd noticed, however.

He gestured toward the chairs in front of his desk while he walked around and sat down in his chair behind it. Levi and I acknowledged his silent command and took a seat.

"Delphi, I'm glad to see that Levi was able to get you on the right path. It's nice that *someone* is willing to listen to the advice of an older man with experience." He gave me a small wink. "Levi here could learn a thing or two from you about dominance. He only listens to the D/s sex part, never about the true bond between a Master and his sub."

"I don't need to learn about a bond right now, dad. Delphi is the one always looking for advice 'cause he's crazy about one girl." He ran his hand down his chest trying to show off his frame. "NSU has too many females for me to let all of this glory go to waste," Levi said cockily.

"What about Terri?" Master B asked skeptically, leaning back in his chair.

Levi stiffened in his. "What about her?"

Master B stared at his son for a moment, and then shook his head. "Never mind, you're not ready." He turned his attention to me, clearly dismissing his son's remarks. "In any case Delphi, I heard how Asha reacted during your class last week. Tell me, did she show signs of gratitude with the fondling, like she wanted more?"

I looked at Levi and smirked. "No, she got pissed off at Levi and accused him of setting her up."

"Mmm," Master B said thoughtfully. "It's interesting that she focused on Levi." He touched his fingertips together in front of his face. "It sounded like submission is not necessarily a turn off, but rather like she doesn't trust you yet with submitting over her power. It scared her. Until she comes to realize the true power she actually has, you will have to demonstrate patience with her. In the meantime, you need to also strengthen your own control so that when she is ready, you will be too. You must be the rock she can hold on to." He stood up and walked around to sit on top of his desk directly in front of us. He crossed his arms over his chest.

"In order to get stronger, you should practice so you can perfect your skills, Delphi," he said, staring watchfully in my eyes.

"What do you mean?" I asked. A feeling of trepidation peeked through. I had a feeling I already knew where he was going. I just wasn't so sure I wanted to follow.

"I mean you should take a submissive to train until Asha becomes ready."

I sat back in my seat, blowing out the breath I didn't realize I was holding.

"With all due respect," I said hesitantly. "I really would prefer to focus all of my attention on Asha."

"I understand your reluctance," offered Master B. "However, the type of hold that will keep Asha to you requires a level of control that you don't have yet. Do you wish to win her, only to eventually lose her because you are unable to give her what she truly needs?"

"Of course not." I said dejectedly.

"I didn't think so." Master B uncrossed his arms and laid his palms on his thighs. Your foundation must be whole before you start breaking off pieces to give to someone else. Otherwise, there will be nothing left to support you." Levi looked over at me and gave a confirming nod to his head.

"I don't want to lead anyone on, especially when I know it's not going to work out in the long run," I still countered. "It'll be hard to find a girl that's willing to just be a plaything until the real deal is available."

Levi gave me a crooked smile and leaned over to slap me on the shoulder. "Don't worry about it, my friend. You'd be surprised at how much available ass there is on campus. Trust and believe. Besides, you don't have to look at all. I know for a fact Tanya wants to get with you. She'd be perfect."

Tanya Lewis. Major Bitch #1. God, just the thought of her made my skin crawl.

"Tanya is too high-maintenance. She doesn't have a submissive bone in her scrawny conceited body. I don't even know if I could get it up around her. She's just not my type, man."

"I'm not saying you have to have sex with her, just go all Dom on her. She'd love it. You'll be giving her the attention she evidently needs and can practice your control all at the same time." Levi snapped his fingers. "Plus, Asha would see the control you're giving to Tanya and may decide she wants a little bit of that for herself. Maybe she'll finally give up that joke of a man she's got."

Master B looked at his son and shook his head as he rolled his eyes.

"I want Asha to choose me because she wants ONLY me, not because the grass is greener," I scoffed.

"And she will. But how will she even know there's grass on the other side of the fence when she's been eating sand for so long? You and I both know she needs to graze in much richer pastures, my friend. She's hungry and tired of having a lead stomach," Levi retorted with a straight face.

Master B and I stared at Levi for minute before we both burst out laughing. "You know, your sense of reasoning is truly fascinating, my friend. Really dude? That's the best you can do?" I manage to get out between chuckles.

Levi gave both of us his patented smirk. "Just wait and see. I'm telling you it's perfect."

40

Chapter Four

Riding the Trace
Junior Year

Asha

"So tell me about Austin's father," Delphi casually asked as he leaned back in his chair.

We'd just finished an intense study session that evening in the campus' student library. We both had midterms coming next week, and we knew that Dr. Kennedy was no joke when it came to administering his finals. Our classes were now focused on our chosen field of study; so every test passed was a victory. Our study group consisted of Delphi, Nate--Delphi's roommate, Jackie, Levi, and myself. Midterms also just happened to coincide with homecoming week, so we were all feeling the pressure of crunch time.

The others had just left and it was now just Delphi and I lounging back. I was waiting around until Terri finished her work-study shift at the library so we could walk back to our dorm room together. I'd guess Delphi just wanted to keep me company.

I shook my head as I tried to organize my thoughts. We were now in our third year and I was still amazed at how well I was still handling the experience. The ending of my sophomore year was still a huge blur. Terri finally convinced me to pledge her sorority, and the entire event was an eye-opening experience. I decided to pledge because I believed joining my sorority would open doors for me both economically and socially. I'd gained a legion of sisters all across the world. Growing up as an only child, I was proud to be a part of the organization. I'd also secretly hoped it would bring me out of my shell a little more; but those thoughts I kept to myself. So far I was batting 50-50 with that one.

Ramon wasn't too thrilled about the new wave of jocks and fraternity guys that now seemed to flock even harder around Terri and me. To counteract his jealously, I tried my best to be the doting girlfriend I knew he expected me to be. I did this all with the exception of Delphi. I just didn't have the heart to push him away. In all honesty I didn't want to. It seemed the attraction I felt for him grew more intense with each passing week.

Delphi ended up pledging as well. He decided to join his fraternity around the same time I joined my sorority. Neither of us saw much of each other during those last few weeks last semester. We were both happy to finally finish so we could devote our attention on serving the local communities and towns around campus.

With all the things I was involved in that kept me busy, it still didn't deter from the void I sometimes felt when I thought about my handsome little boy. The nightly phone calls to Austin helped however; and he kept me focused on the real reason I was here.

I felt a finger graze my cheek.

"Hello?" Delphi laughed. "Get out of your head, Asha. Pull the thoughts from your head and form the words on your lips. Speak it out loud so I can hear them; that way I can be there with you, too. It's OK to let your defenses down around me. I'll keep your thoughts safe and would never use them to hurt you, so feel free to share. I'll treasure anything you want to release to me."

My heart filled with affection as I smiled at him. This was why I couldn't distance myself from Delphi. I was drawn to him more than anyone I had been before. He was my safe place, my refuge. He was so unlike Merritt in every way. I took a deep breath and tried to start from the beginning to answer his request.

"Merritt and I started dating my freshman year in high school," I began. "I met him during my third period study hall. He was the All-American, typical basketball jock. I thought he was wonderful at the time. I was so excited that someone like him could have been interested in me." My head dropped a little and my gaze slid to the floor with my next thoughts. "His parents didn't approve of me, though. They didn't like the fact that he was dating a black girl."

Delphi slid his finger down my cheek again. "I'm sorry you had to experience that," Delphi said regretfully. "My parents went through something similar, but my dad said he told my grandfather he could either get on board or get out of his life because mom was here to stay." He chuckled reflectively. "Granddad knew my father didn't play, so he eventually came around-but all of that occurred long before I was born."

"Well, Merritt's mother still to this day has never accepted Austin. She once chanted right in front of me: *Mother's baby, father's maybe* over and over again like it was some sort of sick nursery rhyme."

Delphi bristled. "And what did Merritt do?" he said between clenched teeth.

"Nothing. Merritt never said anything. He never once tried to defend Austin or me. I eventually just got used to the insults. It wasn't worth getting myself worked up from someone with that kind of hatred. Besides, Austin was too young at the time to really understand what was going on."

"I wouldn't discount a child's comprehension on any event that he sees taking place right in front of him…especially a child from your genes," he said.

Puzzled, I glanced over at him. "What do you mean?" I asked.

"I mean your son has to have inherited that beautifully strong spirit from someone. It sounds like it's all coming from you. Not to mention those beautiful eyes of yours-I saw the pictures you keep of him, remember?" Delphi gave me his patented sexy-as-sin-so-come-rub-your-cheek-against-my-beard-and-feel-the-softness-grin. I felt my heart rate quicken.

Man, this guy really did it for me. What would it be like to be the focal point of all that sexiness? I licked my lips and noticed Delphi's eyes following the movement of my tongue. My daydreams and nightly fantasies often centered on those eyes and how they might look heated in a moment of passion. I shook my head again. *Get out of your head, Asha,* I reminded myself once again.

"What about you?" I asked, trying to steer the conversation away from me. "What about your twins' mom?" Delphi previously confided to me that he had a set of twin boys during his senior year of high school. His parents were justifiably disappointed, but still wanted him to pursue his dream of law. Instead of denying him the opportunity to go to college, they decided to pitch in and support both the twins and their mother back home while Delphi was in school. His father founded one of the most prestigious law firms in Philadelphia, so luckily they were able to afford to do so.

Delphi venomously denied that the relationship with his sons' mom continued after the conception of his children. His usually bright and cheerful demeanor always seemed a bit forced whenever we discussed his kids. To put it simply, he exhibited mental and emotional blockades, like he was bothered by the mere thought of them. His behavior really agitated me. Feeling determined, I decided to push him a little more to see if he would open up to me like he was constantly insisting I do with him.

"Felicia is fine," he answered curtly. Once again, his face started to close. Once again, I bristled. How could I give him the honesty he demanded of me when he consistently refused to be straightforward about what he was feeling?

"What does 'fine' mean?" I pushed.

"She's enjoying the benefits of being the mother of my sons," he answered shortly.

I didn't know how to take that. "Well, how are your sons doing?"

"They're fine, too." Once again, a short answer.

I didn't understand this. How could he seem to be so interested in Austin all the time and still have such a small tolerance for his own children? Did he not like his kids at all? It was times like this when I questioned the logic of my attraction to him and was glad I'd kept it a secret. For certain, logic told me I shouldn't become romantically involved with someone who did not like his own kids. I refused to place Austin in a no-win situation like that because I knew how it felt.

But then again, Delphi always seemed *so* interested in hearing anything I had to say about Austin. He asked about him all the time and even spoke with him a few times on the phone. Well, Delphi spoke and Austin kind of did one or two word responses. Was I completely wrong? Thoroughly perplexed as my heart and mind went to battle against each other, I sat in silence for a few moments. I think Delphi too was thankful for the small reprieve.

"I'm here now, my shift is finally over *mi amiga,*" Terry said, breaking the silence as she walked over to us. "Let's go. My bed just sent me a message that he's feeling extremely neglectful. I vowed to give him all the attention he's been craving for the next eight hours."

"Ok," I said. I stood up and gathered my things to prepare to go. I bit my lip and looked back at Delphi. I didn't want to leave the conversation like this between him and me. I hated any type of tension between us.

"Delphi, would you be able to do me a favor tomorrow night?" I asked sincerely.

"Sure," he says. "What's up?"

"I need to stock up on my food supply. I'm running short of ramen noodles and microwave popcorn." I smiled. "Would you be able to drive me to Port Gibson so I could go to the grocery store?"

"I'd love to," he said as he stood to gather his things as well. "I can take you after I finish practice, say around 7 p.m."

"Sure thing, " I said, relieved we were at least back to being buddies again. "I'll see you tomorrow."

He looked down at me. "Yes, you definitely will," he said somberly, and we all left the library.

∧∧∧

"Hey Delphi, give me just a sec," I said. He called my room from the lobby phone in my dorm. "I'll be down in a minute."

I checked my outfit one last time. "Looking good chica!" I heard Terri say as she walked out of our bathroom blow-drying her hair.

"Why you dressed fo da Piggly Wiggly? You got an affair wit da cashier we don't know bout? Better not let Ramon know. I hear he gets a little overly possessive when it comes ta you, ya erd me?" said Jackie jokingly as she draped herself across my bed.

Jackie Merlot was a part of my study group. She was also my sorority line sister, or my SHIP, having pledged at the same time as me. Like Terri, Jackie was full of life and always had a healthy supply of both energy and side jokes. She was a gorgeously stacked Creole girl from New Orleans like Ramon—but her upbringing was entirely different. She was raised in the Ninth Ward, an area known for lower income residents with a high crime rate and an even higher high school drop-out average. It was a testament to Jackie's resilience that she'd made it out of that lifestyle and was driven enough to attend college. However, some of those New Orleans traits were harder to let go of. She always tended to end her sentences in "ya erd me"; which I later realized was short for "you heard me." It was the equivalent to my neighborhood's "I know, right?" slang. She had the best sense of humor, however. Being around her always left me laughing—unless, like right now, that humor was directed at me.

I looked down at my blue jean mini skirt. I'd coupled it with a frilled yellow-laced tunic with matching flats. I curled my normally straight hair so it fell in rolling locks around my face. I wore my gold loop earrings and applied vanilla-flavored lip-gloss across my lips. I thought I did a decent job cleaning up; now I wasn't so sure.

"You look fine, *carina*," Terry said as she looked disapprovingly at Jackie, silently willing her to be quiet. "Go on now and bring me back some Oreos."

"Will do." *Ok, I can do this,* I thought. *It's not like it's a date. We're just going to the store.* I grabbed my purse and headed out.

I got on the elevator at the end of our hallway and pushed the button to take me down to the lobby. I made a mental note to not only look for Delphi, but Ramon as well. I wouldn't put it past him to do a surprise visit just to check on me. I'd told him earlier today while we ate lunch where I was going this evening and who was taking me. I didn't want him to get the wrong impression about Delphi and I leaving together.

Ramon, of course, didn't like it one bit. He grilled me about why Delphi couldn't take me during the day so it wouldn't seem so much like a date. I told him I had to wait until Delphi got out of practice, which usually ended around 6 p.m. I told him if he was so concerned, he could ride with us, but he just rolled his eyes at me. He finally conceded after I reminded him since he didn't have a car, Delphi was the only person I knew on campus who both had a vehicle and who would be willing to take me without bargaining for my last dollar. People with cars tended to auction their livery services to the highest bidder, and my money was tight. By promising to pick up a few items for him as well, Ramon finally agreed.

I looked down at what I was wearing again as I rode the elevator and thought about what Jackie had said. Delphi could unquestionably get the wrong impression given the fact I ditched my normal baseball cap and t-shirt for a miniskirt and dress shoes. The question was: Did I care? *Hell no.* I shrugged to myself. *A girl can look good for herself, can't she?* The elevator doors opened and I walked into the lobby.

"If you're looking for Delphi, he just walked outside," said the resident dorm monitor on duty that evening. People always seemed to know that the only reason Delphi came to this building was to see me.

I thanked her and walked outside to the parking lot. The Fall air was still a bit muggy for my taste. I was used to October feeling like October—meaning, a crisp 55 degrees easy. It was still 85 here in Mississippi. I paused. *Wait, am I crazy?* I shook my head as I let that fly right out of my brain and started walking again. It might be muggy now, but I'd take this over the winter season at home. Give me a cool 40 degrees in the middle of January like it tended to be here anytime.

I caught sight of Delphi and felt my heart lunge all too familiarly against my ribcage. I felt myself smiling a little too hard as I took in his attire. Somehow he had managed to run back to his room, shower, change his clothes, and get his beard and hair trimmed right after practice in time to be here by seven. My lust was so appreciating his effort.

He donned a pair of dark jeans with a muscled NSU FOOTBALL t-shirt that stretched across his wide shoulders and fabulous pecs. I also saw the tattoo I loved peeking underneath the sleeve on his left bicep. I'd discovered while going to see Levi one day during his band rehearsal at the school's stadium that the tattoo was actually an intricate pattern of blades, thorns and roses. It stretched from the middle of his bicep and ran all the way around and completely covered his left shoulder. Delphi had been on the football field shirtless at the time. I can't describe the internal fainting and lusting session I'd had in that moment.

My eyes scanned his face. His hairline was perfectly cut along his forehead. His beard had that sharp razor's edge that always drove crazy thoughts into my head; like running my tongue along his cheekbone, slowly making my way down his strong jaw line, moving toward those lips...

"Get out cha head Asha and put it on your lips," Delphi laughed, quoting his typical line to me. "Let's go get you some food. I want to go to Sonic and get a chili cheese coney while we're there. I'm starving and I know you didn't eat dinner at the Café yet."

"I'm hungry too," I said, placing my hand on my hip. "And how did you know I didn't eat yet?"

"Because I know you," he responded, smiling. "You were going to ask me to take you there because you're tired of eating cold salisbury steak slopped in grey sauce."

I snorted. "And you would be correct." I continued smiling and walked over to him. Delphi bent down to pick me up and gave me his usual hug. Since Ramon wasn't standing right behind me, I gave myself over to the sensation of being in his arms. He smelled just as sexy as his looks. Issey Miaki was earning his money this evening. I felt my pussy clench. *Damn*, I thought. *I should have packed an extra pair of undies and put them in my purse.*

"There," he said after he let me go. "Now, we can leave." He opened the passenger door to his car and I slid in. He closed the door after me and I reached over to unlock his driver's side door as he walked around the car.

48

"Do you want to eat first or go to the store?" he asked as he opened the car door and slid in the driver's seat.

"Let's go to the store first. Then we can eat and take our time at Sonic."

"Sounds good," he responded, starting the car.

We pulled off campus and began driving the long stretch of miles on Natchez Trace toward Port Gibson, Mississippi. Port Gibson was the closest rural area around school, but I would never classify it as a city. I wouldn't even call it a town, actually. If you sneezed, you could drive right through it. However at the moment it had what I needed, so I would call it my rescuer.

Delphi and I chatted about the past few weeks of class and our upcoming midterm exams as we drove along the Trace. Unlike Levi, Delphi and I actually had to study for our exams to make sure we did well. For Levi, getting an "A" in a class was like waking up to take a piss in the morning. It all came naturally.

"So the frats are throwing a party after the coronation Friday night," Delphi was explaining. "They want to relax after the 'Adopt a Big Brother' campaign we're holding at the middle school earlier that morning. I'm not going because I need to be ready for the game on Saturday, and Tanya has to go home that weekend. Do you have your dress already picked out?"

Tanya was the latest girl Delphi was currently dating. There had been so many girls over the past couple years Delphi had been involved with; however, Tanya seemed to be the one who's held on the longest. She was also, unfortunately, just like the others when it came to me. None of his prior girlfriends liked me; no matter how hard I tried to befriend them. They always cut their eyes at me and smacked their lips whenever I came around. I thought Tanya would be different seeing how she and I were also sorority sisters; but it seemed she was even more vicious and hateful than her predecessors. Tanya pledged the semester after Jackie and I did. I'd once hoped to draw a closer relationship with her, but over time eventually gave up, realizing that you just can't have a close relationship with all of your sisters.

"I probably won't be going to the coronation," I said. I didn't mention the fact that I didn't have any money to buy a formal gown. The few dollars I had were going to be spent in less than 30 minutes at the grocery store.

"Of course you are," Delphi said.

"Probably not," I said, cutting my eyes at him. He was not going to order me around like Ramon. I wouldn't put up with that shit.

"Let me rephrase," Delphi said, glancing at the expression on my face as he turned into a parking space at the store, a small smile forming on his beautiful lips. "If you haven't already picked out your dress, I have a surprise for you in the trunk."

"What sorta surprise?" I asked, quickly swapping out my irritation for excitement as he put the car in park.

"Something that will please both you and me," he said indulgently. He opened his car door and I remained seated as he walked around the front of his car over to my side. *Damn, that man could work a pair of jeans,* I thought wistfully as I watched him walk.

He opened my car door and took my hand as he pulled me out and around to the back of his car. He took his key and unlocked the trunk. Inside I saw a red covered box wrapped in a satin white bow. I squealed and jumped up, clapping my hands.

"Thank you, thank you!" I said, throwing myself in his arms. "No matter what it is, thank you! I'd stopped getting presents a while ago. It's been so long I'd forgotten what it feels like—so whatever it is, it will always be special to me!" I put my arms around his waist, grinning like an idiot.

My grin started to slide when I felt a hard bulge pressing against my stomach. "Um, sorry," I said. "Sometimes I get carried away." I lowered my arms and moved out of his embrace. I already felt the loss of his body heat.

"You mean Ramon doesn't get you gifts?" Delphi frowned. "I work all summer long so I can have spending money during the school year. It's nice to have the flexibility to splurge on anything I want without having to ask my parents for anything. I know we're in school, but surely he has to have gotten you something these past years." I wasn't sure whether he was frowning because I moved or at the thought of me not getting presents.

"Never. He's always said that we weren't that type of couple to show off to others how we felt toward each other."

"What about showing YOU how he feels about you?" he asked offensively.

I shrugged. "It's fine. I know he cares."

Delphi shook his head as he handed me the package. "I wanted to get you this for a few personal reasons. The main one being I wanted you to feel like the most beautiful girl at the coronation. To me, you already are; but I wanted you to feel that way too." He handed me the package.

My heart did its normal tug at his words. I felt my eyes begin to water and quickly looked down so he wouldn't see how much his caring affected me. I looked at the box in my hands and untied the bow. Lifting the lid, I saw one of the most luxurious blue satin gowns I'd ever seen. I gasped as I pulled the dress from the box. It was a floor length, and was cut with a sweetheart neckline. Sparkling sequins ran across the top and extended to the waist, along with a thigh-high slit running on the right side that was both sexy and sophisticated.

"Delphi, I can't accept this," I said hesitantly, putting the dress back inside the box and closing the cover.

"You can and you will." He growled darkly, but not in a threatening way. "For once you will see yourself as I've always seen you...beautiful."

This time the tears did start to fall. "Delphi, I ..." I began.

"Enough. That's it, that's all." He took the box and placed it back in the trunk. "Let go shopping so we can eat. I'm starved." He lifted his hand and rubbed his thumb across my check, wiping my tears. He gave me a lopsided grin. "I promise no more emotional digressions from my end."

I can't promise them from mine, I thought, wiping my face. "Ok, let's go."

We completed our shopping in record time and fell back into our normal routine of laughing at the silly things we always seemed to find in the country store. Like the old man that always sat outside and sang songs to every woman who walked in. He'd always claimed he taught James Brown all his moves, but I could have sworn James Brown was from South Carolina. Then there was the local booster who always tried to get me to buy his latest self-made cassette tape. He claimed he was already signed to Def Jam records and his mix tape was, of course, the latest unheard hit; so he would sell it to me for a steal at $5. When he'd eventually try to press his pitch a little to close to my body, Delphi always managed to jerk me away from his conversation.

As we finished with our purchases and walked out of the store, we ran into an older gentleman I had seen around campus from time to time. He always caught my attention because of his questionable fashion sense. Today he wore too tight polyester knit pants and a linen button up shirt that was stretched across his round stomach with weathered cowboy boots. Delphi stopped and shook hands with the gentleman.

"Asha, this is Mr. Elwood. Mr. Elwood, this is my friend Asha St. Claire. She goes to NSU, too."

"Pleasure to meet you ma'am." Mr. Elwood tipped the Stetson that adorned his head. "Delphi, you let me know whether or not you want it, here? I wanna get somebody in derr quick and I want somebody I can trust not to trash the place," Mr. Elwood said in his thick Mississippi accent.

"Will do, Mr. Elwood," Delphi answered. "I'll definitely call you tonight and let you know."

"Sounds good. Nice meeting ya, Asha." He tipped his hat toward me.

"You too," I said as Mr. Elwood walked past us into the store.

I turned to Delphi. "What was that about?" I asked curiously.

"I was thinking about renting one of the trailers he owns along the Trace," Delphi said. "It's a double wide with three bedrooms. I'm really tired of living on campus and I think it would be cheaper than paying those dorms rates. It's not required to stay on campus for my scholarship

52

and since I have a car getting to class wouldn't be a problem. Besides, you know I like my privacy and New Men's just doesn't allow that," he said, referring to the men's athletic dormitory.

I nodded my head. I understood, but I didn't think I liked it all that much. I liked knowing my Delphi was close-by. I shook my head. *He's not YOUR Delphi, Asha,* I scolded myself.

"Let's go eat," I said, trying to break up my thoughts. "I'm famished."

Delphi grinned and grabbed my hand, dragging me to his car.

We placed our groceries in the trunk, got in the car and drove the half-mile to Sonic. We ordered our food and fell once again back into idle chitchat that was uniquely our own. My thoughts began to wander again as I thought about his moving off campus.

"Aren't you nervous?" I blurted out.

Delphi turned those blue grays on me and raised one eyebrow. "Nervous about what?" he asked.

"Moving off campus on the Trace," I replied.

He laughed in response. "Not at all. I'm actually kind of excited. It will be the first time I'm really on my own outside of my folks' house."

"I guess," I said reluctantly. "I hope you'll still hang out on the YARD." I smiled faintly.

Delphi grabbed my hand and closed his fingers around mine. It was a move we've practiced numerous times in the past, but somehow the heat was intensely higher at this moment.

"I can't stay away," he said quietly and kissed the back of my hand. I felt my heartbeat race as that kiss went straight to my pussy. My breath hitched as I dropped my head so I was looking at the floorboard.

"Don't," he said and used his finger to lift my chin so I was looking directly in his eyes. "Don't retreat inside your head, Asha," he whispered. "Never be afraid to tell me how you're feeling. I'll always be here for you, no matter the physical distance or..." he took a deep breath. "...whether you or me are in other relationships. I'm not a sometime friend. I'm your always companion. Yours. Never forget that."

I sighed and took a deep breath. "Okay," I said.

The waitress walked up to Delphi's window at that moment with our food order and we fell silent as we ate. I wolfed down my coney and tater tots and chugged down my strawberry limeade like it was the last meal I would every have. After taking the last slurp of his slush, he put our trash in the bin next to his window and started the car to head back toward campus.

The sun was going down as evening descended upon us. I had to admit the Trace was really beautiful at night, with the dusk's sunrays kissing the tree limbs in a fiery glow. It was pretty as long as you were in a moving car. Otherwise the darkness that blanketed the two-lane highway could be incredibly scary.

The radio was on and one of my all-time favorite songs began to play. Luther Vandross had that type of voice that instantly called to me. His sweet melody quickly began to invade the car's interior.

"Oh my god!" I said breathlessly. "I LOVE this song!" I turned the volume up so that Luther's remake of "*Superstar*" permeated through the speakers and washed through my soul. I threw my head back, closed my eyes, lifted my arms, and began swaying to the music, completely forgetting where I was and who I was with. I twirled my wrists in a circular motion as I began to sing the lyrics with a passion that generally only came out when I was alone. I don't know what it was about that song that did it for me, but every time I heard it some type of emotion always swelled within me-bursting to be set free.

"Beautiful." I heard a whisper say to my left, breaking my trance. I opened my eyes. Delphi was staring at me with a look of wonder across his face. He'd slowed the car down to a snail's pace and was watching intently as I went through my moment. Embarrassing heat began to creep up on neck and onto my cheeks as I realized I had an audience to my one-woman show.

"Come here Asha," he said softly. Still feeling my heart racing from the effects of the song that was still playing, I scooted closer to him. I felt myself needing that personal and physical contact because of the emotion overwhelming me. I could feel the heat radiating off him as we sat thigh to thigh. He kept his left hand on the steering wheel while circling his right hand around my shoulders.

"I need to share this moment with you, love. Please." His eyes pleaded with me and he turned my shoulder, pulling me closer to his chest.

"What do you want me to do?" I whispered. The chemistry between us was lighting up like a torch.

"I want you to ride on my lap while we drive back." He looked directly into my eyes with the intensity of a lion ready to pounce on its prey.

I licked my lips as my pussy clenched at his words. How often had I thought of doing just that, except not in a moving vehicle? What would it be like to feel his body pressed that tightly against mine?

"Isn't that dangerous?" I asked cautiously, looking around outside and then back at him with longing. I wanted to straddle him so badly and Luther's voice was calling me to a paradise that was just a lap dance away.

"No more than it is driving through here at high speed. I promise I'll drive slowly and if I see a car I'll pull over so you can slide off."

"Ok."

I moved to my knees and turned around in the seat so that I was facing the back window. Lifting my right leg, I slid it over his lap underneath the steering wheel. I felt him gasp as my knee brushed against the erection pressing tightly against his jeans. I moved my body across his chest so that my back was pressed against the steering wheel and my breasts were rubbing against his chest. I felt his dick twitch through the denim rubbing against my pussy as I settled down unto his lap. I placed my cheek against his neck so I could make sure I wasn't impairing his vision and took a deep breath to inhale his scent. It felt so good to be connected with him like this, so right.

"Sing to me, little one. I want to hear your passion," he whispered in my ear.

I picked the words back up to the song as it continued to play. Once again, I became lost as I heard Luther's voice called to the siren inside me. She responded willingly, blending her harmonized voice with Luther's. I felt my hips moving back and forth to the rhythm. Feeling the hard press of Delphi's dick against my clit as my skirt rose higher across my thighs, I gasped. A tremor of lust took hold of me while I still tried to maintain my voice. I began riding his lap as he thrust harder against my pussy, grinding into me. I wound my arms around his back and placed my cheek against his beard. My pussy was so wet I could feel my panties easily sliding against him. I felt his growl from deep in his throat as he continued to push into me. I continued to sing as I turned my face toward his neck, breathing in his scent. Finally, I couldn't take it anymore and let my tongue run along his jawline in a slow, needy lick. He groaned.

"Damn, I can smell you." He exhaled, "Let it go, sweetie. Release it. I'll catch you. I'll always catch you." His right hand wound around my thighs to my ass and he pulled me harder, if possible, against his body. He began to thrust faster against me and I let go of the song to concentrate exclusively on him. He held my ass tightly as he continued driving.

"Oh!" I felt my pussy clench as I moved frantically up and down on his jean clothed dick, trying to put as much pressure and friction against my clit as I could. "Delphi, Delphi," I moaned over and over.

As Luther crooned out his last lyrical wonder, my vagina performed a wonder of its own as it sent me spiraling over the cliff of the biggest orgasm I'd ever had. I screamed and threw my head back, clutching his shoulders tightly as the tremors took control of me. I shuddered against his body.

"That's right. Let it all go. I got you. I got you."

"Delphi," I said, my voice hoarse.

"I got you, baby," he whispered soothingly. "Rest, I got you." I closed my eyes, laid my head on his chest, and did just that.

When I finally opened them again, we were parked outside of my dorm.

"Did I fall asleep?" I asked lazily as I slowly extracted myself from his lap to move over to the passenger side. It felt so good snuggling against him that I hated to leave.

He smiled crookedly at me. "Yes, but don't worry. You don't snore and didn't drool on my shirt, so I can knock that off the list of things to find out about you."

I mockingly hit him in the shoulder. "I know I don't snore!" I exclaimed. My eyes turned down as I thought about the past few hours. "Delphi, I'm not sure what happened back there, but…"

"No buts, no regrets." He cut me off. "Don't beat yourself up thinking about the shoulda coulda wouldas. Nothing has changed for me sweetheart. I'm still your Delphi."

But everything DID change! At least for me it did. *Maybe he didn't feel the same way I did,* I thought. Maybe I was just like the rest of the girls he's dated where he just made out with them and then left like nothing happened. Maybe it was once again, all in my head. Maybe, wait…did he just refer to himself as mine?

"I'll help bring your groceries to your room," he said, opening his car door.

I paused and looked at him, not quite sure how to proceed. He walked around the front of the car to my passenger door and opened it. He then leaned in and waited, as I remained seated, still confused. He stared down at me, a small frown shadowing his face.

"Asha," he said slowly. "I never wanted to…"

"It's about time!" yelled Terri as she jogged toward us. "I need my Oreos chica! I'm going through withdrawal!" She got to the car and hit Delphi in the shoulder. "What took you so dang long?" She then caught sight of me still seated and frowned back at Delphi. "What did you do, *pendejo*?"

"He didn't do anything, Terri." I sighed, trying to put on my best face. "I just woke up. You know I tend to look crazy when I first wake up from sleep."

Terri laughed. "Yes, you do." She pulled me from the car. "Get out girl."

"I'll be up in a minute with your groceries," Delphi offered. I looked at him and nodded. He had a pained looked across his face that I was sure was triggered by a lot of regret. I forced a smile on my face.

"Thanks for giving me a ride, Delphi." I didn't want him to regret what happened. I know I didn't. I never would.

"I'm here anytime you need one," he said seductively. His pained expression was quickly replaced by a look of relief.

"Yes, get to it worker bee," Terri joked as she snapped her fingers at Delphi. He rolled his eyes as he walked to the trunk to get our groceries. They had a love-hate sort of friendship similar to Levi and me.

"Yes Diva Queen." He shook his head and smiled as he gathered our things. He handed me my red box. "I hope you'll still wear this," he said softly.

"What's that?" Terri asked curiously, peeking over my shoulder.

"Mine, nosey," I said pushing her back. I didn't want to discuss this in the parking lot.

We went up to our room where Delphi unloaded our groceries. He then walked to the front door to get ready to leave. Before opening the door, he turned to look at me.

"Nothing has changed, Asha," he said pointedly to me. "I mean it." With that, he opened the door and left.

"What was THAT all about?" Terri asked as she flounced herself on her bed. She folded her legs in a cross position while she opened the pack of cookies, munching away. I sat down on my bed with a deep sigh. I leaned back on my pillows and stared up at the ceiling, biting my lower lip. Terri stopped chewing and stared at me when I didn't answer right away.

"Nothing," I responded eventually with a shaky voice. I didn't know how to even express the hurricane of feelings that were going on inside me, so it was best not to get started.

Terri didn't say anything. She continued to stare at me for a couple of more minutes. "That's OK, honey. You'll let me know when you're ready to chat, eh? In the meantime, what's in that box?"

"Go ahead and look Terri," I resigned myself, breathing a little easier at not being pushed right away. "You're going to look anyway when I leave the room. Delphi said he wanted me to have it."

Terri opened the box and regarded the dress inside it. "Asha, this is beautiful," she whispered.

"I know."

"Why did he give you this?"

I shrugged my shoulders. "He said he wanted me to wear it to the coronation next week," I replied.

She paused. "Surely you said yes."

"I admit I was surprised, I'm just not sure I should. It's really expensive."

"Are you kidding me?" Terri exclaimed. "You are wearing it and you will love it. I have the perfect shoes to go with that too!" Terri ran excitedly to her closet and pulled out a pair of sexy 5-inch silver Badgley Mischka heels. "You know you're my size, so don't even try to say you can't fit these. Come on, Asha, give in to it for once in your life."

I laughed at the seriousness in her face. "Give it to whom?" I asked, getting off my bed. I began removing our groceries out of the paper bags to store in our closet and mini refrigerator.

"Give a big 'fuck you' to the idiots who can't appreciate how incredible you are and a humongous '*Yes, I am THE Shit*' to the admirers who've been waiting to see you shine." She snapped her fingers.

I paused in storing the groceries and turned to look at her. "Why would you say something like that?" I asked, stunned. Terri rarely cursed. She often left that type of rhetoric strictly for Levi.

"Look, Asha," Terri started, putting her hands on her hips, the shoes dangling from her fingers. "I'm your friend and I love you to life. I also know that you would hide in this room all day if I didn't drag you out of it. For some reason you've got it in your head that you shouldn't seek happiness for yourself because you had a little boy too young. That somehow denying yourself any sort of pleasure is the appropriate punishment for shaming your family. I know that you've been listening to your mother's voice in your head for way too long. I also know that you subject yourself to undeserved negative verbal abuse and who knows about the physical impacts from your psychotic boyfriend." She stomped her foot in a mini tantrum.

"I've had enough. You will go to that coronation wearing that dress. You will put those heels on. I will do your makeup. I will do your hair. You will be the most beautiful, the most breathtaking, and the most bodacious bitch to ever grace the doors of NSU's auditorium. Now suck it up and get ready, damnit. The chapter meeting starts in half an hour." With that, Terri tossed the shoes on my bed and strolled into the bathroom.

I sat down on my bed, completely taken aback. Apparently all these years Terri had seen through all my bullshit and was able to read me like a book. Things that I had been holding close to my heart she'd just ripped away and threw back in my face--all through the course of a mini temper tantrum. A feeling of awe began to surface within me, warming my blood. It felt good. It felt nice to have someone actually care enough about me to make an effort to see past all the blockades. It felt like someone actually gave a damn. I liked it. I liked it a lot.

And I guess I was going to the coronation next week.

Chapter Five

Homecoming
Awakening the Bond

Asha

"Wow, it's so pretty in here," I said, looking around the auditorium. The homecoming committee had really done a fantastic job transforming the usually smelly, rancid auditorium into a sanctuary of beauty and elegance. Overhead lights sparkled along the ceiling while some sort of sparkle, glitter maybe, adorned the floor. Maroon and gold streamers lined the walls along side white and yellow balloons. Grey folding chairs that were usually hard and unrelenting were covered in a sophisticated maroon and gold pattern with cushioned seating. Yellow roses lined each seated row, and were cased in a delicate array of maroon and gold ribbons. It was magnificent.

"Yes, yes. Let's hurry up and get a good seat," Terri said as she grabbed my arm and pulled me toward the front of the room so we could get a prime view.

The crowning ceremony was lovely. I'd seen the young lady who was eventually crowned Miss NSU around campus several times over the past semester, campaigning and handing out fliers. She had refinement and poise that was envied by many; but I looked at her as if she were the saving grace our school needed. I was personally excited that she was able to walk away with the title. Tanya had also run for Miss NSU and I was secretly happy when the decision that she'd lost was announced. Had she won, she would have assuredly torn the peacefulness of campus politics apart.

As the Queen and her court got ready to leave the assembly, everyone stood and applauded, as was tradition. They descended the stage platform and started marching out of the auditorium. Everyone turned and watched them parade by. I turned around as well to face the back of the room. The view behind me caused me to stagger a little, forcing me to grab the seat behind me.

Delphi stood next to Levi near the back of the room. He wore a pair of simple navy dress slacks and an opened collared dress shirt, which stretched across his wide shoulders. His eyes bore through me as if he could feel every desire, every sensuous craving, and every passion-filled emotion that coursed through me. He broke eye contact and smiled politely as Miss NSU and her court passed him on their way out of the room. Once the coronation party left, he turned back to face me with an intense expression plastered on his face as he and Levi began walking toward us.

"Oh shit," I heard Terri whisper. "*Ay caray* tonight was going so well. Levi better not start his shit with me this evening. I was planning on being a great night."

Levi and Delphi pushed themselves through the crowd and finally made it to where we were standing. "Hey guys," Levi said. Delphi just nodded, but didn't take his eyes off me.

"Hey yourself. Did you guys get a chance to see the coronation?" Terri asked casually.

"We sure did. It was really nice. Speaking of nice, that dress is wearing you quite nicely, Terri," Levi said with a predatory leer.

Terri rolled her eyes. "I make the dress *chilito*; the dress *never* makes me," Terri scoffed.

"You certainly do, little one; although I have to admit I've never been accused of having a small dick before. Why don't you come see for yourself if what you called me is actually true?" Levi offered, raising one eyebrow.

My mouth fell open as I looked at Terri. "Terri!" I said, shockingly. "What is wrong with you?"

Terri shrugged her delicate shoulder that peeped above her strapless red chiffon gown. "Nothing," she said nonchalantly. "Levi just brings that side out in me."

"And you," I said turning to Levi. "Since when did you learn to speak Spanish?"

"Since our freshman year," Levi responded casually as his eyes roamed across Terri's frame. He shrugged it off as if the question were as simple as when did you learn to spell your name. "I needed to understand all the things Terri was spouting at me."

Terri looked at him with what could be considered as grudging respect in her eyes.

Their banter did nothing to stop Delphi from getting his fill staring at me, I noticed. His eyes never swayed from me. Instead, I saw him slowly rake his eyes from the top of my head to the bottom of those achingly high, tight for no reason stilettos Terri made me wear.

"You look lovely, Asha." Delphi acknowledged. "I'm pleased more than you can ever know that you decided to wear the dress."

"Is that right?" I said, mockingly. "And why is that?" Inside I was beaming he thought I looked good in it. After Terri finished her beauty makeover on me, which was nothing short of painful, I had to admit I liked the end results. She fixed my hair in a classic chiffon style that highlighted my slim neck and high cheekbones. She also filled in my eyes with a smoldering eye shadow that accentuated them; making them the most dominate feature on my face. She finally topped it off with a plum lip color and adorned my neck with a simple silver charm locket. I felt pretty tonight. Scratch that; I looked pretty damn good and I was feeling slightly cocky.

Delphi leaned over and murmured in my ear so only I could hear. "Because I know that the dress you're wearing is a representation of me stamped all over your beautiful body. It's me cupping your breasts; it's me that's sliding across your hips, and me hugging that fabulous ass of yours."

My breath hitched as he leaned away from me. Just like that, my pussy started to throb as if it knew exactly who was near it. He placed his hand at the small of my back and began to rub seductively through the material.

"Hey Terri, I'm going to take Asha back to her room tonight. Do you mind? I know you guys came together," Delphi asked innocently, like he hadn't just rocked my world.

"Ah, yea I mind. I don't want to walk back to the room by myself," huffed Terri.

"Don't worry, I'll walk you back. I won't let anything happen to you," Levi countered. He looked over at Delphi and nodded his head. "Catch you tomorrow, man."

"C'mon," Delphi said, grabbing me by my hand and rushing out of the auditorium. "I have a surprise to show you." With a quick wave of goodbye to Terri, I followed him out of the building.

"Can we at least slow down a bit?" I said, finally feeling the affects of walking from our dorm all the way to the auditorium in 5-inch heels. Terri and I tried to be divas earlier as we strolled the Yard on our way to the ceremony. Now I realized how that was so not a good idea, especially since I forgot to bring flats with me.

Delphi didn't slow down. He simply turned, picked me up like I was completely weightless, and began walking again toward the parking lot where his car was parked.

"What are you doing?" I said, feeling self-conscious about the load he was carrying. "I can walk; just let me take off my shoes."

"Nah, I like carrying you."

We reached his car and he set me on my feet so he could unlock and open the passenger door. I slid in, reached over to unlock the driver's side, and immediately began taking off my heels, rubbing my aching feet. Delphi slid in the car and turned the ignition.

"Oh that feels so good," I groaned as I rubbed the heel of my left foot.

"Let me," Delphi said as he reached for my leg. He drew it over his lap and began massaging my leg and calf at a sensual and leisurely pace.

"That feels wonderful," I said, leaned against the door and gave in to the relaxing sensations his hands were causing.

Delphi chuckled. "I'm glad I could help. So, where's Ramon? Why didn't he escort you to the coronation tonight?"

"Ramon said he wasn't going to waste his time bolstering someone else's ego. He said he refused to be among the mere peasants in the audience while the royals looked down on us," I snorted. "He hitched a ride home with Jackie, and she's dropping him off at his house for the weekend. Jackie told me Tanya left with her too because she was a sore loser and needed to eat some humble pie," I said with a straight face.

Delphi stopped massaging my calf to stare at me. After a few seconds he threw his head back and let out a loud laugh. After a moment, I joined him as well.

"Wow," he said, still chuckling. "Yea, Tanya called me right before she left and told me she was outa here till Sunday night." He paused for a moment. "His loss for missing out on this." He let go of my leg and I smoothed by dress back to a respectable position. The slit had risen further up my thigh when my body twisted to give better access for my massage.

"Missed out on what?" I asked curiously.

"On this." Delphi reached over and grabbed the back of my neck, pulling me closer to him. He lightly brushed his lips against mine in the sweetest of kisses. I melted a little more as he continued to hold my neck in that possessive manner as I tried to lean away from him. *God, I loved....*

"Anyway," I interjected, trying to shake off those thoughts. "I thought you told me you wouldn't be able to make the coronation. What happened?"

"I told you I wouldn't be going to the frat party. I never said anything about not going to the coronation. I thought you would be attending with Ramon, but clearly that's not the case." Delphi released my neck and grabbed the steering wheel. "Come on. I told you I have something I want to show you."

Delphi pulled out of the parking lot and began to drive toward the campus entrance. He drove for about 10 minutes down the highway when he suddenly pulled onto a dirt-covered road right off the Trace.

"Where are we going?" I asked, looking around. I still hadn't gotten used to being on the Trace at night.

"You'll see, hold on." Delphi grinned at me. He drove another minute or two before he finally pulled into the carport area next to a well-lit trailer home. The trailer was in pretty good condition, with its tan siding and black shudders surrounding the front windows. A chain-linked fence began on the left side of the home and continued toward the front of the house for about 10 yards, making a nice area one could consider to be a front yard. There were small, planted bushes in the front, and potted plants lining the front walkway leading up to the door.

"I wanted you to be the first person that see this," Delphi said as he turned off the ignition. "I moved in here last weekend. What do you think?"

"I think it's fabulous," I said in awe. And I did. "It's nothing like what I expected."

"Come on, I want to show you inside." Delphi got out of the car and walked around to my side to open the door. He took my hand and walked me up the bricked pathway to the front door.

"Welcome to my humble abode," Delphi said in his most serious Dracula voice. I looked at him and rolled my eyes as I stepped over the threshold. Inside the trailer, a large couch covered in a brown floral pattern sat in the middle of the living room. A large 48-inch television sat on a small glass cocktail table in front of the couch. *I hope that table holds out,* I thought absently. The living room expanded into a small kitchen with what appeared to be a newly installed refrigerator and stove appliance set. There was a small dining room table and chair set that sat in the center of the rooms' walkway.

However something was off and I couldn't put my finger on exactly what it was. Then suddenly it hit me.

"It's so clean in here," I realized. "I thought this was supposed to be a bachelor's pad," I mocked jokingly. "You're always complaining about how junky your dorm room is--I would expect this place to be messier."

"Ha ha, very funny," Delphi mocked, joining in the amusement. "Nate is not moving in until next week, so the place will stay spotless until then."

I laughed. "Nate is moving here, too? Man, I can already see the wild frat parties and spade tournaments happening." Nate Kerr had been Delphi's roommate since their freshman year, like Terri had remained mine. Nate was a fellow Chicagoan as well. We often rode the train home together during Christmas and summer breaks. He reminded me of a young Lawrence Fishburne in that movie "School Daze" in both mannerisms and looks. He was always all about the people, for the people, every day, all the time. He was also Delphi's SHIP.

I'd noticed something else as well. "Did you cook?" I asked, realizing the knot in my stomach was not just about anxiety.

Delphi pulled out one of the dining room table chairs. "Have a seat, sweetie. I admit I was actually thinking of a way to steal you away from Ramon tonight, but he did me a favor with his no-show. I'm happy about that actually. I think it allowed you a better opportunity to let your light shine a little brighter." He smiled at me warmly.

"Okay..." Not sure what he meant by that. I walked over and took the seat he offered as he took a sweeping bow. "You are so silly." I laughed; basking in the attention he was showing me.

Delphi gave me a lopsided grin. "I didn't cook, but I do have some food for you. I know how you detest eating in the Café; and I know you didn't eat before the coronation tonight. All you were thinking about was trying to look good in that dress-which you do by the way. You look absolutely perfect, if that was even possible. I hope you know that." He turned and walked into the kitchen.

"Thank you," I blushed. "And yes, I'm starving. I'm not even going to ask how you knew that." I leaned over to peep into the kitchen to see what he was doing. "Did you want me to help you?"

"No, I got it. Let me serve you this time. It pleases me."

"Oh, ok." Why were my cheeks heating?

I heard plates and glassware moving around as Delphi continued to ponder around. Finally, he walked over to me and sat two plates on the table along with a bottle of grape juice, my favorite.

"Oh yeah!" I exclaimed excitedly, doing a fist pump in the air as I took in the plate's content. "Jeannie's! Right on time!" Jeannie's Restaurant was the local diner all students went to when they wanted a good, semi-home cooked meal. Well, if one considered a greasy pork chop sandwich, ribs slathered in hickory barbeque sauce, or thick wedge cut home fries. Jeannie's food was the highest quality a student could expect out here, beating out both the Café and the SUB hands down. It was also much closer than driving to Port Gibson. It sat about two miles off campus, so it was a rare treat when a person without a car was finally be able to indulge.

Delphi laughed. "Yes, I knew you'd appreciate it. You're so easy to read. I hope you like it." He'd bought us both shrimp baskets with fries and soda bread. I felt my mouth water as I took my first bite. Heaven!

We sat in silence as we savored our meal. Delphi finished before me and leaned back in his chair to wait for me to finish. "I have one final treat for you, little one."

I looked up at him, a question suddenly burning in my gut at hearing his endearment. "You know there's something I've always wanted to ask you."

"You can ask me anything. I want you to ask me. What's up?" Delphi asked curiously.

"Why didn't you ever give me a nickname?" I asked. "I know people labeled you with 'Delphi' a long time ago because you're from Philly; but you told me at one point that you would give me a nickname. What ever happened to that?" I asked.

Delphi let a sly look come upon his face. "Well, let's just say I decided a while ago that the name I will call you will be uniquely for you. No one else will have the privilege or the honor to call you that. For now, calling you Asha is fine for me. I haven't earned the right to call you anything else." He paused and glanced at my lips. "But I have every confidence that I will."

That threw me. "OK... everybody, including me, calls you Delphi all the time. So are you saying it bothers you when you hear it?" I asked bewildered.

He shook his head. "No, not at all. Most people on campus call me Delphi like we're the greatest of friends; but they really don't know me. It's the only alternative they have to feel a connection to me. They then try and link that connection to something they can relate to, like my hometown. I've found that very few people try to make a real honest effort to get to truly know a person, inside and out. Most prefer the superficial association rather than the deeper connection. They believe there's less risk of having to make themselves just as open and vulnerable."

His face turned serious. "I don't need to attach a label or try to link you to Chicago because I'm too weak not to have taken the time to get closer to you. I think I've earned the right to call you Asha for now. Like I said, soon I'll earn the right to call you something else— specifically for me."

I let his words sink in. "Okay, then. Well, when I've earned it, what will I call you?" It seemed he had taken a lot of time to ponder this issue, more than I would have previously thought. Now I was even more intrigued about what his response would be.

"Sir Jaymes," he said simply, staring directly into my eyes.

Confused, I stared back for a beat. "Isn't that your name already? And what's with the sir?"

"Yes, but no one calls me that, not even my parents. My friends at home call me Jimmy and my parents still call me Junior because I'm named after my father, even though I passed his height during junior high school." He leaned forward in his chair, reached out and let his finger slide down my cheek. "The SIR is a significant detail, but we won't go into that right now. We'll discuss it more when you've earned it."

"Oh." And for some reason, I was okay with that answer. His finger brushed against my cheek once more before moving away from my face. That I wasn't okay with.

"Okay." Delphi smiled at me and leaned back, steering the conversation to a lighter topic. "Ready for your last surprise?"

"Yes."

Delphi stood and walked over to the refrigerator. He pulled out a maroon box and walked back to the table. He placed the box down, grinning knowingly in my direction.

"Oh my God!" I squealed, clasping my hands together. Inside the box with the Baker's Square logo sat my favorite pie in the whole world, a French apple cream cheese cake. I looked at Delphi. "Thank you so much," I said, feeling the tears welling up.

"Don't thank me. You're well worth the trip to Jackson to buy this. I wanted your special night to end with a special sweet treat," he said indulgently.

Suddenly I had an impulse. "Wait. Close your eyes for a minute," I said as I scrambled to the kitchen to grab a fork.

Delphi did as requested as I walked back over to the table. I opened the box and took out the cheesecake. "Open your mouth," I murmured near his ear. He opened his mouth slightly, still keeping his eyes closed. "Wider." I coached. He opened it just a fraction more. "Wider." He finally opened his mouth fully, waiting for my next command. I took my fork and dipped it into the cheesecake. Once I had a large scoop, I placed the fork in his mouth.

"Now close your mouth," I whispered. Delphi closed his mouth over the cheesecake and moaned a little at the flavor. I leaned even closer so that my mouth was right next to his ear. "Now you know exactly what I taste like," I whispered seductively.

Delphi growled and kicked his chair back as he turned and grabbed me faster than I could ever imagine. He picked me up and I wrapped my legs around his waist as we walked down the hallway past the kitchen. I held onto his neck as we passed a smaller bedroom and a bathroom until we finally reach a larger master bedroom at the end of the hall. Inside the room was a large king-sized bed with a small dresser next to it. A lounge chair holding a cd player sat next to the window facing the bed, with a collection of cds lined against the wall.

I didn't have time to take assessment of anything else as Delphi tossed me on the bed. He stood over me as we both drank in the sight of each other, longing in both of our eyes, before he crawled on top of me.

He grabbed my neck and pulled me to his mouth. I was expecting the same gentle touch he'd always displayed in the past, so the roughness he was using now mimicked the same urgency I felt. His tongue caressed my lips and licked the inside of my cheeks in hungry strokes, leaving nothing untouched. He then gently began sucking my tongue through a series of pulls and tugs that seemed to have a direct line to my pussy. Each pull created small spasms inside me and caused moisture to drip from my pussy and spread across my thighs.

Delphi flipped me over onto my stomach and slowly unzipped my dress so that my back was fully exposed. "Beautiful," he whispered as he trailed his finger along my spine. "Get on your knees." I pulled myself into a sitting position so that he could slide the dress over my shoulders. He unhooked my bra and I felt cool air brush against my hardened nipples as it along with my dress fell down to my hips.

"Turn over," he said hoarsely and I did as he commanded. He pulled the dress from my hips and I was left with nothing but my black-laced G-string underwear. He leaned over to suck one nipple into his mouth as his hand tweaked the other. I began to writhe and whimper, silently begging for more.

"Gotta taste you…" he whispered to himself as he slid the underwear from my body. He placed his nose directly on my pussy and took a deep breath. "You smell so good," he whispered. The next thing I felt was his tongue taking a long swipe up my slit. My thighs began to quiver as I tried to catch my breath. His tongue was so soft and wet. I moaned at the sensation.

He took a strong suck on my clit that caused my back to jolt off the bed. I came back down panting even harder as my hands reached and grabbed his head to pull him closer. I whimpered in frustration as he stopped licking to glare up at me.

"Keep your hands above your head or I'll tie them down," he growled. "You do not control this, my Asha."

My pussy gushed even more at his threat. *God, yes…* my mind screamed. I didn't want to be in control. I wanted to give him the full submission of every part of my mind and body to handle, to manage, to cherish, to love, to bring to ecstasy.

"Delphi," I pleaded, letting my thighs spread further apart while placing my hands above my head to grip his headboard. He dipped his head down again to drag his tongue across my opening. Suddenly I felt a finger piercing my pussy, slowly fucking me.

"Yes, yes, yes," I chanted wantonly as he began sucking my clit harder, still fucking me with his finger. One finger became two, then three as he plunged in and out of my hole, causing my hips to grind up to meet each thrust. I heard the slushing sound of my wet pussy each time he pulled his fingers out. When he curved his fingers slightly and pressed down, hitting my g-spot, I exploded. My body began to buck wildly. "Fuuucccccckkkk!" I screamed as the exquisite orgasm racked through my body. My vision blurred as I rode the wave.

As I came down from my high, Delphi chuckled seductively. "No baby, not yet. But we will now. For the time being, I'll allow you to yell out profanities when ecstasy is gripping your body. Next time, only my name is acceptable."

I looked at him with lust-filled eyes as he began taking off his clothes. He unzipped his pants and tossed them in the chair, his erection tenting a dark pair of boxer briefs. My mouth started to water at the thought of holding him between my lips, tasting every inch of skin. He then began unbuttoning his shirt.

"Wait," I said breathlessly. "Can I do that?"

His eyes filled with some sort of emotion I didn't recognize. "Yes, my sweet. Come here." He held his hand to me and helped me up as I scrambled off the bed.

My fingers shook as I started the task of unbuttoning his shirt. I stopped halfway through and let my hands run across his pecs, feeling the hardness there. I caressed his six-pack and felt the muscles quiver underneath my strokes. I resumed unbuttoning his shirt and finally pushed the material from his shoulders. My fingers traced the tattoo etched across his shoulder as I marveled in its pattern. I stretched on my toes to place a heated kiss on his erect nipple, and then slid my lips across the puckered skin. He hissed and held my head in place.

"Bite me." He growled and I did just that, taking his nipple in my mouth to bite down hard. I felt his cock jerk in his underwear against my stomach as he panted heavily. I moved my head to lick and caress his other nipple, and then slipped my hand down to feel his erection through his underwear. I felt a damp spot where his dick was already weeping as I stroked him hard through the material.

"Enough!" he shouted pushing me back on the bed. I opened my thighs and arms to welcome him. He slipped his underwear over his lean hips and reached over to grab a condom from the dresser next to his bed. After he sheathed himself, he nestled his body between my legs.

Delphi took his hand and slid it underneath my hips, cradling me. "I love you, Asha. I always have, I always will no matter what. I will always be here for you," he whispered as he took his cock in his other hand to push himself into me.

I groaned as he stretched me with his girth. He was so wide and felt so good. As he continued to push, I felt his dick drag over my spot. Incredulously I came again, this time so hard I must have lost consciousness for a moment because all vision and sound was lost to me. When my mind cleared, I felt him thrusting in and out of me, pounding against my flesh, while he held my ass in a firm lock. "God, your pussy is clenching me so fucking tight. It's so good, so good," he moaned.

"Please, I need to taste you, too," I pleaded, still holding to the headboard.

"Yes..." he panted. I placed my arms around his neck and pulled his face to mine. I let my tongue run along his beard, savoring the softness and the flavor of his skin. I ran my nose along his neck, basking in the smell of Issey. My tongue ran along his shoulder, outlining his tattoo.

"Asha…." He groaned as his hips began to buck and lose its rhythm, signaling his pending climax. He gripped me tighter as his heartbeat quickened against my chest as he groaned his release. I felt his dick twitch in the condom as it filled with cum. Finally he collapsed on top of me, panting heavily.

We laid like that for a long moment as our heart rates slowed to match each other. We were both in deep thought as we contemplated what we had just done and its possible ramifications.

"Let me get rid of this," Delphi said in a raspy voice, sliding out of me and walking out of the room. I then heard water running in the bathroom as I stared up at the ceiling. He returned a moment later with a warm washcloth. "Open for me." I slid my thighs apart and he gently washed me. Once completed, he tossed the towel on the floor and crawled next to me, pulling my back against his chest as he wrapped me in his arms.

"That was amazing," I whispered. I felt his arms tighten around me. "I never knew making love could be that intense."

He chuckled softly against my neck as he placed a soft kiss near my ear. "I knew from the moment I saw you that it would be this way with you. Only you."

Happiness flowed through me as I processed his words. My mind began to race with the possibilities of truly being with Delphi like I'd always imagined.

"What now?" I asked hesitantly. "I mean…I know you're still seeing Tanya. I like Ramon enough, but compared to this…" I reached down to caress the steel thighs that still held me captive in his embrace. "There is no comparison."

Delphi turned me around to face him as he stared intently into my eyes.

"I am serious about you, Asha. I always have been. There will only be us. No one else. No one can come between what we have. When we graduate, we will go and get Austin, and after that we can settle

74

down wherever you want. I can start my practice anywhere. I just need you and Austin by my side."

At the mention of Austin, I sat up, pulling the sheet close to me to cover my breasts.

"What about your boys?" I asked cautiously. "Wouldn't you want them, too?"

"Felicia can handle them," he replied irritability, rolling out of the bed. He reached over to pick his pants from the chair and put them on.

I sat there, unwilling to let it go. "Felicia shouldn't have to take care of your boys by herself. It's hard to be a single mom, believe me. And she has two to take care of."

"She's got my parents support, so she doesn't have to worry about struggling to make sure they have what they need."

"What about your support?" I asked.

"What about it?" Delphi replied tersely.

Coldness washed through me, washing away all prior feelings of warmth and protection. "They need you too, Delphi."

"They have my parents." He still replied stubbornly.

"But they still need their father."

Delphi lowered his head and bit his bottom lip angrily, so hard I thought he might draw blood. He clenched his fists and then looked at me through narrowed eyes.

"I don't want to talk about them," he said through gritted teeth.

"Well, I do," I said, just as persistently. I kicked the sheet off and turned away to put my dress back on. When I finished, I turned around angrily. "What type of man refuses to be a part of his sons' lives? What makes you think I would want Austin around that type of individual?"

"I am the same man. Nothing has changed, Asha," Delphi said crossing his arms across his chest. "They are not a factor here."

I looked at him incredulously. "Not a factor? How can you say that? Don't they mean anything to you?" I clutched my chest as a painful throb raced through me.

"I know they definitely mean more to Felicia. Look, this isn't something I want to get into with you. Let's just call it a night and tomorrow we can act like this conversation never happened."

"Never happened..." I choked, still holding my chest. My heart hurt so badly it felt like a knife were stabbing me over and over again, twisting and turning. "Could you dismiss me and Austin so easily too?" I whispered.

Delphi looked at me with a panicked expression. "Asha, look. It's not that, it's just...." He hesitated. He then stopped and dropped his head again, his fists clenched at his sides.

His refusal to acknowledge his sons had me suddenly seeing red. "I don't understand, Delphi and I don't think I ever will. I care about you. I always have, and unfortunately for me I probably always will. But I won't let my feelings for you make me blind to the type of person you may be when it comes to dealing with my son. I have to do what's best for him. He needs to be exposed to someone who will be there for the long run, not someone that could easily dismiss him at the drop of a hat like he did his own children."

"Asha, please," Delphi said, reaching out to me. I stepped back to avoid his touch. He was breaking my heart.

"I can't Delphi. Please take me back to my room," I said. Hot tears finally began to burn through my anger as they coursed down my cheeks. I needed to distance myself from him. I couldn't believe this was the same man I had just slept with.

Delphi nodded briskly as he led the way out of his trailer and back toward his car.

The ride back to campus was quiet as we were both lost in our thoughts. Silent tears continued to stream down my face as I wrapped my arms around my torso to try to ward off the chill of disappointment and anguish. When Delphi pulled up in front of my dorm, I reached over to open my door, not waiting for him to walk over. He sat and silently looked at me, a sad pained expression on his face. Some other emotion I couldn't name was there, too, but I wouldn't take the time to figure it out. I had to let him and the dream of us together go once and for all.

"I'll see you around campus," I said softly before getting out of the car. I couldn't bear to get anything else out. I closed the door and hurried up to my room.

As I opened my room door, I breathed a sigh of relief when I saw that Terri was still out. I hurriedly got out of my clothes and went into the bathroom to take a shower. As the warm water caressed my skin, I began to sing in-between sobbing breaths the words to Boys II Men's "End of the Road." I tried to lose myself in the melody and lyrics so I could give voice to the pain that was ripping me apart.

After bathing I slipped into a t-shirt and a pair of basic black undies. I turned the light off and slid into my sheets, pulling my comforter tightly around me. The blackness of sleep blissfully came, sweeping me into a land where I heard and felt nothing that could further tear my grieving heart apart.

Chapter Six

The Choice
Senior Year

Delphi

"Man, you have got to let that go," Levi whispered to me as we sat under our fraternity tree on the YARD. It was a beautiful mild day and we were enjoying the sunshine.

"Yea, Delphi. You have to move on. You can have your pick of any of these hunnies out here. Hell, you could get Tanya back if you were really that desperate. I hate to see you wasting all your energy on somebody who obviously couldn't give two shits about you." Nate shuddered dramatically. "It's like it's a man-law violation."

I glanced at Nate and rolled my eyes. Nate and I decided to hang out with Levi on the YARD since we were finished with classes before heading back to our trailer for the weekend. It was a warm spring Friday afternoon in April, and finals were just around the corner. We were now in our final semester of our senior year at NSU; and soon after, Asha would be gone for good. I'd have no way to keep up with her or to make excuses to try and see her everyday.

Last year after homecoming was rough. Asha didn't speak to me for a couple of months after our fallout. Finally, after Terri physically dragged her to our table one day in the Café, Asha slowly began to acknowledge my presence. By acknowledge I mean she gave me one or two syllable words to show she saw me. Over time she began to open up to me a little more, but she still held herself apart from me. It drove me crazy, but I didn't know how to break through to her. I still loved her. I was suffocating without her and I didn't know how to get air.

I also noticed she clung to Ramon a little harder whenever she saw me pass her in halls or outside during school events. It was like she was using him as a shield against me. Ramon, the prick, took full advantage of her distance from me by draping himself over her every chance he got.

"I can't tolerate Tanya anymore," I said absently as my eyes locked on Asha as she approached the Café. "Tanya has always made my ass hurt. I only put up with her to train for D/s. She got upset every time we played because I wouldn't fuck her, and she finally broke it off with me. Not that I cared. I am *not* trying to entertain that type of headache."

Asha was walking to the Café slowly with her head hanging low and her arms crossed in front of her chest. She looked like she was in pain. I wondered what or who had made her upset.

"Yeah well, all I'm saying is that you have other options my friend," Nate said as he watched a group of freshman girls walk past our tree. "Crabs," he murmured, "Fresh meat." He quickly jumped up to greet the pack. He took a deep bow and the girls began giggling as he started shooting his game of one-liners.

"Nate's right, Delphi," Levi said. "You have to try and let Asha go. She's my friend, too, but she's going through so much right now that I don't think she can handle any more emotional drama."

That caught my attention. "What's she going through?" I turned my head to pierce my eyes at Levi. I knew Levi and Asha were still friends; but he was my boy too. He was supposed to be looking out for me as well.

Levi shrugged his shoulder. "It's her story to tell. Just don't push her, man. She won't be able to handle it right now. Even submissives have their breaking point. I don't know if she's reached hers yet, but I guarantee you if you don't back off, you will end up being her point of contention instead of her saving grace."

Frustration welled inside me. "Fuck this!" I jumped up as I saw Asha entering the building. I started walking toward the Café in quick steps, trying to catch up with her.

"Hey!" I heard Nate call out to me. "Where are you going?"

"I'll be back." I tossed over my shoulder.

I quickly reached the glass doors and headed inside. I looked around the bench seats and finally spotted Asha bent over her food tray, swirling a fork around in a lumpy batch of mashed potatoes. Her shoulders were hunched over and her hair was hanging low, covering her face.

I walked and sat down across from her. She didn't even notice me sitting down. "Asha," I called quietly. Would she even talk to me?

She quickly lifted her head at the sound of her name. When she saw me, some of those same emotions swept over her face that I'd saw that first day of class: sadness, gratefulness, lust, apprehension, and finally her patented shield of indifference. But this time, they were all contained behind a pair of red, swollen eyes.

"Delphi," she said, acknowledging me. Well, at least she said my name. Usually I just got nods or nothing at all.

"What's going on sweetie? Why are you so sad? Is there anything I can do to help?" I asked tentatively. I knew she probably didn't want or need my help, but I had to offer anyway.

Asha took a deep breath and straightened her posture, causing her round breasts to push tightly against the t-shirt she sported. I felt my dick stir at the thought of those dark nipples hardening under my tongue. I shook it off. I needed to focus on her mind right now, not her body.

"I'm fine, Delphi. I'll be fine. Don't worry about it," she responded politely. She stared at me for a moment, as if making some sort of decision before she spoke again. She pasted a fake smile on her lips. "Graduation's just around the corner. I know you're excited about getting into Harvard Law with Levi. Congratulations."

I was startled. Those were the most words she's spoken to me in over a year. "Thanks." I felt myself blush for some reason at her compliment. Truth be told, I didn't even know she knew I had applied. Hmmm, maybe she's been keeping tabs on me? Hope started to blossom in my chest at the possibility that she might still care.

"What are your plans after graduation?" I had to stop myself from mentioning Austin. I didn't want to bring up any past hurt feelings between us.

80

Asha lowered her posture again and started swirling her fork back around in her mashed potatoes. I waited for her to answer, but it didn't seem as if she wanted to.

"Asha?" I nudged. I didn't think I'd asked a hard question, did I?

"Austin and I will be moving to Texas with Ramon. He's landed a job as a junior actuary for this Fortune 500 company when he finishes his degree."

All of my breath left me at once. "Texas?" I managed to get out. "Why are you going with him after graduation? I thought you were going to apply to graduate school in Chicago when you've finished here?"

She looked at me sadly. "I was," she said slowly. "But things changed. People change." She looked down at her plate. "I have to do what's right for my kids."

"Kids?" I asked, even more confused. "It's just Austin. Ramon has kids?"

"He does now," she answered quietly, a look of pain crossing her features.

I sat for a moment as I tried to interpret her facial expressions. Realization suddenly dawned on me as my jaw dropped. Stunned, I felt my stomach drop. "You're pregnant?" I asked disbelievingly.

"Yes."

Time stood still as we both stared at each other. Her eyes filled with tears and she bit her bottom lip to keep it from trembling. Finally, she broke eye contact with me. She stood up and began cleaning her plate of untouched food with shaky hands. She walked over to the trash area, dumped the uneaten food in the can, and placed her tray in the bin. She then walked back to me. I sat there, my eyes following her movements as I struggled to let her confirmation penetrate my brain.

"I know you've never cared for Ramon," she said as another pained expression crossed her features while she gripped her stomach. After a few moments, it looked like she was able to compose herself enough to mask whatever it was she was hiding. "But I believe this is for the best. Austin can have a chance for a real family, and this baby will get to know his father. I have to give this baby a chance." She started to reach over to touch my shoulder, but let her hand fall to her side.

"I still care about you Delphi." I heard Asha murmur through the ringing in my ears. "I always have. But I have to think of my kids. I have to try." With that, she quickly turned and hurried out of the cafeteria.

I'm not sure how much time passed as I sat there in stunned silence. I felt a hand close around my shoulder and I looked up in a daze. Nate and Levi came and sat down across from me. Levi wore a sympathetic look on his face while Nate wore a look of indifference.

"She told you," Levi said softly.

"Yea."

"Fuck her man," Nate scoffed. "It's obvious she didn't give a shit about you. Move the hell on. No telling how many other guys she's been leading around by the tip of her clit."

I reached across the table and snatched Nate up by his shirt, fisting it tightly in my hand.

"Say another fucking word about her, and I swear I will leave your lifeless body on the Trace for Port Gibson's finest to find you." I snarled as I released him. Nate tumbled back into his seat, looking flustered.

"Hey, no disrespect. I'm just saying," Nate stammered, holding his hands open in the air as if trying to ward me off. "No woman should be worth this much angst, man. You and Levi will be going out East soon, and you don't need to have any ties holding you down. You'll have enough to worry about trying to get through law school."

Levi shook his head at Nate, and then turned to me. "Despite the fact that Nate is an idiot, he does make a valid point. You've got to stop running after her and start living man."

I was sick of everyone telling me how I should feel. I slammed my palms on the table. "Yea, the same way you've stopped running from Terri. I know for a fact that you got into the University of Texas School of Law just like Terri got into their MBA program," I sneered. "Yet who's the one running way across the country cause he's too much of a pussy to admit he cares about the girl?" Nobody was immune from my rage right now. My hurt needed a victim.

Levi's eyes glazed over as he stood up. "Hey, just trying to help out." He bit out. "Asha's my friend just like you. I'd hoped she would eventually see the light; but since that didn't happen, I have to lay my bets with you. You can either wallow around like a hurt puppy or man up and move on with your life." With that he turned and left.

"I'll see you outside whenever you're ready to head back to the trailer," murmured Nate and he quickly got up to leave Levi behind.

I slumped down in my seat. I groaned from the ache in my chest and placed my head in my hands. Maybe it was time for me to let go, I thought. I never wanted her to have to make a choice between her kids or me. But I knew that if I pushed her, in her mind I would be doing exactly that.

I thought about that day last year after homecoming. Everything had been perfect then. I almost had all of her, but my past came crashing down too soon on me. I wasn't prepared to answer her questions yet.

Now it seemed like it was too late.

∧∧∧

I looked behind me at the sea of graduation caps until I found her. Asha sat near the back looking flawless in her gown. As if she could feel my gaze, she turned her head and stared back at me. Eventually she gave me a little smile and nodded her head. I turned back around in my seat, not wanting her to see how much I still ached for her.

"And now, introducing the graduating class of 1994 here at Natchez State University!" announced Dr. Kennedy. He and Dr. Wilson were on stage with the rest of NSU's professors and grad assistants to distribute the degrees to the students. Master B was also there as an honoree, being one of NSU's largest alumni contributors over the years. "As I read your name, please make your way to the podium to receive your degree."

"Jaymes Allen." I heard my name called. I stood to make my way up the stairs to the stage where the professors were waiting. I greeted

Dr. Kennedy first as he shook my hand. "Congratulations, son," he said as he handed me my degree.

"Thanks," I said as I moved on to shake hands with Dr. Wilson. Finally, I reached Master B.

"Delphi," he said, clasping my hand in a strong grip. "You should feel proud, son. Remember that everything is done for a reason. Don't be discouraged if you have to travel on the path you wouldn't have necessarily chosen to take. Just know that your eventual destination is well worth any bumps you may have along the way." He looked over my shoulder into the crowd of graduates. I knew he was looking and referring to Asha.

"Thank you sir," I said and walk down the stairs. I looked out and noticed Asha looking at me with a wistful expression on her face. When she realized I could see her, she immediately dropped her gaze. I walked back to my seat and sat down.

Dr. Kennedy continued to move through names and eventually called Asha. I stared straight ahead. I saw her in my peripheral vision as she walked past me to get to the stairs. She climbed the steps and walked over to Dr. Kennedy to receive her degree.

All other thoughts fled my mind as I drank in the sight of her. My chest expanded as I thought about all that she had accomplished over the years. Despite the many obstacles thrown her way, she was still able to graduate on time and with honors. I was so proud of her.

She made her way down to Master B. He leaned over and whispered something in her ear, which caused her to drop her head. Master B took his index finger and lifted her chin up. He said a few more words to her. I then saw her straighten her posture, holding her head a little higher. She smiled at him and then made her way down the stairs. She looked over at me with a teary expression as she walked toward my row. She then quickly wiped her eyes and gave me another small smile as she continued to walk by.

I let out the breath I didn't realize I was holding as I felt my hands shake. I gripped my palms together to try and get control. The rest of the ceremony went by in a blur.

Suddenly I was jarred from my thoughts as I heard Dr. Kennedy say, "Congratulations again to the Class of 1994!" Hooping, hollering and shrieks of laughter went up all around me. I stood up a little panic driven and turned around, looking for Asha. I had to say goodbye one last time.

"Junior! Junior! Over here!" I turned and saw my mother rushing toward me with open arms. I bent down and squeezed her small frame. "Thanks, mom," I said.

"We are so proud of you son!" bellowed my father, walking up behind her. He patted me on the back. "Very proud, indeed."

"Thanks Dad," I said. I glanced over my shoulder into the crowd of students that now swarmed the aisles. Parents hugged and greeted their students everywhere, blocking my view of Asha. I turned back to my own parents and saw Master B walking up to us.

"You must be Delphi's parents. Hello, I'm Bryce Blackburn. So glad to finally meet you both," Master B offered, extending his hand to my father.

"You as well," my father greeted, shaking his hand enthusiastically as my mother nodded her head. "I understand you've been a great influence over Junior during his time here. I'd love to hear how his progress has been coming along." He looked pointedly at Master B.

My parents have been in the D/s lifestyle since before I was born. I knew my dad was curious about Master B's training. Every summer he tried to grill me on what Master B went over during the school year. I finally let him know that I was fine and he didn't need to pester me with details. My mom would often try to play referee between us when I got so frustrated I felt like I would blow. She always found ways to subtly suggest to dad that he needed to leave me alone. She topped from the bottom so smoothly I often hinted she should try and patent her technique. She then would laugh at me and ask what I talking while she found ways to redirect dad's attention.

Right now dad's attention was solely on Master B. He raised one eyebrow and waited for Master B's responses. Since I had grown accustomed to interpreting my father's looks over the years, I knew what he was saying. The look he was giving now said, 'Tell me what I want to know right now.'

Master B wasn't moved. Instead he smiled ruefully as he nodded his head toward my father. "I'd love to go over his progress with you. I also have some progress of my own that I'd like to share as well." Master B paused, looking around. "I notice Ms. Felicia is not with you."

"No, she couldn't make it," mom offered. "She and the twins decided they would wait until we brought Junior home to celebrate. They wanted to stay behind so they could have the time to organize a huge graduation slash welcome home party."

I so didn't have time for this conversation.

"Dad, Mom, if you'll excuse me. I'll be right back." I looked back again to see if I could find Asha. I found what appeared to be the back of her head and moved in that direction.

"Oh, ok son. Well, hurry back. We have reservations at Deb's tonight," mom called after me, referring to the swanky restaurant in Jackson as I rushed away. I pushed past other students, throwing out "excuse me's" along the way, until I finally found Asha. I then abruptly stopped in my tracks.

Asha was standing next to a shorter, older version of herself, which I quickly concluded was her mother. She had short curly dark brown hair, streaked with grey, and a weathered, tight smile. She would be an attractive woman if not for the harsh frown lines marring her face. The pearls she clasped around her neck seemed too tight along with the short heels she wore. Her dress was stretched across an ample bosom and she held her purse in a firm grip. She definitely gave off an intimidating vibe.

But that's not what stopped me.

Asha was holding a little boy, who looked about 5 years old. He had on dark blue jeans and a red polo shirt with a Chicago basketball cap pulled low on his head. He was grinning from ear to ear and patting his mother's face with his stubby hands. Asha leaned over to nuzzle her cheek against the little boy's face, causing him to break out in a fit of

86

laughter. He had his mother's hazel, Asian-shaped eyes and full lips. I felt my heart break at that moment. I realized in that instance I wanted this little boy as much as I wanted his mother, and felt sick that I couldn't have either.

Asha must have felt a presence behind her because she then turned and saw me. A look of surprise displayed across her face as we stared at each other. The sound of a throat clearing broke the hypnotic spell we were both under.

"Hello, young man. And who are you?" I heard faintly from the buzzing in my ears.

I shook my head and tried to clear my thoughts. "Hello, Ms. St. Claire. My name is Jaymes Allen. I'm a friend of Asha's." I extended my hand to her and she shook it warily.

"Delphi! It's Delphi Mom!" The little boy shouted as he tried to lunge from his mother's grip. Asha put the squirming child on the ground and he ran over to where I stood. I bent my knees and lowered myself so I could try to be within the same height range. However even bending, I still towered over the little boy.

"Hello, Austin. I'm glad to finally meet you," I said, giving him a little wink. Austin grinned at me shyly and clasped his hands behind his back.

"Hi Delphi," Austin said bashfully.

"It's nice to meet a *friend* of Asha's," Ms. St. Claire said skeptically. I stood back up and looked down at her, ready for whatever critique she was going to throw my way. It didn't much matter now if she liked me or not. Asha had made her choice, so I wasn't trying to win favors with someone who I knew unceremoniously dumped guilt trips on Asha at every given opportunity.

I couldn't be disrespectful, though. My mom's home training had been too ingrained in me. I attempted to at least be polite.

"Yes, ma'am. Nice to meet you, too," I said.

"Mom," Asha said, rolling her eyes. "You know perfectly well who Delphi is. He's called the house numerous times over the past years to talk to Austin."

Ms. St. Claire didn't say anything. She just pressed her lips into a tight thin line. *No wonder Asha seemed so beat up at times,* I reflected. Does this woman have any softness at all? She seemed like she was all hard edges, all the time. I briefly wondered what events in her life could have made her that rigid.

"Delphi, did you know I'm having a baby sister?" Austin spoke up to me, grinning proudly.

I looked at Asha who then cast her eyes down. "No, I didn't know she was having a girl," I replied to Austin, still looking at his mother.

"Well, I don't know the sex yet, it's too early. Austin wants a sister because he said he's going to protect her when she gets older. He told me boys didn't need protection like girls did," Asha said indulgently, looking at Austin.

"Well, I don't know about that. Sometimes boys can hurt just as bad as girls can," I said regretfully.

Asha jerked her head back to me and let out a small breath.

"Asha, there you are." I heard behind me. I turned and saw Ramon walking toward us. He paused a moment when he saw me, then hurried his steps to quickly get to Asha's side.

"Delphi," he said curtly.

"Ramon." I responded just as briskly.

"Hi Ramon!" Austin said enthusiastically, waving at him as he walked back to his mother to grab her hand.

"Austin," Ramon nodded at the little boy, and then focused his attention back to me.

"Well, Asha, we better get going. The traffic on the Trace will be forever to get through. We still have to go shopping for your wedding dress before you leave tonight," Ms. St. Claire said haughtily.

"Wedding dress?" I stilled and looked at Asha. A nauseated look came over her face as I felt my stomach plummet.

"Ramon asked me to marry him this morning," she whispered, clutching her stomach with a shaky hand.

"And she said yes," Ramon offered, looking at me with narrowed eyes.

"I see," I said. My vision started to blur and my breath was coming out choppy. I was feeling lightheaded all of a sudden. "Well, congratulations Asha." I felt like I was going to throw up. I needed to get out of here.

She looked at me pleadingly with tears in her eyes, but I didn't have anything left to give her at that moment. She had chosen. I would respect her wishes unquestionably now. I nodded my head to her and I turned around to leave.

"Bye Delphi!" I heard Austin call out to me. I refused to turn around. I felt my eyes blur as I walked back into the crowd toward my parents.

There was nothing left for me after all.

Chapter Seven

A New Life
Tyler, TX

Asha

It was just after midnight when I finally picked myself up from the floor of our bedroom in our small two-bedroom apartment. I slowly walked toward the bathroom; the pains in right my side hindering any fast movement. I reached over and turned on the light, closing the door behind me. I tried to stay as quiet as possible so I wouldn't wake up Austin or Alanna.

Opening the mini side cabinet behind the bathroom door, I picked up a small washcloth and ran it under the cold water of the tap. Gently, I placed the cool towel against my swollen cheek and mouth, wincing at the brief moment of contact. Taking a deep breath, I lifted my head to stare at my reflection in the mirror.

The woman staring back at me wasn't someone I recognized anymore. Her once silky, healthy brown hair now lay limply against her cheek. Her eyes were baggy and swollen from lack of sleep and hours and hours of crying. Her healthy skin tone now held darkened bruises and discoloration. She'd also lost at least 20 much-needed pounds from skipping too many meals.

Five years had passed since I graduated from NSU. Five years had passed since I held out hope that Austin could have someone he could look up to and emulate. Five years had passed since I felt the love of a man instead of his scorn and abuse. Five years since I felt like I wasn't alone in the world. Five years...

I shook my head, took a deep breath, and turned the light back off. I decided to try and lay down for a bit before I needed to get up in a few hours to get the kids ready for school. I opened the door and walked back toward my room. Crawling between the sheets, I briefly wondered where Ramon went tonight after giving me his little love gift for my face. I sighed. Not that it mattered. He usually didn't come home for a couple days at a time during the week anyway. Quite frankly I cherished that time he was gone because there was peace in the house. The kids seemed happier. I was happier.

I pulled a pillow closer to me as I closed my eyes and let my mind drift to the imaginary happy place I'd created to try and calm my nerves. It was in that happy place where his beautifully trimmed beard and blue-green eyes caressed my face as he kissed me sweetly on my lips. That place where he held me in his arms as I hummed a song specifically made for him. A place where he still loved me...

∧∧∧

Sounds of the alarm ringing woke me from my twilight rest. I reached over and hit the off button, and every nerve and muscle in my body protesting from the abuse of last night. I briefly glanced over at the empty spot next to me on the bed before pulling myself up and sliding into my house slippers. Reaching over to grab my robe, I pulled it around my shoulders and took a brief glance in the vanity mirror at my face.

At least some of the swelling has gone down, I told myself. Hopefully it will be enough that Austin won't notice. I was pretty sure Alanna wouldn't be able to tell. Her main priority would be whether or not the television station was tuned to Bananas in Pajamas so she could watch it during her morning oatmeal.

I gathered my remaining strength and walked confidently in the kid's room. Austin was sprawled across the top half of the bunk bed set, his Spiderman pajamas rumpled and half off his body. Alanna was curled in a little ball in the lower bunk, her thumb sitting halfway in her mouth while a small drop of drool slid down her cheek. My heart melted at the sight of them. God, I loved my kids. I would do anything for them. *I AM doing everything with them in mind,* I reminded myself. I was even continuing to put up with the jackass so they could have a home with both a mother and a father. I couldn't let them grow up wishing they had the love of a father like I did...

I bent down to lightly shake Alanna. "Wake up sweetie," I called to her. "Rise and shine." Alanna took her thumb out of her mouth and rolled over for a long stretch. I then reached up to pat Austin's cheek. "Wake up Momma's little man. Breakfast will be on the table in 20 minutes. Up and at 'em."

That was all Austin needed to hear as he jumped from the top and hit the floor--running for the bathroom. I smiled as I bent down to pick Alanna up to help her get dressed. Whenever food was mentioned, he was the first one in line. That kid ate like he had a tapeworm.

After finishing getting Alanna ready, making sure her teeth were brushed and hair combed, I went about putting on my own work clothes for the day. I walked into the small kitchen to fix the kids their oatmeal along with my regular bowl of cold cereal.

"Okay, name this movie line, "Austin started. "He... is the Chosen One. He... will bring balance... Train him." Austin spread his arms wide and tried to roughen his pre-teen voice as if to emphasize the greatness of the phrase.

I pretended to think long and hard. "Umm, I'm not sure. It is the Matrix?"

"No!" he said exasperatedly, rolling his eyes and throwing his hands in the air. "Star Wars the Phantom Menace!"

Alanna giggled as she kept her eyes glued on the singing and dancing bananas on television.

"That's right! I forgot, love. Next time I'll do better. Now hurry up and eat your breakfast. I don't want you guys late for school." Austin and I always played "Guess Which Line is from What Movie," games during breakfast. This morning, however, my tiredness didn't stand a chance against his energy.

We finished eating and I cleaned up the kitchen while the kids gathered their books and backpacks. I double-checked to make sure Austin had his lunch money and homework assignments ready to go, and that Alanna had her favorite snack items tucked away in her backpack. I then stuffed a few items along with my wallet inside my purse. I herded the kids out the door towards our 1985 Hyundai in the apartment complex parking lot.

I placed the kids in their safety seats and started the car, driving the short couple of miles toward their school. One of the best things I've found in East Texas was its fabulous school system. The school my children attended was a far cry from anything I'd ever seen back in Chicago. It housed classes ranging from full-day kindergarten until their entire junior school years. Coupling that with the highest quality before and after daycare around, I was extremely grateful my kids had a good foundation for their education.

I pulled up in front of Edgars Elementary and double-parked so I could get Alanna out of her child restraint. Austin was already out of his seat and opening the door when I walked to the other side of the vehicle.

"Bye Mom!" he yelled, not bothering to look back as he ran toward the cafeteria doors where other fifth graders were already lining up. "Bye sweetie," I called after him, pulling Alanna out of the car. I then walked her over to where her teacher stood waiting.

"Hi, Ms. Nelson. Alanna's got her lunch today and I put some extra snacks in her bag just in case she gets hungry," I said. Alanna walked over to grasp her teacher's hand with her little fingers, while her right thumb still hung loosely in her mouth.

"Thank you, Mrs. Towers." She paused as she studied my face. "I don't mean to seem rude, but are you okay? You look a little out of it today."

I brushed off her concern. "I'm fine. Just need to get a little more rest. Having two young children can wear you out sometimes, you know what I mean?" I said, trying to make light of the fact I knew she could see my bruises, despite the makeup I tried to cover it with.

She didn't say anything for a moment. "Okay..." she said tentatively. "Well, we'll see Mr. Towers around 5p.m. at the center?"

"Sure thing." I bent down and gave Alanna a kiss. "Bye Momma's boo. I'll see you this evening." I ran my thumb down her cheek as she smiled at me through her thumb-filled mouth.

"Bye, Momma."

I got back in the car and drove home. Having only one car between the two of us, Ramon usually drove it to get to his job at the insurance company. Since the kid's school didn't have local transportation, I usually drove them every morning, and then brought the car back home so Ramon could take it to work. The kids would then stay in the afterschool program until Ramon got off work in the evening. Some mornings, like today, I wasn't sure if he would be back from whatever he was doing the night before in time to get the car. Somehow however, the car always managed to go missing around the same time he needed to leave.

Ramon told me I needed to work close to home in case the children needed me for anything. Since the only business even remotely close to our home was the local gas station, my claim to fame after securing a four-year degree was a job as a cashier at the Seven Eleven around the corner from our apartment. Ramon allowed me to keep $75 from that paycheck every other week to buy the kids' school supplies, clothes, groceries, or other toiletries they needed. Since often times I didn't have enough money to buy food for both myself and the kids, I would often skip meals so I could make sure they had something to fill their bellies.

Ramon also told me I needed to be home by 4 p.m. so I could have dinner on the table waiting for him no later than 5 p.m. each day. That was the latest he would tolerate his dinner being late. Anytime after that was subject to discipline.

I was late last night.

I pulled into the parking lot of our apartment and turned off the car. Walking in the front door, I breathed a sigh of relief as I realized Ramon hadn't made it home yet. I dropped the keys on the tray next to the door, and then walked back out to hike the trek to my job.

"Hey Ernie!" I called as I pushed open the doors to the store.

"Hey yourself. That backorder of cigarettes we ordered last week just came in. Come on back so we can do inventory."

I tossed my purse in the closet in the back room designated for employees only; then walked to the storage area to help the owner sort through the day's tasks.

Time seemed to drag as I counted each hour until my shift was up. Three thirty couldn't get here fast enough.

"Hey Asha, do you mind sticking around until 4p.m. today? Daryl called and said he was having car issues again. I called Mary to see if she could cover his shift and she said could, but she won't make it here until that time. Do you mind?" Ernie asked, peeking his head out of the office, the phone handle glued to his ear.

"Sure Ernie, no problem," I said, trying to mask my weariness. *It's just an extra 30 minutes,* I told myself. I should still be able to make it home on time to whip something up for dinner. I'd just micro-zap some ground beef and throw together a quick pasta dish.

Unfortunately, Mary didn't come rushing through the door until 4:50 p.m. "I'm so sorry Ernie! I tried to get here sooner, but my son had an episode, so I had to wait for my sister to come over so we could calm him down," she apologized. Mary's son was autistic, and she sometimes needed extra help in handling him if he had an attack.

That knowledge didn't quench my nerves, though. I was a wreck. I'd realized there's no way I'd be able to walk all the way home AND have dinner ready by 5p.m. Walking quickly to the employee closet to retrieve my purse, I felt my trepidation quickly building within me. I tossed goodbyes to Mary and Ernie and raced out of the door for the 30-minute hike home.

When I finally reached my apartment complex it was 5:15 p.m. I also saw our car in the parking lot, signaling the fact that Ramon was already home. I made my way to the front door and pulled out my purse to retrieve my house keys. SHIT! I'd left my house key still attached to the car keys when I dropped them in the tray earlier. Hesitantly, I knocked on the door.

"Momma's home! Momma's home!" I heard Alanna calling through the door. I hear her soft footsteps running toward the door.

"Hey sweetie," I said loud enough to make sure she heard me. "Can you go tell your father to open the door? I forgot my key." We taught her a long time ago never to open the door, no matter who it was, so I figured she was waiting for my instruction to tell her what to do.

"Okay, Mommy. I'll tell daddy right now." I heard her running away from the door to tell her father what I'd said. I leaned my forehead against the wooden doorframe as I tried to get my rampant breathing under control. My anxiety was at an all-time high.

A few moments later I heard heavier footsteps approach the other side of the door and stop. Nothing was said for a long moment, making me wonder if anybody was still there.

"Ramon?" I call tentatively. "Can you open the door? I left my key inside."

"You are late," Ramon called out in a low, monotone voice.

A cold wave of fear shot through me as I adjusted to his tone. When he spoke with no feeling like that, it always spelled trouble.

"My manager asked me to stay and cover the shift until a replacement could come," I responded timidly. "I didn't think I would be this late, I promise. Otherwise, I would have told him no."

"How do I know you weren't still at work? How do I know you aren't lying about meeting up with someone else for a quickie right before you came home?" He snarled from the other side of the door.

"I didn't, I swear." I laid my palm against the door. "Please. Just let me in." I pleaded.

"No, I don't think so."

"Whh...What?" I stammered.

"I don't think I'll let you in. You can stay out there and sleep with the stray dogs tonight." He laughed humorlessly. "Hell, tonight you can let your true bitch fly. You need to reflect on how important you believe this family really is to you."

"What are you talking about? This family is my life. It's all I have." I cried, tears welling in my eyes.

"Obviously it's not. I'll order the kids some pizza and let them know you decided stay out tonight."

"NO!" I shouted, panic now threatening to overtake me. "Let me in the house right now!" I start slamming my fists on the door. "LET ME IN!"

"Stop causing a scene!" he hissed.

I heard footsteps approach the door. "What's going on?" I heard Austin asking from the other side.

"Nothing, just some salesperson that won't take no for an answer. Go on back to your room and watch Alanna," Ramon answered sternly.

I stopped my shouting because I didn't want to frighten Austin. He couldn't know about the things that happened between Ramon and me. For all of Ramon's issues, he never took his anger out on or in front of the kids. I alone held his focus for abuse.

After a few moments, I heard Austin's lighter steps walk away from the door.

"See what you've done?" snarled Ramon. "Now, leave. The door to this home will be open to you tomorrow morning."

"WHAT!?!" I cried. "Please Ramon. Pleasseee! Where am I supposed to go until then?"

"Go back to whatever caused you to be late it the first place. I see last night didn't teach you anything. Let's see if this lesson will help you remember who's in charge." With that, I heard his footsteps move away from the door.

I braced my back against the door and slumped to the ground, my energy spent. It seemed like all my fight went out with Ramon's last words. I pulled my legs under me and put my head in my lap. Silent tears streamed down my face as I tried to think about where I could stay the night.

Ramon brought me to Texas a week after we graduated. I didn't have any family or friends to speak of in this town. He wouldn't allow me a cell phone so I couldn't call anyone for help even if I did. Everyone I knew here was through an acquaintance of Ramon's, outside of Mary and Ernie. I couldn't ask my boss; and Mary had enough to deal with. I lifted my head and realized the sun was starting to set, causing the crisp evening air to grow even cooler. I took a deep breath and pulled myself to my feet. I needed to find somewhere safe to sleep tonight.

I walked away from my building and turned down the stoned walkway that led to the forest preserve park on the other side of the complex. I looked around for some type of bench I could lay on when I spotted an old, weathered looking shed behind a garbage dumpster. I quickly walked over and tried pulling on the handle to see if it was locked. SUCCESS! I tugged on the rusted handle until the door finally creaked and gave way a few inches—just enough for me to squeeze in. I pushed through, slid inside and pulled the door closed behind me.

Darkness descended as the night air chilled me through the thin work shirt I wore. I leaned against the door and slid down to the floor, trying to get into a comfortable position for the night. I wrapped my arms around my legs to try and maintain as much body heat as I could. Still feeling cold, I stuffed my hands in the pocket of my jeans and felt the tip of my mini mp3 player I'd absently shoved in earlier that day as I took the kids to school. The player had been a late graduation gift from my mom a few years back. I pulled it out and placed the ear buds over my ears, leaned my head back and closed my eyes. Luther Vandross' "A *House is Not a Home*" wafted against my eardrums. I began to sing along to the melody while a river of tears fell down my cheeks.

Chapter Eight

Old Memories
Houston, TX

Delphi

The downtown view of Houston had always been a gorgeous sight to me. The sun was setting beautifully against the city's horizon, causing a gorgeous display of orange and brown color to dance across the evening sky. I glanced around the small empty office space with pride. This would soon be the headquarters of Allen & Blackburn LLC. Our dream was finally becoming a reality. Initially we'll start off renting this small area. Next we'll build our multi-level high-rise office structure, complete with our marquise as a beacon of light across the Houston horizon.

A knock on the door broke me away from my wishful thoughts. "Come in," I called, still gazing out of the window.

Levi strolled in wearing his infamous cocky smug.

"What are you doing?" he asked knowingly.

"I'm thinking about the future, man," I answered, not at all ashamed of being caught daydreaming.

"Yea, well let's take one step at a time. Our first client is all set to go. She'll be here next Wednesday. It's a domestic abuse case. Not really our specialty, but the girl is really desperate. That means we need to get our office setup and looking halfway decent before she gets here."

"I'm on it already. Dad already donated some of his old office furniture from one of his Philadelphia offices. It'll be here on Monday, along with some extra office equipment. We're all set up on that front."

"It was cool that your dad was willing to give us a break on this loan to get started," Levi said reflectively. "It made things so much smoother. By my projections we should be making a profit in less than a year's time, then we'll be able to start paying him back."

"Dad's not in a hurry to be paid back. He just wants us to be smart and stick with the business plan. He has confidence in our abilities." I reassured him.

Levi shook his head. "I just don't like to be indebted to anyone for too long. You know how I am."

I chuckled. "Yea, I know sometimes you just need to slow down and take time to appreciate what's right in front of you. Stay in the moment for once and appreciate what you have."

"I hear you, *Dad*." Levi said sarcastically as he shook his head. Anyway, I came in here to see if you wanted to go get some dinner. I'm starving."

"Sure. Let's go. My treat."

"Damn straight it is. Didn't I just tell you we wouldn't be profitable until next year? My kitchen is stocked with ramen noodles and peanut butter and jelly."

I laughed outright and shook my head. "Let's go, Blackburn."

We locked the door behind us and headed out to my car. We drove along the Katy Expressway toward the Good Co. Seafood Restaurant; one of our favorites spots to eat since we moved here a couple years ago. I glanced at Levi as I exited the freeway. He'd slumped down in the seat with his head thrown back against the headrest, lost in his thoughts.

Driving always allowed me time to let my thoughts drift and reflect too; although not always in the direction I wanted them to go. These past few years seemed to have flown by and now we were finally starting to live our dream. The time spent at Harvard showed me how to stay focused. Passing the Texas BLE showed me how to perfect my self-discipline techniques, not to discount any of Master B's training. And being ultimately rejected by Asha showed me I never needed to give my heart away to another female again. I should be content with going through scenes and get fulfillment that way. But I could never open my heart again like that to another woman.

I sighed heavily as I turned into the restaurant's parking lot and cut off the engine. *Who was I kidding,* I thought to myself. My heart was and will always belong to one woman. The one woman whose jazziness snatched my attention on that first day of Crabology and whose submission I still craved to dominate. She would never leave my heart no matter how hard I tried. Sometimes late at night when I was alone in my apartment, and my dick was throbbing and aching for release; I could still hear her moans and gasps, calling me by the one name I craved to finally hear on her tongue...

"Come on, man. Let's go inside," Levi said, jumping out of the car. I shook my head free from my wayward thoughts and followed him inside.

We were seated pretty quickly for a Friday night. After placing our orders, Levi leaned back in his seat and looked intently in my direction.

"So, what are your plans this evening?" he asked, raising one eyebrow.

"Not sure yet," I answered, not really wanting to get into it. Levi had been pushing me to go to a local club he'd recently visited, but I was just not in the mood.

"It's been nine years, man," Levi said softly. "Don't you think it's time to let it go and move on? I mean Asha not only kicked you to the curb, but her friendship with me, too. I've never told you this, but a few months after she got married, I was still trying to call her to see how she was doing. At first I'd always ended up getting her voicemail. Eventually her line just came up disconnected altogether. It pissed me off when I heard how it went down after graduation. And then when she told me what that idiot did when they got married I was even more irritated."

"What are you talking about?" I asked, my ire immediately rising. "And why are you just now telling me about this?" I demanded.

"I never told you..," he started calmly, after accurately realizing his close approximation for an ass beating. "...because you had enough on your plate with her leaving."

I felt my jaw twitch and my eyes start to bug out of my head as I grabbed the table to stop myself from choking Levi. I tried to take a breath to calm myself.

Levi continued on, completely ignoring my obvious frustration. "Anyway, she called me the day after they got married, crying on the phone and shit. Ramon didn't want a big ceremony so he convinced her it would be a good idea to elope so they could get their family started right away. She told me Ramon didn't even respect the day enough to at least take the damn day off from work for them to get hitched. The bastard just came home on his lunch break, took her to the courthouse, did their thing, and then dropped her back home as if they were just running a fucking errand. What kind of moron does that? And it pissed me off even more because she LET him do that, and she kept refusing to listen to anything I had to say. I tried to convince her the entire setup was wrong, but it seemed like the harder I pushed, the more she wasn't trying to hear it. Like I said, eventually she just stopped all communication; but after a while, I figured it was ultimately her choice and her decision." Levi lowered his voice solemnly. "You have to let it go, too."

"I have!" I spit back, more forcefully than I'd intended, startling a couple from the next table. I was seething. I *knew* pushing her would only make her cling to Ramon even harder. That beautiful, stubborn, pig-headed woman. Now it seemed that I'd been right all along.

"Sure you have," Levi replied with that same irritating tone. "When was the last time you were involved with someone? I mean really involved, other than a quick hit?"

"That's all I have time for," I answered defensively, but feeling my fight slowly leaving with each labored breath.

"Bullshit. That's all the time you're willing to give it." His eyes grew serious. "I'm concerned about you, man."

"Well, don't be. I'm fine," I said, more in an effort to convince myself than trying to convince him.

He shrugged his shoulders. "Okay, if you say so," he said unconvincingly.

Our conversation ended for a moment as our waitress came back with our meal. After setting our dishes down and refilling our drinks, she left us to dig into our food. We ate with gusto, feeling the effects of skipping lunch earlier in the day.

Levi finally put his fork down, after having inhaled half of his shrimp etouffee.

"The NSU reunion is coming up next year," he started. "You planning on going?"

"I hadn't thought about it." I lied. Truth was it was all I could think about. I tortured myself daily with thoughts of whether or not Asha would come and if I'd get a chance to see her again. I hadn't heard anything from her since graduation, and I felt hungry for any information I could find about her.

"Well, you should consider it. It'll be 10 years since we've seen our old stomping grounds. It'll be nice to go back and catch up. I know dad would be thrilled if I could drag you back with me," Levi said wryly. "Sometimes I think he'll be happier to see you than me."

"That's only because he gets frustrated with you because you keep dodging his questions about trying to settle down with one girl." I looked at him, a judging tone tinting my voice. "Much like you're trying to do with me right now."

Levi rolled his eyes. "The difference here..." he said, wagging his finger between the two of us "...is that I don't believe there is just one woman out there who could possibly give me everything I require. That's why I spread my love around to make sure all of my needs are met. In fact, I consider it a service to the community by offering my skills to those in need." He wagged his eyebrows up and down while I made a barfing gesture.

"You, on the other hand, have been trapped in a self-made purgatory over one female for far too long. It is my job as your long-time friend to try and give you the life preserver you desperately need. Come to the club with me tonight."

"Fine," I said exasperatedly, throwing up my hands in defeat. I just wanted him to shut up.

"And if you happen to find that preserver in a well-fitted hour glass package with a set of double-D breasts along the way, I'll be more than happy to take her off your hands for you." He grinned at me.

^ ^ ^

We pulled up to a small, red-bricked two-story building right outside of Cypress just before midnight. The parking lot was full and a line to get in was already forming outside the club's entrance. The bass from the music permeated through the walls into the night air.

"It looks like it's already jumping in here. Let's go," Levi said.

We walked up to the door of "Escapades" where a large, muscled bouncer stood waiting.

"What's up, Levi. Back for round two?" the burly man snarled as he cracked his knuckles together.

"Yeah, you wish. Tell Nate I brought Delphi here." The man nodded his head and disappeared inside.

My head snapped around to stare at Levi.

"Nate?" I asked. "What the hell is he doing here?"

"Ahh, he owns this club, clueless. You would know that if you pulled your head from your ass every now and then and got out more. Nate opened this spot a few months ago. He won some lawsuit against the Chicago Police Department after they beat his ass for smarting off. CPD ended up throwing his ass in jail for a couple years on some trumped up charges. His lawyer found out the beating was actually caught on tape and submitted it for his appeal."

The bouncer came back to the door, waving at us to go ahead inside.

"Nate got the case overturned and sued the shit out of the department," Levi shouted as I followed him through the club. "His settlement was large man, and he came up. He called me about a year ago to let me know he was in town and looking to get into some property. We've kept tabs off and on over the past few months. He asked me not to tell you he was in town until he was finally on his feet. He bought this

104

spot from the previous owner who retired, and he's turned it into a real money maker."

The Bose speakers blasted DJ Quick lyrics throughout the club, making it extremely difficult to hear, let alone hold a conversation. I nudged my way through the swarm of people, trying to keep up with Levi as he searched for Nate. A couple of times I felt somebody grab my ass as I pushed my way through the crowd and found myself having to push a couple of groping hands off me. I used my height to my advantage and looked over the top of people's heads in search of Levi, finally spotting him standing next to someone with his back turned.

"Man, it's packed in here," I said, walking up to the two men. The man in the suit turned around and I had to take a step back.

Nate ditched his college attire of t-shirts and ratty jeans for a well-fitted suit and power tie. His Ferragamo loafers shined against the tiled floor and his gold cufflinks glimmered against his light brown skin. The black silk shirt he wore under the suit lay open at the neck, hinting at a strong physique.

"It's about damn time you finally brought your ass here! I was beginning to think you were just avoiding me." Nate grinned as he walked up to me. We gave each other a brief hug before I stepped back to take another assessment.

I grinned widely at my friend. "My mouth is like wide open! Look at you! You clean up nice, man! I am so proud of you! And this place is awesome!"

"Thanks, Delphi. It came with a cost, though. Levi filled you in?" Nate said, glancing around at the patrons before turning his gaze back to me.

"Yeah, he was just telling me about it and I'm sorta pissed at you right now. Why didn't you let me know sooner what was going on and let me know you were here in town?" I said accusingly as I gave him a mock punch in his shoulder. "And why didn't you tell us about all the shit that happened with CPD?

"That's something I've been trying to get answered for a while too," Levi said frowning at Nate. "We would have been there to support you, for real."

A gorgeous caramel-skinned waitress sporting a wild mane of dark, curly textured hair walked up to Nate at that moment to hand him a drink. She was obviously uncomfortable in the snug, all black satin mini-skirt and deep v-neck lace top she wore. The outfit exposed more than an ample view of her breasts as she nervously tugged at the hemline with her free hand. Nate accepted the drink from her shaky fingers. She nodded her head slightly and turned away to quickly walk back to the bar. Nate's eyes followed her the entire way, forgetting for a moment that we were standing there. I cleared my throat noisily.

Nate broke his stare and turned back to Levi and me. "At first I was too embarrassed to let anybody from the YARD know that I got sent up," Nate said, picking back up his earlier explanation. "Then, the anger set in and all I could focus on was getting my case through. Now, I'm good and can finally breathe; but I eventually had to leave Chicago. Suing and winning against CPD ain't exactly good for your future health, if you know what I mean."

"I can imagine," I said. "But damn Nate, we should have been one of the first people you called. Hell, you know we studied Criminal Law specifically for that purpose," I grumbled.

"See, that was exactly why I DIDN'T want to call you. You're my friend, not my lawyer. I didn't want you to guilt trip about the 'what if's' just in case it didn't turn out the way we wanted it to. My mouth got me in that situation, and I wanted my brain to get me out. Plus, your head wouldn't have been focused on the issue anyway. Look, it all turned out for the best. Tonight, let's just celebrate the three of us together again." He pointed to a secluded seating area toward the back of the club. "Now c'mon and throw back a couple of Hennessey's with me."

I cringed a little because I knew he was referring to Asha. I quickly pushed thoughts of her from my mind as I followed him and Levi toward the VIP area. This was a time to celebrate, not dwell on the past.

Yep, getting lost in some Hennessey sounded perfect right about now.

Chapter Nine

Class Reunion
Lorman, MS

Delphi

"Man, it feels good to be back," said Levi as he threw his arms back against the bleacher seats to take in the crowds around him. The Sounds of Fire marching band just finished their halftime performance at this year's homecoming football game and was now headed off the field. NSU was up 12 to 4 over Meridian College. The stadium was filled with old and new generations of NSU and MC students who were rocking and swaying in time to the band's rendition of Lakeside's "*Fantastic Voyage.*"

The campus and surrounding areas had really gone through dramatic upgrades since the last time I was here. The nearby town of Port Gibson had now manifested into a small metropolitan community, having not only built a McDonald's, but also a local Wal-Mart, several nationally recognized hotel and restaurant chains, and a couple of strip malls within a sort driving distance from the school. Alumni now could enjoy a comfortable hotel stay while still being close enough to partake in the campus reunion festivities.

"I promised dad we'd stop by before the alumni picnic later on tonight. Come on, let's head out of here before the crowd gets too bad. I'm in the mood for some good old-fashioned gumbo and I know dad hooked it up," Levi said, getting up and starting down the bleachers.

I followed him out of the stadium to the full parking lot toward his jeep. We'd actually driven to Mississippi from Texas because Levi wanted to let the drive 'relax his nerves'. I was in total agreement. We'd just finished defending a young woman in a high-profile murder case in which she'd been accused of murdering both her father and older brother.

Over the course of the trial it was later revealed that the young girl had actually been defending herself against years of sexual and physical abuse against both relatives. She was essentially acquitted with the assistance of Levi's expert knowledge of judicial law and my courtroom examination skills. Unfortunately the trial took a toll on both of us, so we were looking forward to the reunion as a vacation escape.

Nate decided not to come because he was in process of finalizing the renovations on the building and casino expansion on his club. He'd said he was going to be the Donald Trump of nightclubs and that required his full attention.

I sat back and relaxed as Levi drove the miles along the Trace toward Pearl River. Looking out of the open window at the swaying magnolia trees in the October afternoon, my thoughts drifted to that one incredible night Asha and I rode together along these same roads.

"Do you think a lot of people from our class will show up at the picnic?" I asked casually. I didn't want to give away the fact I was secretly wishing and praying I'd get a glimpse of Asha.

"Who knows? I hadn't really thought about it. In any case, I heard she moved out West after graduation instead of going to Texas." Levi responded, tapping his thumb against the steering wheel in time with the music playing on the radio.

Confused, I turned to look at him. "Who are you talking about?"

"Terri. I heard she moved to California after we graduated to attend grad school out there. She went there instead to get her MBA."

A smile started to creep over my face. "Is that right? And how would you know that?"

"Dad mentioned it to me. He told me she went to live with her aunt to save on expenses." He frowned. "He wouldn't tell me what she's doing after that though, like it's some CIA secret."

I turned my head back around so he wouldn't catch the smirk I couldn't keep off my face. Apparently I wasn't the only one who was hoping for more than just a friendly reunion too.

We finally pulled up in front of Master B's home, tucked away in the deep back roads just off the highway. The Blackburn house was a quaint, country-style ranch home with a modest wrap-around porch with a small wooden white swing. Levi told me his dad installed the swing for his mom when they first got married so they could sit outside and watch sunsets together. Now it sat unmoved and still in the afternoon sun.

"LEVI! DELPHI! Just in time. Get over here and help me with this!" Master B called as he stirred the pot over the open fire pit sitting on the side of the house.

We hurried out of the jeep and ran over to help Master B lift and carry the large pot inside house toward the kitchen and onto the stove. When we reached the kitchen, we saw a familiar face we hadn't seen in years sitting at the table.

"Dr. Wilson! What are you doing here?" I said, walking over to the man to embrace him in a friendly hug. He stood and welcomed me, then turned and gave Levi a similar greeting.

"It's good to see you boys! You're looking good and apparently I hear doing well for yourself." He grinned and sat back down.

"Dad, I didn't know you knew Dr. Wilson!" Levi said, throwing questioning glances at his father.

"Of course I know him. He's a well-respected member of Finesse," Master B said cockily. "You don't have to know everything, boy. All those years you thought you were watching Delphi, I had Charles watching you."

Wait, did I hear that right? Feeling amused, I pulled out a chair at the table and sat down facing Dr. Wilson. "Your first name is Charles?" I asked, my lips tugging upward.

"Yes," Dr. Wilson said with an annoyed look on his face.

"Your name is Charlie Wilson?" I asked again, this time with a full-blown smile.

Dr. Wilson rolled his eyes. "Yes..." he said.

"As in Charlie who also sung with the group the GAP BAND, mister *Yearning for Your Love* Wilson?" Levi choked.

"Yes," Dr. Wilson said, looking even more irritated.

Levi and I looked at each other for a moment before we both burst out laughing.

110

"Laugh it up boys. You think I haven't been mocked about it before? I'll have you know I am older, better looking, can sing far better and am much smarter than that man. So in reality, he took his talent after me, not the other way around," Dr. Wilson huffed.

"Most definitely, Dr. Wilson," Levi managed to get out. "We can so see that."

Dr. Wilson rolled his eyes as Master B chuckled lightly, placing bowls and spoons on the table.

"Come on now, dig in," Master B announced.

"EXCELLENT!" Levi said. He grabbed a bowl and pushed his way over to the stove, with me right behind him. We found ourselves shoving each other out of the way to get to the food like we used to do in college. As we sat down and began eating, Dr. Wilson made his way to the stove to fill his bowl as well.

"You guys act like you haven't eaten in weeks. You don't have to pig out. Aren't you still going to the alumni picnic they're having tonight on the YARD? It'll be food there too." Master B asked as he stood to fill his bowl now that everyone had gotten his portion.

"You don't go to the picnic to eat, Dad. You go so you can drink and talk about how sad your classmates look after all these years. Then you brag about how much better you are than them," Levi said in between bites of the rich stew.

"Oh, I see," Master B replied. "Charlie, were we ever that arrogant when we were at NSU?"

"I wasn't, but you certainly were. I think that's the only reason Mechelle fell for you instead of me; you didn't give her any choice to say no. You just clubbed her over the head and yelled 'MINE' to the rest of us mortals."

Levi turned to look in shock at Dr. Wilson. "You knew my mother?" he asked.

"Knew her? She and I used to date until this lug over here stole her away from me," Dr. Wilson said jokily, pointing at Master B. "That's OK, though. It all turned out as it should have. Otherwise, I never would have met and married my Rita." He smiled warmly.

"Wait, and your wife's name is Rita Wilson?" I said. I bit my cheek to stop the smirk that threatened to spread.

"Yes, it is." Dr. Wilson looked at me with a piercing stare. I acknowledged his silent order that laughing at his wife's name was off limits. He then turned his attention to Levi.

"Your father didn't know what type of woman he wanted until he met Mechelle. At first she couldn't stand the ground Bryce walked on, but eventually she came around, and so did your father. He'd only been skating around his dominant side until Mechelle showed up. After one look at her, it was all over."

He turned back around to look at me. "It's always believed that a truly dominant male is never fully awakened until he meets his true mate. Much as when you first laid eyes on your Asha."

The smile that had been resting across my face fell sharply at his words. I shifted in my seat uncomfortably. "Why would you say something like that? And what do you know about me and Asha?"

"Delphi, I had to watch you two skirt around each other for a whole semester in my classroom. The sheer chemistry between the two of you was unmatched to anything I'd seen on that campus in a long time, except for..." he paused to glance at Levi, and then turned his attention back to me. "The mere fact that you allowed her to go off and marry that Ramon young man instead of demanding what was rightfully yours unfortunately also showed that you still had a way to go regarding your training."

I took a deep breath to control the anger starting to simmer. "I've stopped playing years ago. The only sex I have now is vanilla." And I hated it. Just thinking about the last encounter I had made me want to puke. I was so disinterested I couldn't even remember the girl's name afterwards. I treated her just like I did any normal bodily function. *What was her name again..,"* I thought to myself. *Lily, Nellie, Emily, something with a 'lee'.* I shook my head. It didn't really matter. I hadn't had an emotional attachment since...

"Asha was the one who left me, I didn't leave her. She's the one who distanced herself after our junior year," I said defensively, thinking of that night after homecoming.

"And you allowed her to do so." Dr. Wilson shot right back. "She needed your dominance and guidance; yet you allowed her to run free and unchecked for over a year. She fell right into the hands of the enemy. Getting pregnant was only a result of not being in control of anything in her life, and ultimately finding that control with the wrong person when YOU should have been the one to give it to her." He shook his head at me.

"When a person is dying of thirst, a glass full of battery acid will eventually sound appealing if presented in the right light. She was YOURS and you allowed her to call the shots when what she really needed, was in fact BEGGING for, was for you to say you will be there for her, regardless of any obstacle that may come up. Unconditionally. Indisputably. Unquestionably. Unwavering. She needed your honesty and control. She needed to know that you would take her in any condition that she came in, especially having already given birth to one child before. *She. Was. Yours!* That girl was honest in everything she did and said to you. Instead what you gave her was indecisiveness and mistrust, while you hid behind your fear of rejection and your issues surrounding that girl from your hometown. You let it rule you and it ultimately cost you in the end."

I reared back in my seat as his words felt like a slap in the face. The very truth of them shook me to the core. I knew he was right on all accounts. I dropped my head as I felt it swimming in confusion.

I sat there silent for a long moment. Everyone waited for me to allow his words penetrate. "What do I do now?" I said looking around the room, finally surrendering to the inevitable truth that I had a direct impact on how past events had turned out.

Dr. Wilson gave me a half smile while Master B nodded his head.

"You go after and claim what is rightfully yours," Master B replied.

∧∧∧

The YARD had completely filled with people young and old by the time Levi and I made it back to campus. Parked cars were littered down the road stretch toward campus. We parked about a mile from the school and walked toward the festivities. Tents and barbeque pits were set up all around the YARD as well as ice-filled coolers brimming with beer, juice, and water. Small children ran everywhere playing some sort of tag while the older adults looked on indulgently as they caught up with old friends. Music blared from the various speakers strategically posted throughout different areas. Everyone was laughing and appeared to be having a good time.

Levi and I walked over and each grabbed a beer from one of the ice chests. "Let's walk the YARD to see who's here that we know," he said. I followed him as we strolled around for a minute.

"DELPHI, my man! Look who finally decided to show up!" I turned around at the sound of my nickname and saw an old football team player and fellow fraternity brother approaching us.

"Kennedy! What's going on, man! Long time no see." I turned and gave the man a quick hug.

"I figured you'd be here with Levi of all people. Good to see you too, Levi!"

"Nice to see you too, Kennedy." Levi acknowledged, passing him a beer. "Whatcha been up to?"

"Got married and moved to Memphis a few years back. You guys remember my wife Jackie, don't you?" At that moment, his wife slowly walked up to us, rubbing her rounded pregnant belly and looping her other arm around Kennedy. Kennedy slid his arm protectively over her shoulder.

"Hey guys," she said breathlessly as if the journey to walk toward us spent all her energy. "It's good to see ya bof."

Recognition at her deep New Orleans accent hit me. "Your Asha's sorority sister, aren't you?" I asked.

"Ya, Asha was always da sweetie. I lost touch wit her ova da years, tho. I was hoping she'd show up today seeing as how it's been like a decade since we were together, ya erd? But I haven't seen her." Jackie turned and looked around the YARD. "After we graduated, errbody just kind of scattered, but we still come err year. Some years a lot of old classmates show up, and then it's years where we hardly know anybody."

Disappointment washed through me as I glanced over her shoulder. "Who else have you seen from our class?" I asked, still holding out a tiny bit of hope that Asha might show.

She turned back around to look at me. "Not too many to tell ya da truth. Maybe errbody is waiting for da 20 year reunion instead." Jackie chuckled. "Anyway, I'm glad ya two showed up."

"You know we couldn't miss free food and beer," Levi joked, tossing back his second beer and grabbing for his third. I tried to give him a warning expression, but he just ignored me. I sighed. *Looks like I'll be driving back to the hotel room tonight,* I thought observantly.

"I hear you. Man, we had some great laughs back in the day, didn't we? Remember that time we roughed up that one guy behind the athletic dorm cause he tried to grow a pair of balls and tell you to stay away from his woman?" Kenney laughed. "Then we showed him your balls were bigger and you could do whatever the hell you wanted to? Man, what was that guy's name anyway?"

"Ramon," I said, remembering the incident well. "She ended up marrying him, by the way."

"No shit? Really? I hadn't heard that," Kennedy said surprisingly. "Well, in any case, I don't get out as much as I used to now that I have all this..." he nodded his down at his wife. "So I intend to enjoy as many benefits NSU is willing to shove out this weekend."

Jackie nudged him with her elbow. "Watch it now. Dat sounded almost like a jab at me."

"Never, kitten," Kennedy whispered, lightly brushing his lips across her forehead. Levi and I looked at each other at the sound of the endearment, which was a common pet name for D/s play.

"Anyway," Jackie said. "I am glad ta see you guys, especially you, Delphi. I never did get da chance to apologize to ya and da timing never seemed right when we were in school."

I looked at her confused. "Why would you need to apologize to me?"

"For what happened dat weekend Tanya went home wit me during homecoming our junior year."

Still confused, I quickly searched my memory to decipher what she was talking about. All that came to mind was that night with Asha at my trailer.

"I honestly have no idea what you're talking about Jackie," I said.

Kennedy tightened his hold around his wife. "No need bringing up stuff that's already old and buried." He looked down at his wife and gave her a stern look. "Besides, I want to hear all about this law firm I heard you guys managed to open up. And did I hear right that Nate moved out there by you guys?"

Levi rolled his eyes. "And how did you hear that?" he asked, already knowing the answer.

"Your dad came down last year and told us. He was bragging about you guys and that court case you handled. Congrats for the work ya'll did, by the way. News coverage on that story reached all the way up to our city."

"Which is exactly why we are here; to relax and unwind and not think about drama filled cases," Levi muttered, reaching over to grab another beer. I knew part of his irritation had nothing to do with Kennedy bringing up the case, and more so to do with his disappointment that Terri didn't show up, just like I was about Asha.

Kennedy held his hands up. "Hey, no harm intended man. Trust and believe I know how important it is to just relax."

Jackie looked at me remorsefully, as if she wanted to expand further. I gave her a half smile to let her know whatever she wanted to get off her chest; she could lay it to rest. She smiled back at me fully now, her relief lighting up her whole face.

I was done wallowing in regret. From now on, my entire focus was on the right now and hopefully the right future.

And the right future had Asha by my side, no matter what.

116

Chapter Ten

A Revelation
Tyler, TX

Asha

"Bye Mom! We're leaving!" Austin yelled as he and Alanna headed out of the front door.

"Drive carefully!" I called out to them as I heard the front door close.

Austin was of driving age now, so Ramon thought it would be a great idea for him to have a car. That way Austin would always have a ride home after track and basketball practice, and he could also drive his sister to school in the morning.

Of course, I didn't need one since I no longer had a job. I hadn't been employed in over three years, every since I showed up at the 7-Eleven with those dark bruises on my eyes. Ernie had called the police that day and threatened all sorts of bodily harm to Ramon if I didn't come clean and let the police know what happened to me. I'd confessed to the police I'd gotten in a fight earlier that day; I just didn't tell them with whom. I couldn't risk Ramon going to jail because he was the only financial means I had to help me take care of the kids. My pride wouldn't allow me to apply for welfare, and I knew we wouldn't be able to survive on what I made at the gas station.

Later that same night I ended up going to the police station and recanting the entire fight story, opting instead for the typical "I fell" storyline. I'd been too scared of what Ramon would do if he ever found out. I was also too embarrassed to go back to the store after that. I couldn't risk even trying to get another job for fear the same thing would happen, so I just stayed at home. I'd also eventually lost touch with all my friends from NSU as well. Since I didn't have any family in Texas, no one could really say they missed my everyday presence. I felt truly alone at the time.

True to his character, Ramon continued with the physical and verbal abuse. He was always careful to never do anything to me when the kids were around. He would wait until they had gone to school or practice or whatever. I suspected it was because he never wanted to have a witness to his actions, even if it was a minor. So, still attempting to put on a good face for the kids, I kept up appearances like we had a loving and stable relationship. I just prayed the kids would never have to suffer any ill effects from our relationship.

It was only late at night, when my bedroom door was closed and Ramon had disappeared, that I ever let my anguish take control. *A few more years,* I would always coach myself. A few more years until Alanna reached and graduated from high school. Then I could make a break for it and leave. I already knew that if I threatened to leave before both of the kids had reached 18 years old, he would try to petition the courts for sole custody of Alanna. Ramon played dirty. I knew he would make up stories that I was a bad mother and would ultimately try to ban me from seeing her altogether. Since I didn't have the financial resources like he did, I knew he would more than likely win. I couldn't let the kids go through what I knew would be a nasty, long drawn-out divorce battle. However, once she turned 18, any attempt to try and take her away from me would be futile.

I just had to hold on for a few more years...

As I walked into the bathroom to start my shower, a little ping of excitement coursed through me. Ramon had already left for the day, so I was blessed with a rare sense of peace and tranquility. I'd heard on the radio yesterday that Indie.Arie's new cd was coming out today, and I decided to take a quick trip downtown to the record store to pick it up. I hummed contently as I lathered my washcloth and began to bathe.

Lately I hadn't been feeling as trapped inside the apartment as I usually did when everyone left for the day. One day a few months ago I'd decided I would no longer allow this apartment to feel like my jail cell.

Courage to venture out by myself and explore the area took hold of my latent sense of adventure and I loved it.

Now, I'd gotten used to the four-mile hike to the nearest bus stop to venture into the downtown Tyler. My alone time was now a period where I could give myself personal motivation to make it to the next day. Ramon so far has never found out that I'd actually left when everyone else did. I'd made sure that if there was ever a time when he came home before me, I was always at my friend Holley's house as an excuse.

Holley Rune was a girl that moved into my complex about five years ago, but we'd only become close in the last two. One day she saw me after an interesting discussion with Ramon in the parking lot that ended with my lip busted and bleeding profusely. At first I was a little intimidated when she initially approached me, taking into account the sleeve of tattoos on her left arm, star piercings in her nose and one eyebrow, and red and black tinted spiked hair. But when she sat silently next to me and held out an ice pack, motioning for me to put it on my mouth, all anxiety left as I burst out crying. Apparently from her apartment window where she could easily see the park and the parking lot, she also happened to witness the fight between Ramon and me.

After drying my tears on my sleeve, Holley gave me a hug and took me back to her apartment. She helped me wash my face so I could try and be presentable before the kids came home. We've been close friends ever since.

Holley now acted as a small beacon of freedom whenever I needed an escape. She also never questioned why I didn't leave Ramon, which I appreciated. She just gave me her typical reply of "Whatever you need, Asha" if I asked her to look out for me.

And look out for me she certainly did. She would send me a text on the prepaid phone she'd bought me to let me know if Ramon came home early so I could double time it back to the apartment. She stood watch as an alibi if Ramon knocked on her door looking for me. She even made me a spare key to my apartment that I hid in the shed near the dumpsters. Thanks to her, I would never be locked out of my own house again.

Sighing, I turned off the shower and began to dry off. After putting lotion on my body, I slipped into a pair of worn jeans and a faded NSU t-shirt as I continued to reflect on the small positives steps I've made these past couple of years. Looking at myself in the mirror, I took stock on how my jeans were filling back in again. All of my clothes were starting to fit better now, thanks again to Holley. On more than one occasion Holley served me leftovers at her house she always claimed would just go to waste if I didn't eat it. I knew she was lying, but still appreciated her thoughtfulness. I closed my eyes and said a silent prayer, thanking God that at one of the lowest points of my life, He knew to send an angel to help me.

I pulled my hair up in a ponytail and placed a baseball cap on my head. After putting balm on my lips and sliding my feet in my sneakers, I grabbed my purse I'd tossed earlier on the couch and started walking toward the front door.

Suddenly the phone rang just as I'd opened the door. I reached over and grabbed the line, pushing the door back shut as I answered it.

"Hello?" I asked.

"Hello..." a familiar female voice responded.

"Yes, how can I help you?" I asked a little impatiently, glancing at my watch. I had only so much time to walk to my stop before the bus showed up.

"Is this Asha Towers?" the voice asked.

"Yes," rolling my eyes. "How can I help you?" I asked again.

"Ummm, I see you've forgotten my voice. I can assure you, though, your husband has not."

THAT got my attention.

"Who is this?" I demanded, gripping the receiver a little tighter.

"Asha, darling! We used to be such good friends! How is it that you've forgotten me? I've never forgotten you. I think about you all the time. I think about you every time your husband kisses me. I think about you when your husband comes over to MY house every other night and curls up in MY bed. I especially can't forget about you when he makes

120

love to me screaming out MY name," she giggled. "That's when I think about you the most."

I put my hand against the door for strength because I suddenly felt like I was going to pass out.

"What the HELL are you talking about?" I spit. "Who the FUCK IS THIS?" I said hysterically.

"This is Tanya Lewis."

The world began to tip slightly as I struggled to get my breathing under control.

"Tanya," I whispered disbelievingly.

"Yes, bitch! It's Tanya. Did you miss me? God how I've waited for this moment for years! This is fucking awesome!" She laughed loudly in my ear.

"How did you get this number?" I asked, moving over to the couch to sit down because of the sudden lightheadedness washing over me. I felt my hands shaking and wasn't sure how much longer I could continue this conversation.

"How do you think? Ramon gave it to me. Look, I wanted to call you and let you know that Ramon and I have been fucking for years, literally." I gasped loudly in the phone as she continued. "We first got together while we were still at NSU during that weekend I went home with Jackie. Don't you remember?"

My mind raced to try and recall the events she was talking about. "Homecoming weekend our junior year?" I asked unbelievingly. "If that's true, why would he turn around and marry me then if he wanted you all along?"

"Because your dumbass ended up getting pregnant, that's why!" She shrieked. "He didn't want to be separated from his fucking child. Great trick by the way. Should have thought of it myself."

I felt my shock slowly start to lower as red-hot rage quickly rose to take its place.

"A TRICK? Is THAT what you thought I did?" I screamed back at her.

"Of course. Why else would a man like that decide to marry you? After you had his brat, he decided to stay because he wanted his daughter to grow up in a two-parent household." She sighed dramatically. "Even after all these years, I've never understood that. I've been telling him over and over Alanna would be perfectly happy here living with me, but he would never listen."

"Don't you dare let my child's name come out of your mouth!" I spit venomously. "And you can't understand it because you have the morals of a hooker."

"Oh, get over yourself," she said as she easily blew off my rage. "Don't think I'm lying and making all this shit up either, bitch. I can prove I know his body a lot better than you. I have loved every inch of it for years. I especially love that clover shaped mole he has on the left side of his dick." Tanya clucked her tongue in my ear. "He loves when I twirl my tongue all around it."

I put my hand to my mouth to muffle the anguished sob trying to escape.

"Look, the reason I'm finally calling you now is that Ramon thinks he has a shot at this executive position he's been positioning himself for these past few weeks. If he gets it, I plan on being by his side when that six plus salary starts rolling in. I'm tired of being on the sidelines; it's time I moved up just like him. And the only way to move up is to move you out. You don't deserve him. You never did. I moved to Dallas just so we could be together. That's where his new job will be and in case you haven't figured it out by now, that's where he's been sleeping during the week. The board is supposed to give him the final decision next week."

New job? What new job? I thought frantically. Ramon never mentioned he was even looking to get promoted, let alone wanting to move to another city. Not that it should surprise me. *But what about the kids?* "How do you think he'll take it with you calling me with all of this?" I asked, feeling my panic continue to rise. "Aren't you scared he'll get rid of you just because you let me in on your fucking secret?"

122

"Hell, no. In fact, he'll probably be glad the shit is finally out of the bag."

Then, something abruptly clicked for me in my fogged brain.

A sense of eerie calmness grew inside of me. I took a deep, cleansing breath. Then another. I slowly stopped clenching the fist I didn't realize I was holding and loosened my fingers on my other hand holding the phone. I felt the pounding in my head lighten and my blurred vision started to clear. Tanya paused her conversation, obviously waiting for me to continue hitting the ceiling.

"I just have one additional question, Tanya. Why? Why would you do this?" I asked in a monotone voice. I really was curious about her answer. I no longer gave a shit what Ramon's motivation was.

"BECAUSE OF DELPHI!" Tanya yelled venomously, losing her control. I could feel her hatred for me pouring through the phone. "Delphi USED me just to get to you! I loved him! I gave him EVERYTHING and he FUCKING USED ME! The bastard told me I could never be you and he just wanted to *PRACTICE WITH ME,* the son of a bitch! Delphi was MINE! MINE you fucking cunt!"

I sat back on the couch, stunned by her words. "So all this time, all of this scheming, is really because Delphi didn't really want you?" I asked, surprising even myself with the calmness of my voice.

"Of course not," Tanya lied as I heard her try to regain her composure once again. "This is now about Ramon and where he is going. As I've said, I plan on going with him straight to the top. You don't deserve Ramon any more than you deserved Delphi."

"You're right, Tanya. I don't deserve Ramon. In fact, I think he's just the man for you," I replied coolly.

"Damn right he is. This time, I'll be the one who gets the man in the end. Well, actually I've been getting him for a while, but this time officially."

"And you should be proud," I stated blandly. "Is there anything else you'd like to tell me?"

The serenity of my voice rattled her confidence a bit. "No. Just to let you know I told Ramon last night that I would be telling you today.

When he gets there can you ask him to bring back those cookies I love? The ones with the pecans and coconut?" She was referring to the homemade cookies I sometimes baked for the kids.

"I sure will. Anything else?" I asked, not taking the bait.

"No. Goodbye Asha."

"Goodbye. Thanks for calling." I called out, placing the receiver on the hook.

I took one final, deep cleansing breath as I looked around at the apartment that had been my cage for the past 12 years. *Yes, I thought. It was fucking time.*

I picked up the phone again and quickly dialed a number. "Hello, Holley? Can you come over really quickly? I need your help."

∧∧∧

I heard the key turn in the lock at the front door later that evening. I walked out of our bedroom, closing the door softly behind me. I went into our kitchen to sit down at the small dinette table. I looked down at that table where I'd eaten numerous meals alone, crying and willing myself to make it through another day. *No more tears,* I thought fiercely to myself. *Not another damn one.*

Ramon walked in with his briefcase and laptop shoulder bag. He looked at me with a blank, emotionless expression that admittedly in the past would be a signal for me to run and hide for cover. After closing the door behind him, he tossed his bag and case on the couch and turned back to me.

As he started to move toward me I held my palm up to stop him.

"Stop right there," I said. "Don't come any closer to me."

"Who do you think you're talking to?" he spoke quietly. It was quieter than usual. In other words he was moments away from really hurting me.

"I'm talking to you," I said with more bravery than I felt. "I got a phone call today. I think it's time we had a talk. In fact, it's long overdue."

"Yeah? You think so, huh?" he sneered.

124

"I most definitely do."

Ramon chuckled softly, throwing me for a loop. "Tanya is a riot. She told me she would be calling you today. I didn't believe her, but I guess she wasn't lying. It doesn't matter. She's not going anywhere and neither are you."

I raised my eyebrow. "Is that right?"

"That's right. I won't let you take my daughter from me. You and her will stay in this apartment until I say so."

I shook my head. "Ramon, I never intended on keeping Alanna from you. She will eventually know exactly what type of man her father is. Negative judgment on your character won't ever come from me; I can guarantee you that. That's not, nor has it ever been my style. I know what it's like to grow up without a father and would have been grateful for even the smallest bit of attention, even if it were from a sorry piece of shit like you. Besides, I won't have her look at me 10 years from now like I was the one who prevented her from getting close to you. Like I said, I wholeheartedly believe your true colors will eventually bleed through." I leaned forward in my seat a little. "But we will no longer be living here with you. I want a divorce."

Ramon threw his head back and laughed. "And where do you think you'll go? You have no money, no job, and no friends. And I know you won't go back to live with your mother." His hands curled into fists as they shook at his sides. "You have no one but me. I intentionally made you dependent on me so I could make sure something like that doesn't happen. Tanya isn't going anywhere either for that fucking matter, so don't even ask. I will keep fucking that sweet piece of ass I got set up in Dallas and you will deal with it."

A small, humorless smile pushed to break free from the corner of my mouth. "Is that right? I just want to make sure I understand exactly what you're telling me. You DO still plan on continuing this affair with Tanya, correct?"

"Damn straight. And you're not going anywhere either."

"Is that right? What about that promotion she told me you have all lined up? She's expecting for you to leave your family and finally settle down with her in Dallas."

The grin he gave me was so evil and sinister that I felt a small shiver of fear crawl up my spine. I sat a little straighter in my chair so as not to give away how much he rattled me.

"Like I said, she ain't going nowhere and neither are you." I noticed he had slowly moved closer to me so that he now stood only a couple of feet away. "I'm done talking. I've been waiting to give you a present. It's time you got it."

Cold fear now raced through my veins, but I willed myself to stay calm. "What present are you talking about?" I asked trying to sound unshaken, but my voice still came out as a raspy whisper.

"The same one I gave you the other night. Let's see if I can give you a matching set of bruises on your legs just like I gave you on your back. Keep sitting there." Ramon drew his fists high in the air. I felt myself brace for the impact.

"You go one more step near her you bastard and I swear you'll live to regret it for the rest of your life."

Relief poured through me as Holley and Austin stepped out of the bedroom and stepped between us. Holley held up a small handheld tape recorder and clicked the off button. Austin continued walking over to me and stood next to my chair.

"We got enough, sweetie. Let's get the hell out of here," Holley said. Austin didn't say anything, but shot daggered looks at Ramon.

Rage like I've never seen blanketed Ramon's face. "WHAT THE FUCK IS GOING ON?" he roared.

"What's going on, asswipe," Austin finally spit as he placed a hand on my shoulder. "Is that my mom, me and Alanna will be leaving this hellhole starting right now."

I'd forgotten how tall and strong my son had become over the past couple of years since he'd been weight training for basketball. I was quickly reminded as Austin's hands gripped my shoulders in a death lock to prevent him from going after Ramon himself. I placed my hands over his to reassure him I was OK and felt his grip lighten a bit.

"Nobody's going anywhere! And where is my daughter?" Ramon raged, peering around us looking toward the bedroom.

"Alanna is not here. Like I told you before, I don't believe in being the catalyst to let her know what a jackass you are. She's staying at a friend's house. Austin, on the other hand, is old enough to hear exactly what was going on and why we need to leave Tyler."

"And we got everything we need to make sure she can leave without any hassle," Holley said. She walked over to my other side, presenting a unified front. "Your reign of abuse ends tonight, asshole."

"I always thought it was me," Austin's voice wavered as he stared at Ramon, taking one step forward. Ramon wisely took one step back. "I always thought it was me with the problem of why I could never look at you like a dad. Now I know it wasn't me." Austin blew out a long breath and looked at ceiling. "It wasn't me," he said as if to himself. He looked back at Ramon again; and if looks could kill, Ramon would have Freddie Kruger claw marks slashed across his throat. "If you ever touch my mother again, I swear it will be the last thing that you do." It was then that I noticed the metallic baseball bat Austin clutched at his side. I recognized the bat from Austin's junior league baseball days when he was younger. Ramon looked at the weapon Austin held and wisely took another step back.

Ramon gulped. "You can't take Alanna from me." Ramon had a look of desperation now.

I rolled my eyes. "Don't you listen asshole? I won't try to take Alanna from you. I'm filing for divorce. You're a bigger idiot than I thought if you believed I'd stay married to you."

I stood up. "I'd even consider joint custody, although I'm sure once Alanna see's what type of man she has as a father, she may ask that to be changed. But if Alanna wants to see you, I won't stop her. The only positive thing I can say about you all these years is that I know you'd take care of her."

I grabbed the last box I'd packed that was placed on the table earlier and handed it to Austin. Everything else we owned was already boxed and stored at Holley's house.

When I called her that morning to let her know what was going on, she immediately came over and we got to work, packing up everything we owned. We wanted our departure now to be short and quick.

As I was sorting through our things earlier, I'd discovered a box hidden deep in our master closet. After busting open the rusted lock, to my amazement and sheer delight I'd found old letters from Terri and Levi begging me to get in touch with them and asking if everything was alright. Feeling too ashamed to contact Levi after our last confrontation when he begged me to leave, I mustered up the courage and dialed Terri's number, hoping it was still in service.

After many tears and a thorough Spanish curse out, Terri demanded to speak to Holley so she could thank her profusely for being there for me. Holley just nodded her head while she listened on the other end, saying over and over "someone was there for me too." Terri then ordered that the kids and me come to Houston and stay with her so we could get back on our feet. Apparently she now owned and operated some marketing firm there and doing quite well for herself. I agreed and joked with her like I had a choice. It felt so good to laugh and kid around with my old friend again. She made arrangements with Holley to wire her money so we could fly out of Dallas the day after tomorrow.

Holley and I had all of our things packed by the time the kids came home from school. When they entered the apartment, I pulled Austin to the side and explained to him what was going on while Holley sat down with Alanna. After a lot of crying and consoling each other, Austin dropped Alanna off at her friend's house so she wouldn't witness the scene taking place now. Alanna believed we would just be discussing the details of her mom and dad divorcing and I wanted it to stay that way. Holley came up with the plan to get Ramon's indiscretions and abuse on tape to make it easier during the divorce proceedings.

Holley walked toward the door with Austin following closely on her heels. I started after them, but turned around as I got to the entrance. Holley and Austin saw me pause and waited for me in the hallway, giving me anxious looks. I needed to say something first.

"I would like to thank you, Ramon," I said reflectively, moving just passed the door into the hallway where Holley and Austin waited. I didn't want to take a chance of him grabbing me and locking me inside.

"For what?" he scoffed. He'd followed me to the door and now held the knob with a tight grip. He kept glancing between me and Austin. I got a feeling he was finally realizing Austin was two steps shy of being a full-grown man: A big and potentially powerful man who had just witnessed his mother's abuse.

"For the very first time in my life, I have complete and utter clarity about what I want and need. I know I want and deserve to be happy. I know I don't want to be with you or anybody like you ever again. I know I don't have to feel guilty about my past because it's just that—my past. And I know that I need to finally start living for ME and for what I want out of life, not for my children, not for what people may think about me, not for what people may be expecting of me, but just live for ME. That's the best present you could have ever given me." With that, I turned and began walking down the hallway. I heard Ramon slam the door behind me, causing the walls to shake.

As we walked back to Holley's apartment, I felt the pressure in my chest finally open. The feeling of lightness was so profound that I felt an urge to sing it into the atmosphere. I lifted my head and belted out Indie.Arie's *Living,* feeling free and happy.

Stunned, Austin looked at me. "That's the first time I've heard you sing in years, Mom." He reached down and patted my cheek. I want you to know that I love you. Whatever you need, know that I'll always be there for you."

Tears glistened in my eyes as I looked at him. "I love you, too Austin. I love you and your sister so very much."

"Come on guys," Holley said, wiping her eyes with her sleeve. "Who's up for spaghetti tonight?"

Chapter Eleven

The Lady Emerges
Houston, TX

Asha

"Man, I am exhausted!" complained Terri as she slung her blazer over the marbled island in her kitchen. "I hate pitching to new clients, especially people from the music industry. It's such a pain in the ass. You always have to be on your freakin' best behavior. You can't really tell the jerk who spends more time looking down the front of your shirt than listening to your pitch to suck it because he's the one who can make or break your business plan. And then, after it's all finished, you look like you've run a freakin' marathon because you're sweating so damn hard the makeup is sliding off your face."

I turned and appraised her, my eyes slowly taking in her perfect MAC makeup, Christian Dior designer business suit and 5-inch Jimmy Choo sling backs. I turned back around to the stove where I was putting the finishing touches on the chili and homemade cornbread I was making for dinner and let out an overly exaggerated sigh.

"Terri, you are preaching to the choir right now. You look flawless. I'm sure your presentation was spot on. And as far as the jerk you're talking about, I'm sure you had him eating out of the palm of your hands like you always do. He was probably panting like a dog because he couldn't wait to sign with your company."

"Well, the dog part is correct," Terri murmured, walking up behind me to pull out a spoon from the drawer next to me. She dipped it into the chili pot, groaning loudly as she savored the spicy flavors. "And the signing part, too. You know I got the contract, girl." She winked, tossing the spoon in the sink.

"I know you did." I smiled as I stirred the chili pot.

"In fact, one of the agents from the record label is supposed to drop by for dinner tonight. Part of the 'let's get to know each other on a person level' bullshit. Did I tell you that already?"

"Aahh, no!" I grabbed the dishtowel sitting on the counter and swatted her with it. "Thanks for the heads up, Terri. Good thing I made enough of this stuff for extra helpings because of Austin's appetite. That kid is eating you out of house and home." I paused as I thought about my words. "Sorry about that, by the way." I dropped my head, feelings of shame and embarrassment starting to creep up.

"Don't." Terri grabbed me by the shoulders and spun me around so that we were face to face. "Don't do that, Asha. I've told you over and over again, my godson and daughter are welcome here until the day they die, just like their mother." She gave me a hug as she murmured in my ear. "They are as much a part of my family as they are yours. I love you guys. I didn't realize how isolated and lonely I'd become with just focusing on work, work, work all the time until you guys finally came back into my life." She smiled warmly at me.

After the kids and I arrived in Houston that fateful day over a year ago, the four of us spent well over a week just reveling in the fact that we were on the cusp of starting a new life. During that time I had the kids' school transcripts transferred over to the new private institutions Terri sponsored. Over the past few months they both seem to be adapting pretty well to their new school environment. Alanna made quick friends with a couple of girls who shared her same infatuation with Justin Timberlake, while Austin emerged himself with getting acquainted with his new basketball coach. Austin's new coach was ecstatic after reviewing Austin's game average from his prior school and couldn't wait to get his hands on him.

While the kids adjusted to their new life, Terri and I mapped out and executed a plan of attack regarding Ramon. Through Terri's highly connected lawyers along with Holley's recorded evidence, divorcing Ramon and gaining custodial rights to Alanna had been a smooth piece of cake. To add beauty to the situation, all communication had been restricted through our attorneys. I never needed to physically see him to get the ball rolling and documents finalized. I still feared one day he might show up unexpectedly and cause all sorts of hell, but I'd deal with that if that day came.

True to my word, I still allowed Ramon joint custody despite Terri's protests. Our joint parenting agreement outlined the details of how Alanna was supposed to visit with her father every other weekend, every other Thanksgiving and Christmas, and every Father's Day until she turned eighteen. The child support the courts mandated Ramon to pay was set up in a way that funds should have automatically been deposited into an account strictly in Alanna's name. I didn't want to give Ramon any leverage of power over me regarding how and when his support was being utilized.

Unfortunately true to his character, Ramon always seemed to have other engagements that prevented him from seeing her and, according to Alanna, from his support from being deposited on time. Alanna eventually stopped questioning why she hadn't seen her father in over four months. I kept my mouth shut on that front too, not wanting to add to the confusion and rejection she must have been feeling. Instead, I let her know that her father still loved her; he just showed it in his own way. On some days, however, I'd catch her staring lifelessly out of her bedroom window. I wondered how I could help, but knowing no words of comfort coming from me could expel the feeling of rejection Ramon kept showing her, I tried my best to give her love and continued support in all other areas.

The growling of my stomach pulled me out of my daydreaming. I grabbed a mitt and pulled the cornbread out of the oven, basking in its aromatic fragrance. I looked over at Terri, who opened the refrigerator to grab a bottle of fruit juice. "What time is your client coming over?" I asked, glancing at the wall clock.

"It's the owner of the label's son and he'll be here within the hour to pick up copies of the contract," Terri replied casually, as if she just hadn't just knocked the wind out of me.

"An HOUR? Really, Terri?" I cried, wiping my hands along my jeans as I began hastily cleaning up the kitchen area.

"Relax. Chad doesn't care about the condition of my house. His only concern is how fast my company can skyrocket the promotional tour he's trying to launch with his new boy band. Well, that and my killer ass. Like father, like son." Terri laughed.

"Let me at least call the kids so they'll know you're having a client come over. Maybe they could stay at their friend's house until the morning so you can conduct your business undisturbed?" I didn't want my intrusion on her home to cost her potential client relationships.

Terri rolled her eyes. "Fine. I've told you how I feel about it already. I've already done enough ass kissing for one day. Chad is coming to MY home environment, on MY home terrain. I can act like I want to in my own house. Besides, the presentation was already sold to his dad; he's just coming along as collateral damage." Terri grabbed a strand of hair that had fallen loose from the messy bun on top of her head and began to swirl it around her fingers.

I stopped cleaning to turn and really look at her. Twirling her hair was a tell tale sign she was hiding something. "Terri?" I asked suspiciously.

"Hmm?" she answered. She released her hair and turned to sit on a stool near the island table to pull off her stilettos.

"Are you feeling this guy?" I asked, raising one eyebrow as I leaned one hip against the counter and crossed my arms over my chest.

"What? Of course not," she said as a slow red started to spread on her cheeks. She grabbed her hair again nervously and began twirling away.

I gave her a wide smirk. "I haven't seen you this flustered since NSU." I didn't dare mention Levi's name. There had been some sort of tension between the two every since that homecoming night junior year when he took her home after the coronation. She never told me what happened, but I got the distinct feeling in the days that followed that they'd hit it off in more ways than one. I never understood why they never pursued their obvious attraction for one another. Then again, I'd never understood the majority of the decisions I'd made in my own life either, so I really couldn't pass judgment.

"Look," she started, releasing her hair and giving a loud sigh, obviously wanting to steer the conversation in another direction. "I need to run upstairs and get those contracts in order before he gets here. If the door rings, could you answer it for me?" With that, she scooted off the stool, reached down to grab her shoes, and jogged upstairs.

∧∧∧

"This chili is fantastic, Asha. Thanks for letting me crash in on your meal," Chad said as he sat at the kitchen table in front of his nearly empty bowl, placing his spoon down. Chad Forrester was a strikingly good-looking man with dark wavy brown hair that fell just over the top of his ears and killer green eyes. He had a body that looked like it had been bred for football: wide shoulders, thick, massive biceps and large slightly calloused hands.

"Asha is the best," praised Terri. "I would literally starve if it wasn't for her."

"I definitely wouldn't have let you starve, Ms. Cortes. I can make sure any and all of your needs were met. We aim to please at Dove Records, just wait and see." He teased seductively, winking one eye her way as I saw that familiar blush spread across her neck. I struggled to maintain my laugh. That was one the cheesiest lines I'd heard in a long time.

Surprisingly, it seemed Terri was falling for it hook, line and sinker. I bit my lip to control the smile that threatened. It was good to see Terri finally let her guard down enough to enjoy some mild flirtation.

"Let's head up to my office so we can finalize those documents, then I'll walk you out." Terri suggested, clearly suggesting that leaving her home was evident in his near future.

"Lead the way," Chad said, pushing back his chair. Terri glided past him to lead the way upstairs. He followed after her, his head bent slightly as he watched every movement her body made.

Lightness filled my heart as I watched them leave the kitchen, basking in the warmth of feeling happy and alive again. Every day was a gift to be treasured and I vowed to never again take any day of happiness for granted.

As I cleaned up the dishes and put away the food, I began to sing a song I'd made up long ago when the kids were smaller to help them go to sleep:

Good dreams were meant to be shared in love

Good dreams will always come true

Good dreams will find their way to your heart

That's why all my good dreams are of youuu

Sweet child of mine, my love is forever

Sweet child of mine, no love will be better

Good dreams, sweet child are of youuu...

"That was actually quite beautiful Asha," Chad said as he walked back into the kitchen, a look of awe across his face. "In fact, that was fantastic. Did you write that?" I looked up at the sound of his voice; startled I had been caught in my daydream. I nodded my head.

"I didn't know you had talent." He sent a mock look of insult toward Terri, who had also followed him back into the kitchen. "Why didn't you tell me your friend was gifted?"

Terri laughed as she slid onto a stool and crossed her legs. "Of course Asha's got talent. She's my friend after all." She teased smugly. "Besides, I thought you were only interested in boy bands."

"I'm a talent scout. I'm interested in talent, period," Chad replied as he glanced down at her crossed legs. He licked his lips, and then looked back at me. "Asha, have you ever considered singing publicly? I mean as a signed artist?"

"Ahh... that would be a no," I said, smiling, appreciating his flattery. "Singing has always been a hobby, not a life goal. It's a stress reliever for me. I've never thought about trying to make a career out of it. Besides, these past few years I've only really been involved with my kids and taking care of them."

"Asha, I'm serious. I would love to sponsor you and get you in with some of our producers over at the label. They wouldn't be able to keep their hands off you," he said.

Terri cleared her throat. "I mean they would be extremely excited to work with a talent like yours." Chad quickly backtracked, throwing a quick smile Terri's way. "I think she would be amazing. Definite star potential."

I laughed at him, not really believing the line he was telling me, until I caught a glimpse of Terri's face. She was staring at me with this intrigued expression that caused my laughter to slowly die down.

"What?" I asked, my eyebrows knitting together. "Why are you staring at me like that?"

"Sweetie, Chad is serious. And now that I really think about it, I think I'm going to jump on that bandwagon, too." She slapped a hand to her thigh. "I can't believe I didn't think of this before! Asha, you've got an amazing voice. I've told you that for years, every since I heard you singing in the shower back in our dorm room at NSU," Terri contemplated.

"Precisely," I said, pointing my finger at both of them. "I've got a shower voice. Every person in America has a Whitney Houston shower voice. It's when they dry off and throw on some clothes that they soon realize they actually sound like Rosanne Barr at a baseball game."

"Just think about it for a moment," Chad started. "I could launch your career and really take care of you as an artist." He turned to Terri. "And now that we have Ms. Cortes's contract, she could recommend a good manager to make sure you're taken care of properly."

"Recommend? Hell, I'M managing her. I'm not trusting her with a stranger. She's been through too much already." Terri's eyes widened as she clasped her hand over her mouth. "Oh, Asha. I'm sorry. I didn't mean to mention anything."

I shook my head at her. "It's ok, Terri." I looked at Chad. "I got out of an abusive relationship a little over a year ago. That's why me and the kids are staying with Terri for a while; until I can get back on my feet."

Chad walked over to me and grabbed one of my hands, giving it a quick squeeze. "I'm sorry to hear that. By the looks of you now, I'd say you're a survivor. You're a fighter. You look nothing like I'm sure what you actually went through."

He took a deep breath and stepped back, releasing my hand. "Look Asha, I'm not promising the moon, here. But I really want you to take my offer seriously. I believe you have a natural talent and that's something the industry is thirsty for nowadays. People are starving to hear voices that are real, not convoluted with digital technology that seems to be the fad now. Your range is amazing and your tone..." he tilted his head and reached into his suit jacket to pull out a business card. He handed it to me. "Please consider it."

Panic started to set as I realized they were both serious. "I don't know if it's a good idea to be that exposed in public like that." My thoughts drifted to Ramon. An image of him standing over me like Ike had Tina Turner in that dressing room scene in the movie, *What's Love Got to Do With It?*" made me shudder. I blanched. "I really like having my privacy, guys. The thought of singing in front of a lot of people literally freaks me out."

"We could create and release your whole album on iTunes and promote it on that new Internet site that's getting popular," Chad offered and looked at Terri. "What's the name of that site again?"

"YouTube," Terri replied.

Chad snapped his fingers. "Exactly. We could even do it so that your real identity is under a pseudonym. People would never know that

Asha is singing." He bent his fingers as if he were writing quotation marks.

I leaned against the counter, looking blankly at both of them. "Are you for real?" I asked, still unbelievably.

"I don't kid about stuff like this. It's my job to scout out talent, and Asha, you are busting at the seams with it."

Terri stood up and walked over to me. "We don't have to do anything that you don't want to do. But I really think you should consider this. This could really help you a strong financial foundation for you and the kids if it takes off like I suspect it will."

She snorted as I raised one eyebrow at her.

"And don't take this as a sign that I'm trying to force you guys out of here quickly, either. Believe me, I've gotten *very* used to the home-cooked meals. But honey, we've talked about this before. We both know you hate the field you got your degree in because you don't like the corporate and political games affiliated with it. I've been trying to get you to think about possibly joining my company to see if you'd like the marketing aspect of business, but now I think we've both have been way off base."

Terri crossed her arms over her chest and narrowed her eyes at me. "The more I think about it, the more I'm realizing your lyrical spirit is actually your more dominant, if somewhat dormant, trait." She looked over and nodded her head at Chad. "Yes. I think you hit the nail right on the head with this one."

I shifted uncomfortably on my feet, glancing back and forth between them as they both stared me down. Now I knew how a frog felt lying underneath a microscope in a sophomore high school science lab, just waiting for someone to start cutting and dissecting it.

Terri began pacing back and forth, waving her open palms at Chad. Whenever she got passionate about something, she talked with her hands. "I think a pseudonym for her is actually perfect. No one could ever know it's her. The kids could still grow up in a relatively peaceful environment; she wouldn't need to actually sing in front of anyone immediately with the way I would launch and promote her, and we can

138

let her voice take center stage." I could see the creative wheels spinning in her head as she got more and more excited. She continued to pace back and forth.

"And all of her promotions should be under her stage name." She said more to herself than to Chad or me. She stopped and threw her hands behind her head. She looked up toward the ceiling, rolling her neck as she contemplated ideas. I glanced over at Chad again. He'd stopped staring at me to feast hungrily at Terri's chest that seemed to rise and sway as arched her back in a stretch.

Finally, she dropped her hands to her sides, tilted her head to the right and said, "The Painted Lady."

"The Painted Lady?" Chad and I both looked at her curiously.

"Where did that name come from?" I asked, thoroughly confused. "It sounds like some sort of artwork."

"It is art, in a sense," Terri started. "It's the name of one of the most commonly recognized butterflies in the world. It's easily recognizable because..." she paused and stared intensely in my eyes, "...everyone knows someone who hides their true beauty behind a manufactured outer shell and cocoons themselves off from the world. But finally after events and seasons change that affect not only that outer shell, but also the inner transformation, that person eventually manifests into the most glorious, magnificent butterfly the entire world can attest to."

Chad looked at her for a moment, and then a slow smile spread across his face. He nodded his head approvingly. "I like it," he said simply.

∧∧∧

"MOM!" I heard Austin scream as he burst through the front door upstairs. "MOM!"

"I'm downstairs sweetie." I called absently, never looking up from the self-help guide on public speaking I was reading. I pulled my blanket tighter around me as I tried to focus. Stretched out on Terri's favorite chaise in her lower den area, I tried to will my brain to absorb as much of the book as possible. Lately it seemed that I was hell-bent on utilizing every resource available to overcome my fear of being in the spotlight. If my singing career stayed at the current pace it was going, I needed to tackle my scopophobia.

I'd realized long ago that not only did I have a latent fear of Ramon randomly popping up and causing havoc, but I was also extremely uncomfortable and downright petrified of being the center of attention, especially in any public environment. Every time I attempted to sing in front of anyone I didn't personally know or care about, my voice would clam up, my hands would shake uncontrollably, my heart raced a thousand miles an hour, and I swear I felt like I would pass out.

I knew my fear was more than just simple stage fright. Based on my reading, I'd narrowed down that a lot of my issue was related to being placed in uncomfortable positions and feeling out of control. I didn't fully understand exactly what those past positions were yet, but I was determined to both figure it out and master it. I wanted my new path in life to be a success.

The demo work Chad's producers and I wrapped up a little over six months ago had proven to be an enormous hit. The studio executives at Dove Records seemed to really love the initial tracks we laid and were ready to launch the first cd. In addition Terri's strategic marketing campaign, which focused primarily on YouTube and iTunes promotions, really helped my first initial track release, *Are you Listening for Me* get off the ground. The song claimed over 3.5 million hits in its initial launch weekend. Glowing reviews poured in on the romantic lure of the song and the sultry voice behind the lyrics.

The picture displayed on the video cover of hundreds of illustrated West Coast Painted Lady Butterflies also helped to bolster the mystery behind the song's artist. I smiled to myself as I thought about Terri's marketing campaign. Whispers were still flying about who the Painted Lady really was and why didn't she ever show her face? Terri however kept urging me to tackle my fear because sooner or later, the public would demand to see me in the flesh. I intended to be ready to handle it when that day came.

I heard the sound of heavy feet stomping down the staircase and a few seconds later, Austin burst in the room. His eyes were bright with excitement and he was grinning from ear to ear.

"Mom! Guess what! Something amazing has happened."

"What is it?" I asked putting my book down as I felt myself catching on to his excitement. I drank in his tall 6-foot, 3-inch frame, love in my heart overflowing at seeing him so happy. Every day I breathed a sigh of satisfaction knowing the move to Houston was the best thing we could have ever done for our family.

Austin started jumping up and down, almost banging his head against the low ceiling in the rec room. He waved what seemed to be a letter in his hand in my direction. "YES! YES! We did it Mom! We did it!"

Laughing at his antics, I unwrapped myself from my blankets and stood up. "Slow down and tell me what's going on! Exactly what did we do? What's got you this hyped?"

Austin stopped jumping and grabbed my hands, still holding on to the letter. He looked at me somberly and said, "I love you, Mom. I just wanted to tell you that."

I hit his chest playfully. "I love you, too, now stop trying to distract me! Tell me what is going on!"

Austin dropped my hands and held the letter he was holding up for me to see. The letter was postmarked from Lorman, Mississippi addressed to a Mr. Austin St. Claire. The return address was from the Natchez State's Athletic Department.

I looked at him questionably. "Does this mean what I think it means?" I asked slowly, praying this was the response we'd been waiting for the past three months. My heart sped up at the possibility.

"Yes! A full scholarship to Natchez State to play basketball! We did it Mom!" Austin grabbed me and spun around in a circle, both of us laughing and crying at the same time.

Austin finally set me back on my feet and looked down at me. Emotion raged through my chest, cutting off my ability to speak. All I could think of was the fact that my son was going to be able to go to college. My son was going to college. My son was going to college. The son of a teenage pregnant mother at the age of 15 was going to be able to go to college.

Tears coursed down my face as the enormity of the situation came crashing down on me. I staggered to the chaise and sat down, not trusting that I would be able to stand a minute longer. Austin immediately bent down in front of me, concern etched across his face.

"Mom, what's wrong? Are you feeling alright? Do you want me to call someone?" Austin asked, panic starting to edge into his voice.

I smiled at him through my tears. "Everything is perfect."

I then heard another lighter set of footprints speeding hurriedly down the stairs. I swiped my cheeks in an attempt to get some resemblance of control right before Alanna emerged from the staircase.

"Hey Mom! What's up Austin? We got out of debate practice early today and I am starving! Can we go to McDonald's and get something to eat?" Alanna asked as she threw her backpack on the floor next to the chaise. She flopped down next to me and looked between the two of us.

"What's wrong?" she immediately asked, taking quick assessment of our faces as Austin stood back up.

"Absolutely nothing. Your brother just got accepted into Natchez State on a basketball scholarship," I said proudly.

"Way to go, dude!" Alanna said, leaning up to give Austin a high five. "Ok, let me make my list of demands now. I'll need a Mercedes-Benz, the newest model, of course. Not something that's like 20 years old. I'll need Christian Dior's latest fall line and, of course, an American Express Black card."

Austin looked at her confused. "What are you talking about, squirt?" he asked.

"I'm letting you know now what to get me when you make it to the pros." Alanna shrugged her shoulders as she leaned back again, placing her hands behind her head. "It's just a matter of time. I need to make my demands known now just in case you try and bail on me later. Mom's here as a witness so you can't say I never told you. I need to make sure you roll me my money." Alanna teased, rubbing her fingertips together as she burst out laughing. Austin shook his head and swatted the back of her head with the letter, chuckling lightly.

I smiled at their banter, and then looked up at Austin. "Do you know what type of opportunities you can have because of this? The doors to your future are wide open to you now, son. You and your coaches worked so hard these past few months to get you ready for recruiters, and that work has finally paid off. I can't even describe how proud I am of you."

"Not as proud as I am of you," Austin said somberly as he sank back down to the floor in front of me. "I couldn't have done any of this without your sacrifices and support." As I started to wave his accolade off, he stopped me. "I'm serious, Mom. You think I don't know what you've done and put up with for me?"

"For us." Alanna chimed in, sitting up next to me. "Honestly Mom, did you think I didn't know what was going on with you and dad for all those years?" Her words stunned me into silence as I looked into her face. Guilt immediately crashed through me as tears welled in my eyes and began to fall down my cheeks.

"Don't Mom. Don't feel bad." She patted my back as I tried to control my sobs. "We're just trying to let you know that you're our hero. You've shown us time and time again what real sacrifice means for someone you love. I never felt unsafe, but I know that dad took things too far with you." She looked at her brother. "I've always looked to Austin as my role model anyway, next to you." Alanna smiled and turned back to me. "You put up with a lot for us. Honestly at times way too much. Whatever your reasons were for staying together with dad, know that the night you finally decided to leave was one of the best decisions I think you've ever made. I hope you don't regret it. I know I don't. I'm happy now." She turned to her brother. "It looks like we'll all be happy."

I tried to take a deep breath as my eyes roamed her face. My beautiful daughter, I was constantly underestimating how strong her spirit truly was. With her dark blue eyes, dark curly black hair and dimpled chin, she was the spitting image of her father. But she had the spirit of my mother in that once she set her mind about something; hell would freeze over before she changed it. Now it seemed she had made up in her mind that her father was someone she'd rather not have in her life. I sighed. It was such a shame Ramon couldn't appreciate knowing what a wonderful daughter he'd helped to create because he was too caught up in his own selfish and abusive ways.

Austin nodded his head at Alanna in confirmation. "Whenever I got too tired or wanted to quit studying after a rough game, I thought about you and the self motivation you had to keep going. I knew I couldn't quit. I had to keep going, keep studying, and keep pushing myself to do better. Because we needed something better. See, I had a plan." He tapped his finger against his temple.

I looked up at him and he gave me a little wink, causing my guilt to ease just a little.

"And what plan was that, may I ask?" I said, smiling warmly as I wiped my face.

"I had to do well so I could try and get an academic scholarship like you. I would go to college, get a good paying job, and finally get you away from Ramon. It just so happened that you wised up before my grand plan could play out." He laughed drily, "And before I could whip his ass."

"Austin!" I said disapprovingly. Alanna punched him in the chest. "Hey!" Alanna said, frowning.

"Sorry," he said, not sounding apologetic at all. "Anyway, whatever your reasons were for staying as long as you did, I know you ultimately did it for us. I still got the scholarship I was working towards, just in athletics instead of academics. It doesn't really matter what department sponsors me. It's all a means to an end. NSU's computer science department is one of the best in the country." He grinned arrogantly. "I'm going to be the next Steve Jobs."

"And again, run me my money when you do," joked Alanna.

A means to an end...

He sounded so much like Delphi in that moment. Delphi, I sighed. I'd stopped torturing myself with the woulda coulda shouldas of what-would-my-life-be-like-now-if-I-had-chosen-Delphi's speech a long time ago. I couldn't change the past. Everything happened for a reason and I didn't need to keep fantasizing about opportunities lost. I'd resigned myself on knowing that I blew the chance to be with the love of my life. I might very well remain single because I don't think I could ever love someone the way I loved Delphi. However I still had my children and could shower all of my love and attention to them.

I wiped away my remaining tears. This was a time for celebration, not wallowing in regret.

"Come on, guys," I said, standing to my feet. "We're celebrating tonight. Let's go out for a real dinner, not Mickey D's. Terri won't be back from her sales convention until next week, so it will be just the three of us."

"Fine by me," Austin said, standing over me as he licked his lips. "I'm in the mood for some Italian. I dreamed about a plate of lasagna last night. This morning when I woke up my pillow was missing."

I laughed as Alanna groaned at his poor attempt at humor. "Umm, that rated a two out of 10 on the joke scale, buddy. Lasagna and pillows have absolutely nothing in common. Try again, goofball," Alanna said, rolling her eyes.

"It got mom to laugh, though. So my attempt was a success." He smiled down at me warmly as he reached over and patted my cheek.

Chapter Twelve

Recognition
Houston, TX

Delphi

"Come on, man," Levi said as he poked his head in my office door. "I'm ready to go home and relax a bit. I just want to fall asleep on my couch drinking a couple of beers. This has been the week from hell and I need some zoning out time. I'm so tired I don't even feel like trying to get some ass tonight, despite what my dick is telling me." He glanced at his watch. "I heard Evelyn telling someone on the phone earlier the Grammys are supposed to come on tonight. That sounds like some good white noise television to me. Let's roll."

"Here I come, man," I said absently as I shut off my computer. I picked up my suit jacket and briefcase and followed Levi out of my office. As we walked down the hall toward the elevators, I looked around at our accomplishments. Allen and Blackburn LLC had really blossomed over the past few years. We'd ditched the one-room office closet we'd initially occupied in exchange for taking over the entire 48th floor of our building. Our firm now housed three conference rooms, a law library, an employee lounge and break area, mailroom, and four main offices, two of which were occupied by Levi and myself.

"Goodnight, Evelyn," I called as I stepped in the elevator cab as it arrived.

"See you tomorrow Eve," Levi called.

"Goodnight to you, Mr. Blackburn. You too, Mr. Allen. Have a good evening to you both. Especially you, Mr. Allen. I hope you intend to spend it with a nice young lady by your side. I know I don't have to worry about you Mr. Blackburn."

"You got that right, Eve. But I'm laying low tonight. Just my beer and my remote will be keeping me company." Levi called back as he followed me into the elevator car. I chuckled to myself as the doors closed in front of us.

Evelyn Scott was the new paralegal that Levi and I lucked into a few years ago when we finally broke down and admitted we needed some office help. She occupied one of the empty offices on our floor. As our business exploded, so did the mounds of paperwork, court filings and briefs that needed to be completed. Evelyn was our first interview, and we quickly concluded she needed to be the last. She immediately swept us away with her efficient no-nonsense attitude and impeccable references. She was a small statuesque woman with a beautiful bob of all white hair, dimpled cheeks and warm brown eyes that made her look timeless. Her flawless features also made it impossible to tell how old she really was. Evelyn looked to be in her early 40s; but her experience and work history suggested she was at least in her late 50s. She and my mom immediately bonded when my parents came to visit last year to see how things were shaping up with the firm. Since that meeting, Evelyn now has taken it upon herself to try and get me married off for some reason. I suspected it was at the strong urging of my mother after their numerous lunch and shopping excursions.

What Evelyn didn't know was that my wife was already promised to me a long time ago. Her current husband just didn't know it yet.

"What are you going to do tonight?" Levi asked casually as the elevator doors opened to the lobby floor.

"Not sure yet. I might drop by Nate's place to see how he's doing." I lied. I knew exactly how I was going to spend my evening and I didn't feel like hearing Levi's mouth about it. My evening plans consisted of sorting through resident and phone records to try and figure out exactly where was Asha. My last search pegged her living in Tyler, Texas almost a decade back. After that, it seemed like she'd fallen off the face of the earth. I couldn't find any type of paper trail to confirm her current whereabouts--no phone records, leases, car titles, or anything. It was like trying to find a needle in a haystack. However, I wouldn't be deterred. Finding her had quickly become my obsession. I realized a long time ago no matter how hard Levi and I worked, it didn't mean anything if I couldn't share it with someone I loved. And the person I loved was still Asha. But it seemed no one could understand why I still felt that way, so I stopped trying to explain it.

Levi had come to my townhome one evening as I sorted through paperwork, and immediately threw out all sorts of warning red flags. He tried to convince me that all of my focus was unhealthy and unnatural, but I brushed off his concern. He couldn't relate to having the other half of his soul seemingly ripped from underneath him as he stood by and just let it happen. Then to later realize he could have prevented it if he had just been brave enough. It was too much. The realization was killing me. I had to at least try and vie for an audience with her to make things right. To explain myself. Even if she wanted nothing to do with me ever again, she had to know the truth. I couldn't live with myself if she didn't. I couldn't live with myself now knowing she didn't.

After a few years of dead end leads, I finally gave up trying to find information on her and focused on trying to find her son. I knew if I could find Austin, he would lead me to Asha. I'd gotten a hit on a possible lead about him earlier that day and couldn't wait to get home to explore it.

"Okay, well I'm crashing. I'll talk to you tomorrow," Levi said as he walked toward his Jeep.

"Ok," I said as I walked toward my own truck. I jumped into my Navigator and pulled out of the parking lot. Driving south on the West Loop Freeway, I finally pulled into my Afton Oaks neighborhood. Once I reached my townhome, I pushed the button on my truck visor to open the garage door. After pulling inside and securing my vehicle, I opened my mudroom door and took a deep breath, knowing I had a long night ahead of me.

Walking through the mudroom into the open kitchen, I threw my keys on the marbled countertop. I opened the stainless steel refrigerator to grab a beer. Mom spent a fair amount of time decorating my home to her expensive tastes. After continued and repeated arguments that I was perfectly content with just a sofa, bed, and my 72-inch flat screen to be happy in life, I finally just gave in and let her do what she wanted.

Now in hindsight, I can say truly say I appreciated her efforts. Every time I came home, a sense of peace and tranquility washed through me. Right now I needed to maintain that peace to keep me focused as I searched for Asha's son.

I kicked off my shoes and walked into my office near the staircase, carrying the briefcase I'd brought home with me. Flipping on the light near the door, a thrill of anticipation coursed through my body.

This night would be different. I felt it to the core of my soul.

I walked over to my desk and took a seat in my chair. Placing my briefcase down, I hit the power button on the laptop on my desk. I opened my briefcase and took out the paperwork I'd printed earlier and spread everything out before me. As I waited for my search engines to load, I grabbed the television remote laying on the desk. Turning on the TV, I leaned back in my chair flipping idly through the stations until I found the music award show Levi had referred to earlier. *At least I could listen to music as I completed my searches,* I thought.

I reflected on all the past searches I'd done only to come up empty-handed. This time, I knew I'd hit pay dirt when I saw and printed out the web page I'd run across earlier while taking a quick break in my office: "STAR BASKETBALL CENTER AUSTIN ST. CLAIRE LEADS NSU TO ITS SECOND SOUTHWESTERN ATHLETIC CONFERENCE CHAMPIONSHIP."

I put the remote down and began pecking at my keyboard, searching for online web links to the latest NSU sports reports. Finally, I'd found what I was looking for. There he was in large and living color plastered across my monitor. Asha's son. I gazed at his picture as warmth filled my heart. He had grown to be the spitting image of his mother, right down to the hazel slanted eyes and high cheekbones. He stood among his teammates holding up the SWAC trophy with a huge grin across his face. He wore a King Lion t-shirt across his bulky frame, the same symbol of the fraternity I also belonged to. Well, well...

A wave of nostalgia took hold as I remembered the conversations Austin and I had when he was smaller. I'd always have to sprint walk with Asha back to her room from the library after one of our study sessions because she needed to be on time for her nightly phone call with her son. On a few occasions she'd actually invite me up to her room to let me talk to him. He would get on the phone and ask questions like: *Was I his Momma's boyfriend? Was I being nice to his Momma? Could I come visit him when his Momma came to visit him, too?*

It tore me apart when I had to respond each time that we were just friends because I wanted to shout I was indeed the man in her life, and would be there for him as well. Instead, I would ask if he was being a good boy. And as always, he boasted proudly that he was always a good boy so his Momma would be happy when she came home.

Hmmm, I thought as I drummed my fingers on my desk. It looked like I would be making another trip back to NSU so I can have my old friend tell me where his mother was.

A familiar voice rang out from the television that disrupted my concentration. I looked up from my monitor to peer over at the set. An attractive girl with candy red spiked hair and colorful arm tattoos stood onstage to introduce the next artist. Her face was extremely familiar, but my mind was too filled with thoughts of Asha to immediately place her.

"And now, the moment we've all been waiting for! I am here to introduce to some and present to others our highlighted performance of the night! Her vocals have made their way into our minds and her lyrics will be forever ingrained into our hearts. Ladies and gentlemen, I give to you 'The Painted Lady' singing her smash hit 'Are You Listening for Me?'" The woman announced to the screaming audience.

The lights dimmed in the theatre as the audience continued their explosive applause. A lone spotlight shone onstage, highlighting a woman in an all white jumpsuit with light brown hair sitting on a barstool with her back to the audience. It appeared from the camera's side view that her face was covered in an all white, porcelain doll mask. The back wall was highlighted to show an extremely large butterfly that stretched

150

across the entire length of the stage. Lyrical dancers began to jump and leap with poetic grace to the rhythm of the slow, sultry ballad.

Are you there listening for me?
I hear your heart calling
Are you there wishing for me?
I hear your heart calling
It's been too long since I've seen your face
Too long since I've been in your embrace
The choices I made
Did not kill my love for you
The choices I made
Only grew my love for you
I'm sorry
We should have chosen you
Please forgive me
Say you love me
Say you want me
It's out of my head
And placed on my lips
For all to hear
Are you listening for me?

I stiffened. My blood ran cold as every nerve cell froze within my body. My breath caught in my throat and my hands started to shake as my fingers locked around the sides of the armchair I sat in. I forced my body to stand and slowly moved toward television as my eyes strained to get a closer look at the artist onstage.

My eyes followed along the arch in her back and trailed along the curve of her neck as she swayed and sang to the melody. When she lifted one arm above her head and slowly twirled her wrist in a circular motion as she continued her siren call to my inner soul, I knew my mind had finally caught up to what my body already acknowledged. My heart raced like a herd of stallion horses. I knew that voice. I knew that husky timbre echoing from my television speakers. My vision blurred as I thought about what this could mean.

My Asha! I had found her. I looked back over at my laptop. And I also knew out how I could get to her.

Chapter Thirteen

A Cleansing
Chicago, IL

Asha

"It's nice to have you and the kids' home again," Momma said as she sipped her iced tea. We were sitting together on the sectional in her living room of her downtown condo.

After some encouragement from Terri, I'd finally decided to take the kids home to Chicago to visit Momma for the Thanksgiving holiday. I hadn't visited my hometown in over 10 years and hadn't physically seen my mother in over six. The last time we'd seen each other was when she'd come to Tyler shortly after Ramon and I had gotten married. She wanted to "check everything out" in her words. Ramon had been the perfect host, acting like the perfect son in law. It was only after she'd left that he began his familiar antics of discipline because I'd gotten dinner on the table a couple of nights late due to her visit.

I took assessment of her now as she stared over the lake front. When she picked us up from Midway Airport, my eyes grew as big as grapefruits because I almost hadn't recognized her. She'd slimmed down quite a bit and seemed to have traded in her typical cotton t-shirts, blue jeans, and comfortable dress attire for classic slacks, short heeled pumps, and fashionable yet tasteful blouses. Her hair was dyed a dark brown color and styled in a modern layered cut that swept her neckline, making her look years younger. Overall she appeared...happy.

She'd also dumped her small two-bedroom West Side apartment for a beautifully furnished condo over looking Lake Michigan. Momma seemed to have been doing financially well for herself since we last saw each other. A pain of guilt stabbed through me as I thought about our years of silence. I knew I should have kept in touch with her, but I'd let my stubbornness and pride keep me from reaching out when I needed her most.

It kept me from reaching out to a lot of people, I admitted to myself as I looked at her now. Taking a steadying breath, I gathered my courage together. The kids were busy Black Friday shopping at the Water Tower Place, so now seemed the perfect time to try and make amends and put some demons to rest. According to my self-help reading, I should attempt to have final closure and resolution with her.

"Mom, can we talk?" I asked tentatively, nervously clasping my hands together in my lap.

"Sure, Asha. What's on your mind?"

"I wanted to talk to you about my father and what really happened that night. I want to understand." I paused. "I *need* to understand."

Mom placed her glass on the coffee table beside her and turned around to look at me.

"I've been waiting years for you to finally get around to asking me, Asha. I've always wondered what I would say or how I could ever explain..." She folded her hands in her lap and looked reflectively back out of the window toward the lake's rolling waves. We sat in silence for a long time while I assumed she was gathering her thoughts.

She gave me a small smile as she finally looked back at me. "I guess the best place to start is at the beginning when your father and I first met."

I nodded my head, encouraging her to continue.

"I was visiting my friend Caroline here in Chicago for the summer after that first year I'd attended NSU. I'd wanted to earn some summer money, and Caroline had heard that a blues group called *Sensory* was looking for a temporary background singer. She knew I could sing and encouraged me to try out. The audition went well and the band immediately liked me. They told me we would be B.B. King's opening act when he came to Gary, Indiana on his summer tour. I met your father after the concert at this hole in the ground shack called *After Dark*. He played trumpet for B.B. King's band."

Momma gave me a beautiful smile, her face glowing with the recollection of memories. "Sebastian was so handsome! And talk about talented! He was one of the best brass players I'd ever heard." Mom looked at me wistfully. "You have his eyes." She shook her head to clear her wayward thoughts.

"Anyway, we moved pretty fast. Faster than I could say I'm proud of. But I didn't care because he swept me off my feet. I knew he couldn't stay because he had to get back on the road with the band. I fully knew the situation and accepted that it was just one night." She walked towards me, sadness sketched across her face. "One month later when my menstrual cycle never came, I realized our affair would had lifetime affects. When I tried to reach out to your father to let him know I thought I could be pregnant, he laughed at me. He told me I couldn't be pregnant with his kid because it had only been that one time. I tried over and over to tell him that I'd never been with anybody else and that you were in fact his, but he would never listen. He kept telling me that a dumb country girl like me would never trap him into a relationship, and that I should find some other sucker to pin it on. He said I'd come up pregnant too fast for it to possibly be his."

"Oh, Momma," I said, reaching out to grab her hand to offer comfort as she stood next to me. A lone tear fell down her cheek, her eyes glazed over in reflection. "I'm so sorry you had to go through that."

Momma continued on, seemingly in her own space and time. "Eventually I'd stopped trying to reach out. Your grandmother kicked me out when she found out I'd gotten pregnant over the summer, so I moved in with Caroline and her folks permanently. I know you don't think too much of Caroline, but if it hadn't been for her help over the years, I don't know where we would be right now." Momma wiped her eyes and looked back at me.

"Anyway, I knew I was going to keep you. There was never a question in my mind on whether or not I wanted you. But I knew I couldn't afford to go back to NSU. So after you were born I took a job at this textile plant on the south side and started working. I couldn't control the fact that your father didn't want to be a part of your life, but I could do my best to make sure you had the best opportunities available. A few years later, right before you started kindergarten, I'd gotten a phone call from his sister Sabrina. I'd met her when she was traveling with him while his band was on tour. Apparently she'd been searching for us for years. She knew what type of brother she had and when he'd mentioned to her I said I'd gotten pregnant but never saw you or me after that, she put two and two together. She wanted to let me know that you and I would always be welcome in her family, despite her brother's actions.

"But the hurt was already too deep for me to accept her offer. I didn't want to have anything to do with her, her brother, or her family. So for years, we struggled and scraped by not because we couldn't do any better, but because we could and I was just too stubborn to fix it." The corner of her mouth lifted to one side as she tilted her head at me. "Where do you think you get your stubbornness from?"

I smiled at her, conceding and acknowledging her point.

"You and I went on like that for years until one day, your father showed up out of nowhere. I think you were around 10 years old at the time."

I searched my memories to see if something would jar. Recognition hit me. "Was that the time I came home and that man was sitting in our kitchen? You told me to go back downstairs to Matt's house and don't come back until after you called for me."

That memory was clear because I'd remembered being shocked that a man was actually in our upper flat apartment. We'd never had male guests in our home before, so to see a man sitting there when I came home from school took me by surprise. She told me to go downstairs to our landlord's home on the first floor and wait with his son, Matt, who was in my class. I was always happy to go to Matt's because he always had the latest video games, so I thought nothing of it at the time.

"Yes, that right." Momma affirmed. "Anyway, we argued something fierce that day. Sebastian demanded to see you, claiming he was a changed man and wanted to do right by you. But I wouldn't have it. I told him to get out or I would call the police and have him arrested.

156

Our arguing drifted from the apartment into the street, neither one of us paying attention to what was going on around us..."

A startled gasp fell from my lips. "Oh my god! I remember! Oh my god, oh my god!" I cried, tears forming in my eyes at the memory. "I remember Matt and I ran outside when we heard all the commotion! Oh my god, Momma!"

"Sebastian didn't see the truck speeding toward him at all," Momma said, remorse clouding her every word as she sat down beside me. "He was too busy yelling at me. The impact hit him so hard that it broke his neck in three different places and severed his spine. He died about a week later after they took him to Loyola hospital."

Tears fell freely on my cheeks at the sense of loss I felt for the man I'd never know. I leaned over and grabbed her in a fierce hug as tears flooded from both of our eyes, both giving and taking comfort from each other. After a moment, she leaned back and wiped the tears from my eyes, her face still cloudy with her own wetness.

"After Sebastian died, Sabrina came to see me again. She wanted us to put aside our differences and get to know one another again, but I didn't know how to do that. By then I had already emotionally shut down. I didn't know how to bridge the gap of isolation I had put myself on after he died. My parents didn't want to have anything to do with me. I didn't have any brothers or sisters or even cousins to reach out to since mom and dad were only children as well. I felt very alone." She reached over and squeezed my hand. "Except for you. You were the only bright light in my world. I was determined you would have a good life.

"As you got older, you began to question whom and where your father was; but I still hadn't learned how to deal with it. That weekend when you and I had that huge fight, I'd just received a letter from Sabrina. She wrote to tell me that Sebastian actually had another child a couple years after I'd had you. She said she had been trying to tell me for years, but every time she approached me, I'd always rebuff her and anything to do with her family."

My eyes grew big as the impact of her words registered in my brain. "Are you...are you trying to tell me that I have a sister or brother somewhere?" I asked, dumbfounded.

"Yes," she replied. "It's something I'm not proud of keeping from you, Asha." Momma looked apologetically into my eyes. "I'm so sorry, sweetheart. I'm asking you to forgive me from the bottom of my heart." She shook her head. "I wasn't in a good place after I got that letter. I felt such betrayal at the thought that Sebastian had been out there taking care and loving someone else's child instead of his first-born before he died. When you approached me that final time asking about your father..."

"That's why you told me he'd rejected me and everything about me..." I whispered, sitting back on the couch. A deep sadness overwhelmed me at the enormity of information she had kept from me all these years.

"Yes," Momma said regretfully. "I thought I was doing the right thing at the time by keeping you away from your father. But now I realize what a foolish and selfish woman I'd been. I've done a disservice to you and to myself. I'm so sorry, baby. When you got pregnant with Austin and Merritt's family spurned you the way that they did, all those old feelings of rejection came back to me. I let my own feelings cloud whatever choices you would have tried to make for yourself. I knew you didn't want to go away to college. But I was determined that you would finish your education like I didn't so that you and Austin could really have a chance." She took a deep breath. "I also knew that you didn't love Ramon, but I still wanted to push you into that relationship because I believed that having a husband would ultimately give you and my grandbabies a better chance in life."

We both sat in silence for a long moment, both of us lost in our own thoughts. Finally, I broke the silence. "So much time wasted because of guilt and pain of rejection..." I said softly.

"Yes..." Momma added.

I took a deep breath, determined to get my words out. "Momma, I do forgive you. I have to. There's nothing that you can do now to change the past. I've lived with regret about a lot of things already, and I simply refuse to add you and all of this information to that list. You can't bring my father back. I have to keep in mind you did what you thought was best for me at the time. That's enough."

I paused. "I think we've both made past choices that we wish we could take back," I said sorrowfully. "I certainly know I have. Ramon was not a good husband, Mom. He was never a good choice for me. He was abusive and he was cruel. The only thing I'm grateful for is that his brutality was always centered around me and never toward the children."

I dropped my head in shame, mustering up the courage to confess the next words I needed to tell her. "I never told anyone this, but I got pregnant again about a year after I had Alanna. Ramon didn't want me to have it. In fact, he actually ordered me to get an abortion. He said it was just another form of birth control anyway, and we needed to control the size of our family because he could only take care of so much. Since both taking the shot and the pill gave me allergic reactions; it was my responsibility to get it taken care of because wearing condoms was something he simply refused to do. He also wasn't going to get a vasectomy because it was like, in his words, cutting off his manhood. So I took a cab to a clinic I'd found in Dallas and had the procedure done there. But afterwards, I got really sick. I mean, violently ill. When I went back to the doctor's office to see what was wrong..." I grabbed my chest as the pain of what I was confessing still ached like an open wound. "...they did another ultrasound on me. They told me I'd actually been pregnant with two babies...twins. The first time they did the procedure, they missed the other embryo. So they had to perform the procedure again right there or risk me bleeding to death."

An anguished cry wretched from my mother's throat. She grabbed me again, holding me in a death embrace as she patted my head. The act seemed to break something within me, and I let the floodgates open on my wall of grief. I thought about the things Momma had confided on top of what I had just released and even more tears fell. We both held each other as the sobs tore through our bodies. Finally, after a while, the tears began to lessen. Momma gave me a kiss on the forehead as I leaned back and wiped my face.

"Well, let's start right now and make a promise to always be there for each other, no matter how stubborn we may be and want to crawl back into our own shells. I've learned that life is what you make it. And I am determined to make it great from here on out," Momma said.

I smiled at her, feeling an unknown pressure lift from me at her words. "Ok," I said softly.

"So," Momma said as she picked up her glass and walked into the gourmet kitchen. "Tell me how's it going with your singing?"

"It's going well. Surprisingly so, in fact," I said, relieved at the lighter change in topics.

"Why are you surprised? You've always been talented."

"I don't know. I guess I never expected people to appreciate my songs the way they seem to be doing."

"It's reaching them on an inner level, sweetheart. Your songs aren't superficial. They're real because the artist that's singing them is creating from truth."

I snorted. "Now you sound like Terri. I admit I do like the singing part. I'm still trying to get comfortable with the performing piece of it, though. But I'll get there eventually. Now, what's going on with you?" I looked around the condo. "I'd say things have been going quite well."

"Yes, well," Momma said, waving off the compliment as she put her glass in the kitchen sink. "After you graduated, I decided I wanted to go back to school. I was too ashamed to tell anyone because I didn't want anyone to know just in case I wasn't able to do it. I started taking night classes here and there until I finally got my undergraduate degree. It took a few years, but I'm glad I finally did it." She smiled at me. "I finally reached back out to Sabrina, too. She helped me get this great job as a case manager with this downtown rehabilitation clinic. After working there a couple of years I wanted to move up so I could have more of a say in some of the decisions being made with patients. So, I went back to get my master's and eventually my doctorate." She raised one eyebrow at me. "I had a lot of time on my hands since I hadn't talked to my daughter in ages." She winked at me, letting me know there wasn't any malice in her words.

"Well, I'm proud of you, Mom." I stood up and followed her into the kitchen. "Thank you for telling me all of this." I looked at her seriously. "You've overcome a lot to get here."

She tilted her head to the side. "And so have you."

The sound of keys jangling in the doorway paused our conversation as we looked toward the front entry hall. Austin and Alanna charged in, bags stuffed with items they'd raided from department stores hanging on their sides.

"Mom," Alanna started. "I absolutely love Chicago! Do you know who we just ran into on the way back here? Bill Murray! He is so cool! He was out doing his Black Friday shopping, too! How awesome is that?!"

Austin rolled his eyes as he sat the bags he was carrying down on the sectional. "She is such a nerd. She shamed me and everyone in our family when she started screeching and hollering his name like a lunatic."

"What can I say? Groundhog Day is one of the best movies ever made," Alanna defended. Alanna's always had a love affair with the 90s decade of comedy movie classics. "Besides, I didn't say anything when you stalked Joakim Noah in Macy's."

"Joakim is a Bulls' basketball legend, Alanna. A freakin' legend. I pattern all my moves after him," Austin countered.

Momma laughed. "Well, I'm glad you two enjoyed yourselves." She looked at me. "Your mom is just going to have to bring you guys back here so you can experience the city even more."

I nodded my head and smiled, a sense of peace and serenity filling my heart. "Most definitely."

Chapter Fourteen

Fan Mail
Houston, TX

Asha

"That's the last take we're gonna try for tonight, Asha. Let's wrap it up and go home." Chad called to me over the microphone. He nodded his head to the producer who was busy recording and mixing today's session.

"Ok, sounds good," I agreed, looking at Chad through the glass window of the sound booth. "My throat is still feeling kind of scratchy," I rasped. I'd been feeling out of sorts for the past couple of weeks. When I woke up a few days ago, my throat glands were swollen and I had a slight fever. Every time I tried to swallow, it felt like I was inhaling fire. When my fever finally broke, I thought I could try and finish the soundtrack I'd started before I'd gotten sick, but I still wasn't feeling up to par.

"I think I'm just going to go home and curl up with some soup and a nice hot cup of lemon tea," I said, grabbing the sweater I'd brought and pulling it tighter around my shoulders.

"You do that. That raspiness was working for the bridge of the song, but I don't want you pushing it. Get as much rest as possible because I need you ready for next week. We've finally got the platform we've been aiming for. Opening the tour for Indie.Arie is a huge freakin' deal. I need you fully operational and on point," Terri said to me as I stepped into the studio.

I chuckled drily. "Yes, Ike. You know, you're sounding more and more like that workaholic every day."

Terri threw back her head and laughed. "Yeah, well. Just be glad I'm not making you eat the cake, Anna Mae."

"I swear, listening to you two is hilarious," Chad said, looking between the two of us. "I've never heard *What's Love Got to Do with It* referenced in a conversation more times in my entire life."

I grinned. "Just wait. You haven't been around long enough to hear *The Color Purple* quotes yet."

Chad smiled indulgently, looking at Terri from underneath his lashes. "And I hope to stick around for a long time."

Terri rolled her eyes. "*Anyway*, the front desk called while you were recording, Asha. They said you had a package delivered and they need for you to sign for it. You want me to wait for you?"

"No, you go on home. Like I said, I'm headed home myself. I'll just catch up with you tomorrow."

Since *The Painted Lady* premiered, things were really going well financially for the kids and me. The kids and I moved out of Terri's townhome and secured a nice bungalow in the Montrose area. I'd even been able to stow away a bit of savings for the kids. With Terri as my manager, I knew I didn't have to worry about anyone taking advantage of me or cheating me out of any royalties. I also felt more and more comfortable with performing live. It seemed that the conversation I'd had with Momma was not only long overdue, but was the trigger I needed to release my inhibitions about people focusing directly on me. My self-doubt was at an all time low. Although I still felt some anxiety, I was nowhere near where I had once been.

I waved goodbye to Terri and Chad and walked down the stairs of the studio to the main corridor of the Dove building. My eyes widened in awe as I walked to the reception desk and took in the sight before me. Sitting on the desk was the biggest and most extravagant bouquet of roses I'd ever seen. There must have been at least 200 stems displayed in the arrangement. *Someone must really care about someone here,* I thought wistfully.

"Hey Kay, Terri said you had a delivery come for me?" I asked the lady sitting behind the desk.

The pretty Latina woman crinkled her eyes at me. "Yes girl, I sure did. The delivery guy said you had to sign for them personally, but I let him know I'd make sure you got them since I didn't know how long you'd be recording. After all, who could miss them?" She waved her hand toward the arrangement.

I looked at her confused. "What are you talking about?"

"These roses are for you, honey." She clasped her hands together. "Take a look at the card. I've been dying to know who they're from."

"You've got the wrong person Kay, or the delivery guy made a mistake. You should hurry up and try to catch him so he could pick these up and delivery them to the right person. I'm sure whoever sent them will be pissed they got sent to me instead."

Kay shook her head. "No mistake, girl. The envelope was clearly addressed to a Ms. Asha St. Claire."

That got my attention. "Asha St. Claire?" I asked hesitantly.

"Yes, isn't that your maiden name?" Kay asked.

"Yes, but nobody knows that. It's only a handful of people who even know I'm the Painted Lady. Everybody here knows me by Asha Towers because I never bothered to take back my maiden name after my divorce. I was too focused on just hurrying through the proceedings."

"Well, apparently, somebody has been doing their homework. Quit stalling, Asha and opening up the dang card!" Kay all but demanded.

I raised an eyebrow at her demand, but reached over and grabbed the card from her hands.

I opened the seal and scanned through the words. A small gasp escaped my lips. I read the card out loud this time as proof again to my disbelieving ears.

"To the Best Vocalist this world has ever seen.
I always knew you could do it.
I'll be seeing you soon.
Signed, Your #1 Fan (and this is NOT your ex).
P.S. Get some rest and take care of that cold. That is not a
request."

I tried to keep the card from falling from my shaking hands as I felt my heart pounding. I slowly turned my head toward the bouquet. "This is for me." I still had to say disbelievingly.

"Ahh, yeah. That's what I've been trying to tell you girl!"

"It says it's from my number one fan."

"Wow. Stalker much?" Kay said, a small frown crossing her face.

"It doesn't sound stalkerish. In fact, it sounds like it's from someone who actually knows me. I mean, they called me by St. Claire." I paused. "And how did they know I'd been sick?"

"Who knows? Who cares? Take the flowers home, self medicate on tea and antihistamines, and we'll see you when you're ready to come out of hibernation."

I smiled at her as I picked the bouquet up with both hands. It was so large it blocked my immediate walking view. "Kay, can you open the lobby doors for me so I can hold these?" I looked back at the bouquet. "I may need you to open my car door, too. Can you get my keys out?" I turned to the side so she could have access to my purse.

"Sure thing," Kay said as she secured my keys. She sighed as she looked longingly at the flowers. "Someone must care about you a lot."

It seemed so, I thought to myself as butterflies took over my stomach. It seemed so.

∧∧∧

"Are you feeling better Mom?" Austin asked. I'd already had a hot bath, taken enough medicine to knock out a small army, and slipped into the coolness of my bed sheets when I'd gotten Austin's phone call to check in on me. My eyes were slowly drooping as I laid my spinning head back against my pillow. Despite how horrible I felt, my heart always warmed whenever Austin called. No matter how busy I'm sure his life was now with basketball practice and classes at NSU, he still found the time to check in on me every week just to see how I was faring.

"I'm laying down now. Hopefully I'll be on my feet in a few days. I had Alanna fix dinner tonight and she nearly passed out because she actually had to fix it herself. That girl is spoiled rotten when it comes to getting home-cooked meals on a regular basis, I'm telling you." I said, thinking back on the conversation I'd had earlier that evening with my daughter. She chalked it up as being equivalent to the 10 plagues coming down on Egypt.

Austin laughed. "Yeah, that sounds like her. I miss the brat." He paused for a moment. "So, did anything special happen today?" he asked mysteriously.

"As a matter of fact, yes. You wouldn't believe it, but somebody sent me the most beautiful arrangement of flowers today! At first I was kind of afraid that Ramon was making an appearance, but the card in the delivery said it was definitely not him. It also said it was from my number one fan," I said thoughtfully. I'd contemplated all evening and still couldn't picture who would take the time to send me such an extravagant gift. Once I got home and took the time to really study the flowers, I figured they must have cost the sender a small fortune to send to me.

My mind had run through every possibility, including immediate friends who also knew I was sick; but still came up with nothing. Holley, my dear friend who'd followed me to Houston a couple of years after me, wouldn't send something like. Terri would just have demanded I get my ass in bed and get it together. She wouldn't send flowers to solidify her direct order. I didn't think Austin would send something like that, but just in case...

"You didn't send them to me, did you sweetie?" I asked doubtfully.

Austin snorted. "Absolutely not. Not that I don't love you Mom, but you are on the phone with a struggling college student here. The struggle is real in these parts."

"Oh, be quiet," I said. "You are not struggling. Not anymore at least." I snuggled down deeper in my bed, feeling the tug of sleep pulling hard against my consciousness.

"Well, if it wasn't you, I don't know where they came from." I yawned loudly. "Look baby, I need to let you go. I can barely keep my eyes open."

"Ok, Mom. I love you. Take care of yourself, please. Stop pushing yourself so hard. Alanna and I are fine. We want to make sure you are, too. You don't have to work yourself to death to make sure we're okay."

I smiled against my pillow. "I know, baby boy. I know. I'll talk to you later. Love you too," I said as I disconnected the call and fell into the deepest sleep I'd had in a long time.

Chapter Fifteen

The Claiming
Houston, TX

Asha

I still hadn't figured it out. For the past two months, I'd been receiving mysterious gifts and packages from my secret admirer. At first it freaked me out because the tone of each message was so personal, almost too personal. The idea that I'd gained a Kathy Bates' *Misery* impersonator was not too far from my mind. But as the gifts continued, the notes became more and more endearing, almost like a reverence; casting away any sort anxiety about someone actually wishing me harm in any way. Each note always ended with the same salutation:

Because You Deserve It. I'll Be Seeing You Soon. Always, Your #1 Fan.

Now after weeks of flowers, balloon bouquets, a full day's paid spa treatment, a Salvatore Ferragamo Sofia handbag, and a carefully made candy arrangement full of Jolly Ranchers, Twizzlers, Blow Pops, Now and Later Hard Chews, and Starbursts that had me salivating because the person obviously knew I hated chocolate; I was justifiably intrigued as to who my mysterious fan could be. I figured whoever had taken the time to try and get my attention had definitely succeeded. If anything, at least I wanted to thank him or her for their devotion to my music and obvious appreciation for my work.

Now, as I held the latest note in my hand that was sent along with two-dozen pink roses, I felt a thrill of anticipation course through me. The note indicated my admirer would be meeting me backstage after my concert at the Veterans Memorial Stadium in Jackson, Mississippi. I couldn't wait. The concert was next weekend.

I smiled to myself as I thought about Terri's words to me one evening as she negotiated the tour contract. She'd waved off my initial suggestion on passing on the concert. Rolling her eyes, she'd walked up to me in the studio, her stiletto heels clicking on the marbled floor. "You have to go for the stars, Asha. Don't be afraid of where you might fall; or even the *possibility* that you might fall. After all...small dreams, small accomplishments."

Now looking back, I had to admit she knew what she was talking about. The initial concerts opening for Indie.Arie had gone well. Really well. My single already reached 700,000 downloads on iTunes and was continuing to soar. My album continued to move up on the Billboard charts and Terri was already predicting reaching Platinum status in the next month or two. It was hard not to catch on to her wave of excitement.

However Terri didn't want me to reveal my true identity just yet. She wanted to wait until after the Jackson show, where she'd booked a small press conference to make the announcement. She said she wanted to continue building the anticipation to the highest level and the Jackson show would definitely be at an all-time high. So for now anytime I performed, I wore my traditional white porcelain mask that left only my mouth, nose, and one eye exposed along with a pair of Vikky Secret imitation white, black, and yellow butterfly wings when I hit the stage. I was comfortable with that decision, too. By continuing the mystery, it was still affording the kids a certain level of privacy.

I folded the note and placed it on the nightstand next to my bed. Reaching over, I turned off the lamp and snuggled down in my comforter. I was calling it an early night. I wanted to get plenty of rest so I could be at my best tomorrow. Momma was also flying in-- she usually stayed with Alanna in Houston when I toured and I was definitely grateful for her help. We only had three rehearsals left before next week's performance and I needed to be at my best.

As my eyes grew heavy, images of a sexy pair of blue-green eyes invaded my thoughts, lulling me to sleep.

∧∧∧

The dressing room the stadium provided to me was filled with pink and red roses, completely covering one side of the already condensed space. I looked at my reflection in the dressing mirror as I sat and applied the last touches to my hair, arranging it in a sweeping chignon at the base of my neck. The white leather jumpsuit I wore matched my trademarked mask perfectly along with my jeweled encrusted boots and silver bangles.

Taking a deep breath, I stood and forced myself to focus on my warm-up. Somehow the task always seemed to both prepare my voice and calm the butterflies in my stomach. Even though I was feeling more and more comfortable singing live, I still got a little nervous right before a performance. As I prepared to sing the words I'd grown to cherish, I felt my pulse slow and my soul find the peace it needed to go onstage.

Letting my head drift back and closing my eyes, I took a deep breath and began to sing the melody of Luther Vandross' *Superstar* remake. My thoughts drifted back to the night on the Trace where all my inhibitions had fled. I reminded myself how I had felt completely free, powerful, and beautiful. My goal was to then transmit those same conjured feelings to perform for my fans.

My body swayed as I continued to sing, wrapping my arms around my chest and imaging they were his arms as he held me, encouraging me to sing and let go...

A knock on the door shook me from my musing.

"Come on in," I called, shaking myself from my thoughts as I sat back down in my seat.

Terri bustled in, looking every bit the power manager that she was in her crisp, tailor made pantsuit and stiletto heels. She closed the door behind her.

"Hey girl. I wanted to make sure you were decent." She stopped and looked over the room, giving a low whistle at the flowers. "I'd say somebody's been a good girl," she remarked with a smirk.

I laughed. "Trust me; it's not what you think. Obviously somebody's a really big fan of my music. They've been sending gifts like this for a few weeks. It's kind of sweet actually."

"Sure, Asha. Whatever you say." She waved her hand as she regained her train of thought. She looked kind of flustered. "Look, I know you're doing your vocal warm-ups, but I have somebody out here who wants to see you. I told him he could wait until after the show, but he's really insistent."

I glanced at the flowers. Had my admirer changed his mind and decided to meet me before the show instead of after? My eyebrows drew together as a small frown crossed my face. *What was the urgency?* A sudden thought came to me.

"He doesn't look like a serial killer or somebody that might try and hurt me does he?" I whispered, closing my hand into a fist. I looked around the room for possible defensive weapons. My eyes caught on the metal bucket filled with ice near the door. If needed, I could dump the ice and use that. It looked like it had some weight to it.

Terri threw her head back and laughed. "Ah, no. I'd say he was pretty harmless. Well, except for this look he gave me when I told him no at seeing you right now." She visually shuddered. "Something about that look told me I'd better get my ass in here and announce that he was outside." She smiled at me. "I think you might like this visitor, sweetie."

Curious, I nodded my head to let her know it was OK. She turned back around and opened the door.

"Ok, come on in. She's dressed."

Anticipation curled within me as I leaned forward in my chair to peer around Terri's frame. Disbelief followed by excitement ran threw me as I saw who had walked through the door.

"Mr. Blackburn!" I exclaimed, standing up. I walked over and threw my arms around the mountain of a man.

Master B chuckled as he opened his arms to accept my embrace. "Hello, precious," he said softly in my ear as he squeezed me in a paternal hug.

"It's so good to see you after all these years," I said, leaning back to look at his face.

"Same here, little one. It is wonderful to see you looking so well," he said, giving me a warm smile as we released each other. "As well as you, too, Terri," Master B acknowledged, nodding her way. Terri gave him a small smile.

Hugging him had felt like coming home. I didn't realize how much I'd missed hanging out at his house during weekend visits with Levi, Kennedy, and Jackie. Master B would fix his traditional homemade Creole dishes, and we'd all dig in and spend the day just hanging out and playing Mario Bros on Levi's Super Nintendo system. Such great memories...

"Hey! Is Levi here with you?" I asked suddenly. "I'd love to see my old friend again." I looked expectedly at Master B, then at Terri in time to see her face grow suddenly pale.

"As if I'd stay away," said a deep voice from the doorway. I looked behind Master B and grinned as Levi walked in and stood beside his dad.

I screamed and jumped into Levi's arms, nearly sending us both stumbling to the ground. "LEVI! Oh my god! Oh my god! I missed you!" I laughed, squeezing him in a tight embrace. Master B and Levi laughed at my antics. I glanced excitedly at Terri and noticed she'd moved to stand off to the side with a tight smile on her face.

"Man! How long has it been?" I asked breathlessly, looking back at Levi. It was wonderful to see my old friend again. A sweet sense of nostalgia came upon me.

"Too long..." Levi said, a strange expression crossing his face.

"How did you guys even know I was performing tonight? Better yet, how in the world did you figure out it was me?" I asked, trying to regain some of my composure.

172

"Oh, we have our ways. Isn't that right, son?" Master B said, looking at Levi.

"We certainly do." Levi grinned mysteriously.

"Okay...well, after the show we've definitely got to hook up. I need to hear all about what you've been doing with yourself."

"I don't think you'll have time after the show," Levi said. Quick as lightning, Master B's hand struck out to tag Levi in the back of his head. Levi lowered his head to mask his grin.

I frowned hard at him. "Well, why not? You can't expect to just waltz in here after years of not seeing each other and then sashay your ass right back out the door? We need to hang out damn it!" I said a little desperately.

Master B cleared his throat. I looked over at him as he looked back at me disapprovingly, clearly not liking my choice of words. A solitary raised eyebrow leered back at me. I immediately felt chagrined and lowered my head, feeling slightly embarrassed that I could still be reprimanded at my age.

"See!" Terri finally spoke. "That's the look I was talking about! Makes you want to fall on the floor and scream *'I'm sorry your Highness! Is there anything else you need?'*"

I felt a charge in the air as Master B and Levi both turned at that moment to stare at Terri. Both postures straightened slightly, and Levi cocked his head slightly to the side, a small frown on his face. I looked at Terri and she had the grace to look chastened; knowing she was treading on dangerous territory.

She then smiled sweetly at Master B to try and lessen the tension. She walked over to him to lay a delicate hand on his arm. "I apologize, but if you guys could excuse us. Asha really does need to finish her warm-ups. She's on stage in 10 minutes."

"Brat behavior indeed," Master B murmured, turning to look at Levi. Levi just nodded his head in agreement.

I rolled my eyes. "And now you see the life I've been leading with the slave driver over here," I said mockingly as Terri lightly punched me in my shoulder.

"We understand. We'll try and see if we can catch you after the show. If not, well...we'll see you soon." Levi winked at me. "Let's go, Pop. We don't want to miss this star's opening."

Levi turned and started for the door. As he reached for the knob, he turned and looked at Terri, who had all but tried to camouflage herself against the back wall. She shifted uncomfortably from one foot to the other as she met Levi's gaze.

"Terri," Levi said, his baritone voice seeming to have gotten lower as her name came across his lips.

"Levi," Terri said, letting the 'l' from his name roll across her tongue as she met his gaze. She then licked her bottom lip with her tongue. Levi's eyes shifted down to her mouth and his gaze immediately darkened. They stared at each other a few moments more before Levi broke his gaze and walked out of the door.

"What do they say nowadays? Break a leg or something like that?" Master B said, kissing me lightly on the forehead. "Remember to enjoy yourself tonight while you're on that stage, little one."

"Thank you. I will," I said as I walked behind him to close the door. Suddenly, a thought occurred to me as I yanked the door back open. I looked down the hallway and spotted Levi and Master B still walking away from my room.

"Hey you guys! Have you two been sending me gifts all this time saying you're my number one fan?" I called.

Levi turned around to look at me. "No, sweetie. We're definitely fans, but we're not your number one." With that, he winked at me, turned around, and continued to walk down the hallway toward the stage exit, Master B close on his heels.

Confused, I walked back into my room, closing the door behind me. I guess my admirer would remain mysterious for now. At least until after the show.

∧∧∧

I remained seated on the barstool onstage facing the wall, soaking in the crowd's applause. I'd just finished my second encore of the night and couldn't help the sense of freedom that spread through me as the curtain went down for a final time. As always when a show was over, I basked in the pleasure of knowing others enjoyed listening to my music just as much as I enjoyed singing it.

As the curtain hit the man-made stage floor, I stood up and walked over to Terri, who waited for me next to the mock overhang. It had been difficult to negotiate that the stage be built to allow a temporary wall on one side, which I would face during my performance. In addition, we wanted the overhang to partially mask the band area that sat to the right of the stage. The promoters had initially been resistant to the costs associated with the upgrades, but with Terri casually stating that the concert could draw the same amount of coverage if it were held in Vicksburg, we found ourselves with promoters that in the end were more than willing to negotiate to win my contract.

"Fabulous, honey. Just fabulous, as usual." She clapped as she gave me a quick congratulatory hug. I looked at her as I felt my smile slowly slid away. Tears had misted in her eyes as she held my hands tightly in hers. *"Soy tan feliz para los dos."*

I tilted my head at her, confused at her sudden switch to Spanish. "Wow, Terri. I thought you liked my singing. I didn't know it was so bad that it brought you to tears," I said jokily, clearly not understanding what she'd just said and trying to gage her reaction. Maybe seeing Levi again had more of an impact than I'd originally thought.

"Now, will the first time we see each other be a lesson in discipline, little one? I'll never let anyone talk bad about you, including yourself. You were fantastic, love. You will bask in the moment, your moment."

I froze as the sound of that voice nearly sent me to my knees. It couldn't be. It couldn't be. Oh god. My hands shook as I felt Terri release them since they had deadlocked with hers in a death grip. My already dry throat felt even drier as I tried unsuccessfully to swallow the lump suddenly blocking my air. My eyes grew wide. I couldn't breathe. Or at least it didn't feel like I could. I looked down at my chest and watched as my muscles moved air in and out of my lungs at a rapid speed. Okay, it looked like I was breathing. But why was my head suddenly spinning? I'd dreamed of hearing Delphi's voice a million times in the past, but never had I had such a strong reaction as the one I was having right now. I looked at Terri again, knitting my eyebrows in a look of both confusion and panic. Maybe I was having a heart attack? And why was she just standing there staring at me? *Why the hell wasn't she calling someone for help?*

"I am so happy for the two of you," Terri whispered again. Okay, something was evidently wrong.

"Turn around and take the mask off, love. I need to see your face." That voice again. It was speaking to me again.

Dazed, I pulled the mask from my face, but closed my eyes as if I were standing in the middle of a dream and couldn't wake up. I turned around slowly toward the sound of that the voiced order and slowly lifted my lids to peer at the vision before me. There, standing in all his masculine glory, was my dream materialized into flesh.

"Jaymes..." I whispered; my jaw hanging slightly open as I struggled to catch my breath. My shaking fingers dropped the mask on the stage floor.

Before I could utter another syllable, Jaymes quickly crossed the short distance between us. He bent down low, picking me up from my waist in a solid show of strength. I stared into his eyes as my heart continued to race. Confirmation and recognition washed through me as I realized my love was here. My love was here. My love was here and holding me in his arms. My love was holding me in his arms and looking at me like he loved me too. My love. My love...

All other thoughts ceased as Jaymes captured my lips in the most commanding demonstration of possession I'd ever experienced.

Chapter Sixteen

Back at the Club

Jaymes

The moment I saw her singing on stage, my cock had been at attention. Shit, it had been hard for the past few weeks, ever since I discovered the locations of her tour dates with a little help from Austin.

It had been relatively easy to get in touch with him once I'd discovered he'd actually pledged the same fraternity that I had. After a couple of calls to find out who his NSU Chapter sponsor was; I'd finally been able to get patched through to Austin. After letting him know exactly who I was and what I intended to do once I found his mother, he'd been surprisingly cooperative in helping me secure the dates and locations of her upcoming concerts as well as her current home address. He told me he'd remembered the conversations he and I had when he was smaller, and often wondered what had happened to me since he never heard from me shortly after his mom graduated.

He went on to tell me that Asha had divorced some years back and wasn't currently dating anyone right now, much to my relief. I assured him I wouldn't be dropping by unannounced, especially with her daughter still living there. But I did have every intention of making myself a permanent figure in her near future. He seemed ok, almost relieved by that idea.

I stood back and watched from the shadowed overhang as she sang her song with the same passion I'd seen that night on the Trace. God, she was so beautiful. That mask did nothing to hide the warmth of her eyes or the sensuous curves of those lips. And that body suit, damn. I felt my dick twitch at the thought of what was underneath.

I felt someone touch my shoulder and turned around. Terri was looking up at me with the strangest look on her face. I smiled down at her and held my arms open for a hug. Her stance relaxed a little as she walked into my embrace.

"Hey kiddo. Good to see you."

"Delphi...I should have figured you'd be here too since I just saw your partner in crime a few minutes ago."

I smiled wider at her. "Levi made an entrance, did he?"

She nodded her head, but didn't say anything.

"I'm sorry we didn't get a chance to let you know we'd be coming earlier, but things have been kind of hectic over the past couple of weeks..." I started. Hectic with all of the subterfuge and planning I'd done so this night could be absolutely perfect. But I didn't mention that slight detail.

Terri smiled faintly at me. "That's ok. I don't think I would have been able to handle an extra warning anyway," she said. She hugged her arms across her chest. "You're here for Asha, aren't you?"

"I'll always be here for her. I love her. I always have."

"Good. Be good to her or I'll fucking kick your ass, Delphi. I mean it. She's been through a lot."

I chuckled at her threat. "Always the big sister," I leaned over and kissed her forehead. "I promise. I won't let her push me away a second time," I paused as her words registered. "What do you mean she's been through a lot?" I looked at her expectantly.

She shrugged. "That's her story to tell you. But for all it's worth, she and those kids need you in their life. I think you'd be good for all of them." I nodded my head and turned back to Asha.

We stood silently for a moment as we watched her performance. Realizing her song was just about over, I moved back toward the band into the shadows. Having been just as captivated as her audience as she belted out the last words to her melody, I joined the crowd in a thunderous applause. They chanted for a couple of encore performances, which she supplied graciously. Finally, the curtain fell around her signaling the end of her show.

My heart raced as I watched Asha rise from her seat and walk over to Terri. The overhang gave me a small cover, keeping my presence a secret a few moments more so I could continue to stare at her without being detected. Terri leaned over and gave her a quick hug, then murmured something I couldn't hear.

I watched as a look of confusion came upon Asha's face. Damn, I hope that look wasn't because Terri just told her I was here and she didn't want to see me. Fearing she'd given me away; I walked toward them and stopped a short distance away. I was close enough to catch her last words as I heard her downgrade herself, a major thorn in my side. I couldn't let anybody dishonor the thing I cherished the most in my life, including her.

The words were out of my mouth before I could stop them. I heard myself threaten her with discipline if she didn't stop criticizing the thing I loved. I watched as her whole body froze at my words. Terri released her hands and said something else I couldn't quite make out; but I decided I'd had enough of the delay.

"Turn around and take the mask off, love. I need to see your face." I said a little too forcefully. If I didn't touch her soon I was going to lose it.

I watched as she took her mask off and rotated in my direction. She slowly opened her eyes to look up at me as an incredulous look of disbelief swept over her features. Her eyes narrowed, then widened as realization hit her.

"Jaymes..."

The sound of my real name finally being uttered from her lips broke my control. I marched over to her and picked her up, enjoying the weight of her in my hands and the feel of her curves under my fingers. I couldn't speak for a moment as I was caught in her gaze. Everything inside of me screamed MINE. I just prayed she wanted to be claimed.

Her facial expressions were always so easy to read. I watched as she went from a look of confusion, to disbelief, to apprehension, and then acceptance. Her last look of love and reverence did me in as I felt her entire body relax and go limp in my arms. With that final clue, I leaned in to taste the mouth I'd waited years to taste again.

"I'll catch up with you guys at the press conference tomorrow." Terri called as I led Asha toward the back entrance and away from the waiting mob of fans. I threw my hand up to acknowledge her request, but didn't stop walking.

"Where are we going?" Asha asked breathlessly as she hurriedly followed my long strides toward the stadiums' back entrance where I had a limo waiting. I didn't want to be distracted by the task of driving when I'd finally get her alone.

"You'll see," I replied, pulling her along. The driver saw us as we approached the vehicle and proactively opened the door. I waited for Asha to slide in first and then followed her, closing the door behind me.

We sat across from each other for a moment as we drank in the sight of each other while the driver got into his seat and took off. Asha wrung her hands nervously together and I tried deducing what might have her concerned.

"Your number one fan is absolutely thrilled to be with you right now." I guessed, a casual smirk spreading across my face.

"*You've* been the person sending me those gifts?" she cried, looking relieved. "God, I was worried whoever was sending them would be upset when I didn't show up after the concert."

"Oh no, you should still worry. Not about meeting me, but what I will do if you don't hurry up and get over here. I missed you, love."

Asha grinned and scurried over to me. She straddled my thighs and put her hands behind my neck.

"So you're a fan of my music, huh?"

"I'm a fan of YOU, Asha heart."

"Is that right?" she said seductively, wriggling on my lap. I could feel the heat from her crotch rubbing against my trousers. I took a deep breath to maintain my control.

"Damn straight," I rasped.

She leaned in closer to my neck and ran her nose along my jawline, breathing in my scent. The lightness of the touch tickled my beard. She then laid her cheek against mine and snuggled her face into me. I wrapped my hands around her hips in a possessive hold.

I felt her chuckle against my chest. "What is it about you that always has me straddling your lap in moving vehicles? You got a fetish I need to know about?"

I smiled into her hair and said nothing, breathing in her feminine scent.

"I haven't been the same since we've been apart, love. Know this: I will never be separated from you again. Ever. I can't take it." I whispered.

"I've missed you too, Jaymes. So much..." she said as she leaned up to kiss me. I crushed her to my chest as my hand moved up to position her head like I needed it. Gripping her neck, I devoured her mouth, tasting every corner and savoring her unique flavor. I felt her moan against me as she pressed herself further against my frame. We continued to relish each other's mouths until we finally had to break apart for air. Asha then laid her cheek back against my chest, seemingly to listen to my heartbeat as my hands slowly stroked her back.

We sat like that for a minute before I broke the silence. Her earlier words had peaked my interest.

"Babe," I said.

"Mmmm?" she murmured lazily.

"You called me Jaymes..." I started.

"Mmmm," she replied.

I waited a minute to see if she would offer any explanations as to why she changed what she called me. When nothing came out I tried prompting her again. "You've always called me Delphi, love. What's changed?"

She leaned back in my lap and looked at me. She tilted her head and licked her bottom lip as a hint of a smile grew.

"Because you once told me nicknames are superficial connections to people. I want to know you again, Jaymes. The real you, down to every hidden secret, desire and fantasy. I'm willing to open my heart to you and I want you to do the same with me." She paused as a small frown came across face. "I don't know how that relates to terms of endearment, though. How does that work?"

I laughed as exhilaration flowed through me. "Ahh, little one. I'm pleased beyond words that you remembered. And for the record, endearments are meant to achieve the exact opposite. They can represent the strong emotional bond a person can have for another." I bent down and ran my tongue across her bottom lip and heard her gasp. "I for one intend to be bonded to you in more ways than one before the night is through." I watched as her eyes dilated and grew dark at my words. I grinned wolfishly and gave her a wink. She smiled back shyly and lowered her head.

Finally our limo slowed to a stop and I glanced out of the window. "We're here. Come on." I opened the door, pulling Asha behind me.

"Finesse?" she asked curiously, craning her neck up at me as she took in her surroundings. "What's this?"

"This is a gift from Mr. Blackburn. We have the whole place to ourselves tonight. Come on." I used the keys Master B gave me and unlocked the double doors leading to the inside of the club. Locking the door behind us, I grabbed Asha by the hand and led her through the dimly lit rec area over to the stairs leading to the second floor.

Before we got there, a tug on my hand prompted me to turn around. Asha looked back at me, a mixture of nervousness and determination covering her face.

"Jaymes, I...it's been a really long time. I mean, I want to be with you. I do. It's just that I haven't...well, I mean, I haven't been interested since...I mean what I'm trying to say is I need to know...oh man, I'm not sure how to say this."

I turned around to look at her, understanding filling me with warmth. "Get it out of your head, Asha. Put it on your lips. How long has it been, love?"

Asha looked up at me. "Not since my divorce...and a few years before that." Her bottom lip trembled as her eyes misted with unshed tears. "I'm not the same girl you used to know, Jaymes. I've changed in a lot of ways, but in some ways I still question anything that might be good..." She let go of my hand and stepped away from me. What the fuck? Oh, hell no...

"I haven't wanted anyone like this in a long time, but I won't let my desires make me out a fool again. I have to use both my heart as well as my common sense. I've made too many bad choices in the past and I can't afford to get this wrong. I would kill me..."

Her last words faded out as she looked down at the hand that formerly held mine. She then took a deep breath and straightened her posture. She looked back up at me with an unflinching stare. *Ahh,* I thought. There's the bite I was missing. I bit my cheek to keep the smirk off my face and crossed my arms in front of me, waiting for her to go on. I knew she needed to get this out.

"I want you to know that it killed me when we stopped being together back in college. I've loved you since the first moment we've met. You were and still are the man who will always have my heart. But..." She paused as she thought about her next words. "But *my* heart was never the only one on the line. My son really grew attached to you when he was smaller. He would talk my ear off about when his friend Delphi would be able to call and talk to him again. You seemed so sincere and loving whenever you guys would speak on the phone." She took a deep breath as I watched her eyes fill with tears. My heart broke at hearing her confession, knowing what the root of the issue was.

"But you always seemed so closed off about your own children. It was like you didn't even like them or the thought that they even existed. How could I ever expect you to treat us with real love and devotion when it seemed you treated your own blood like they weren't shit? It was the perfect hypocrisy to the connection you always talked about, a poster child example for the superficial. It made me scared to commit to you, of thinking about having *any* type of future with you."

She stared me straight in the eye, unblinkingly. "It's what's stopping me right now from going up those stairs with you. The kids and I won't be a superficial front. We need the real thing. The real you. And

I've come to realize over the past few years that damn it, we deserve it. I deserve it. Hell, it seemed like it took me forever to realize that."

She then let loose a long breath, as if confessing had been a momentous weight off her shoulders. My mind, however, was reeling over everything I had just heard. I struggled to understand and grasp all of the feelings her words had triggered: relief, anger, frustration, understanding, joy, love, proudness, and exhilaration. I was relieved that I finally understood why she walked away from me all those years ago. Anger raged at myself for not having the balls to explain earlier. Frustration stormed at the thought of all these wasted years we'd spent apart. Understanding humbled me knowing that for whatever reason we'd been kept apart, our time had finally come, and I wouldn't be deterred. Joy screamed through me at the knowledge that she loved me as much as I worshipped her. Proudness seeped from every pore at how far she'd come with vocally expressing herself, especially with something that obviously weighed so heavily on her mind. And finally, exhilaration overwhelmed me at the thought that this woman, this goddess, will finally be mine.

I rubbed a hand along my beard, trying to figure out where I should start. I nodded to one of the dinette chairs sitting close by.

"Have a seat Asha. Let's clear the air about a few things." She looked relieved as she nodded her head and took a seat. Did she think I would be mad about what she'd just said? It was time to put this shit to rest once and for all.

I pulled a chair out from the table and dragged it directly in front of her. Sitting down, I slowly reached for one of her hands, praying she wouldn't pull away. To my relief, she allowed me to touch and hold her delicate hand in mine. Curling my fingers around hers, I pulled her hand to my heart.

"Thank you little one for being straightforward with me. And thank you for even coming back here with me tonight." I shook my head. "I guess it was pretty arrogant of me to assume you would just hop on board with my plans without any sort of explanation." I shrugged my shoulder. "But I'll confess that pigheadedness runs strong on my dad's side of the family, so I'd say I got it honest." I gave her a small smile, hoping to relieve some of the tension I still saw in her posture.

It worked. Her shoulders relaxed and her eyes looked at me expectedly.

"But your words have humbled me more than you can ever know." I squeezed the hand I held to my chest. "You are my heart love. You are the pulse of me. I don't work or even function without you." The feel of her soft skin in mine was playing havoc with my hormones, so I let her hand go and stood up again, turning my back to her. I needed to distance myself for a minute so I can clear my head and get my thoughts together to try and explain myself instead of thinking about jumping her and trying to shove my dick in her warm, tight pussy.

I turned back around and stared at her beautiful face. She sent me a smile of encouragement. "Since you've been forthright with me, I must do the same." I took a breath. "I know I told you I had twin boys when I was in high school." She nodded her head. "But what you didn't know was that I had always suspected that those boys weren't mine." I heard her gasp, but I went on. "Felicia and I got together one night after one of my football games. Some of the guys had wanted to celebrate winning our regionals and had heard that she was throwing a house party. She lived on the 800 block of Manor Street and something told me it was a bad idea, but the guys wanted to go there so..."

I felt Asha looking at me with a slightly confused frown. "Consider Manor Street similar to your Cabrini Green housing projects in Chicago before they were torn down," I explained as understanding dawned on her face. I continued with my story.

"So a few of us went over to her house and partied. The party was wild, I mean like Animal House wild. Felicia and I ended up in her parent's bedroom and..." I looked away for a moment, not wanting her to see the anger that remembering that night was stirring in me. When I finally got control of my emotions, I looked back at her. "I don't even remember what the hell happened that night. All I know is that I woke up in her parent's fucking bed the next morning with her laying on top of me telling me she'd just had the best fucking screw of her life and wanted to do it again. It made me sick and I ran the fuck out of there. The next thing I knew a couple of months later she was telling everybody she'd gotten pregnant by me that night. But I didn't remember anything." I clenched my fists to keep them from shaking because of the anger I felt.

I watched Asha as a look of pure outrage crossed her features. She stood and placed her hands on her beautifully shaped hips.

"Where the fuck was your friends? Why the hell did they just leave you there?" she demanded.

My heart soared at her outburst. Even though right now I knew she was still wary of me, she still wanted to protect me. God, I loved this woman.

"They thought I was having a good time. They said they kept hearing Felicia moaning all night and thought I was enjoying myself. I can definitely say none of those guys and I are friends anymore. Since she was convinced I'd fathered her baby, I didn't want to seem like the jerk that just fucked her and left. After all, I did wake up naked with her straddling me that morning, so I very well could have been. But I always still had my doubts." I shrugged my shoulder.

"Anyway, when I got to NSU and got to talking with Master B one weekend, he got really suspicious, especially when I told him the circumstances of how Felicia got pregnant. He and my dad teamed up and did some digging on their own. They petitioned the courts to push for a paternity test after I left NSU as a condition of continuing the hefty child support she'd been receiving. The test results showed there was no way I could have fathered her sons. Turned out she was just looking for a meal ticket to put her on easy street. I just ended up being the poor sucker who got caught in the trap."

I walked back over to her and laid my palm against her cheek. Asha leaned into it and I rejoiced at the connection.

"I didn't want to taint you with my issues at the time, that's why I never wanted to talk about. I can see now that was a huge mistake on my part and for that I'm sorry. The last thing I ever wanted to do was hurt or confuse you."

186

Tears broke free of Asha's lids and slid freely down her face. I swiped my thumb across her cheek as she placed her hand on top of mine. We stood there in silence, digesting all that we'd confessed to each other.

"We've wasted so much time on bad assumptions, haven't we?" she said softly.

I nodded my head, unable to speak due to the level of emotion running through me.

Asha looked up at me, a gleam of hope and love shining in her eyes. "I don't want to waste anymore time, Jaymes. Make me yours. I need to feel you." She turned her head and captured one of my fingers in her mouth. She then began gently sucking it.

I groaned as her sucking went straight to my dick. "Damn," I said. Reaching down, I hauled her over my shoulder in a fireman's grip and raced up the stairs to the waiting dungeon room I'd prepared earlier. It was time to claim my mate once and for all.

Chapter Seventeen

Mine

Jaymes

I trotted up the stairs with Asha over my shoulder feeling like the ultimate caveman as I heard her giggle against my back. Adrenaline pumped through me at the thought of finally touching the skin I'd longed for all these years. I felt a lightness that wasn't there a few hours ago as I walked into the room. Placing Asha on her feet, I turned to shut the door behind me.

A soft seductive glow filled the room from the dimmed overhead lighting above, causing her beautiful mocha skin to radiate and shine in the pale light. My dick twitched in my pants with an urgency I'd never felt before, but I commanded myself to calm the fuck down. I'd waited too long for this moment and if I didn't control myself, it would be over really quickly with only my pants getting a taste of my essence.

I turned around to face Asha. It was time for another moment of truth. "This is how this is going to play out, Asha," I started, ready to confess my need. "I am a Dominant. I can't control who I am anymore than I can keep the sun from shining. Maybe my past has something to do with wanting to be in complete control in the bedroom, but whatever the reason, I need it. If you think it might be too much for you, tell me now and we'll go the vanilla route. But know this, I mean to end out like I start out. If you submit to me, I'll want your submission forever. I'll crave it. To be honest, I need it now. Let me know if you can handle that. Tell me what you're thinking, love. Put it on your lips."

Asha stood looking around the room, her eyes wide as she took in the view. A large mirror hung on the ceiling above the wrought iron bed that sat in the middle of the room. The king-sized bed was covered in vibrant royal blue satin sheets. The paneled wall was covered in a dark mahogany that set the mysterious tone of the playroom. Brand new packages of toys, lube, and condoms lined the shelf next to the dresser. A small spanking bench was also perched to one side of the room, complete with built-in handcuffs. I didn't bring any paddles or personal small whips a lot of Doms liked to carry in their kits. I'd discovered quite a few years back that I wasn't a fan of many of those types of devices, preferring my hand to dish out any discipline that I would give to my submissive. Levi tried to turn me on to it, but I liked the feel of my skin against the flesh of my sub's heated ass. My sub. God, I needed her to say yes.

"Put it on your lips, love," I whispered to her again, my heart racing with fear that she might say no and walk right out of the door. But I had to be upfront about what I wanted. No more hiding shit. We've wasted enough time already.

Asha finally let her eyes rest back on me. A look I couldn't quite discern crossed her features as she slowly lowered the zipper on the side of her leather jumpsuit. Once fully unzipped, she reached down and removed her boots, then stood back up to pull the leather from her shoulders and down over her breasts. I stood frozen as I watched with lustful eyes, taking in the white-laced bra that set the perfect contrast against her mocha skin. She continued to pull the suit down her body and over her hips, exposing the matching thong underneath. Pulling the suit down her legs, she gracefully stepped out of the material. She straightened before me as her eyes slowly roamed over my body. Finally, she sank down on her knees before me, whispering, "I am here solely for your pleasure, Sir Jaymes. Use my body as you see fit."

I nearly choked as my already aching cock could have spewed right then. Did she realize what those words did to me? She was about to release my inner beast. "Asha, *meu curacao*," I murmured. "My heart." I repeated again, walking over to her and laying my hand on her head. "You have no idea how much your submission means to me. Thank you for this gift. How did you know?"

Asha bowed her head slightly, but I could still see the evidence of a smirk skating across her features. Little brat.

"I read a lot of BDSM books. How do you think I've stayed sane all of these years without having sex? I wanted to be dominated, but couldn't stand the thought of anyone but you touching me. Terri and I actually visited a club once, but it didn't feel right, so we left."

I felt my nostrils flare at that piece of news. "You are to never go into a club again without me, do you understand? It's not safe for a woman to go alone, especially *my* woman."

"Yes sir."

"And Terri better not go alone, either. You make sure you tell her that."

"I will, sir."

"Now spread your thighs wider. I want to see my pussy."

"As you wish, sir."

Asha spread her soft thighs as I walked behind her. "Bend over a little more, palms facing up on your thighs. That's it. Now arch your back just a little. Yes. Now, remember this position, *meu curacao*. This is how you will greet me in our bedroom each night. I want to see you spread out like this with your pussy on full display for my pleasure."

"Yes, sir."

I sighed my satisfaction as I looked down at her. Such beauty. Even from where I stood I could see the glisten of her own moisture on her labia between the material of her thong. "Now stand up and remove your bra."

Asha stood up gracefully and put her hands behind her back to unclasp her bra. I watched as her full breasts spilled out, my mouth watering for a taste. Her nipples were like milk chocolate drops waiting to be devoured. My eyes roamed across her torso. God, even her navel was sexy to me, with its small indention pinching across her belly. I licked my lips. "Now your underwear, love." She obeyed and slid her last piece of clothing from her body, showcasing her neatly trimmed pubic hair.

I lifted her chin so she could see my face. "You are beautiful, my heart. I love you. I am yours forever. Know that even as you submit to me, I am ultimately your slave. We don't need a unique safe word for

190

you to use when we're playing if it becomes too intense for you. A simple 'no' will do for me. Then we'll stop and talk about what's bothering you. My only desire in life will ever be to please you. You're my everything, Asha. I want to give you everything, too. I need to give you your heart's desire."

"You have already," she whispered, her eyes brimming with tears. "You've given me the real you. That's all I ever wanted. I love you too, Sir Jaymes."

With that, I leaned over to suck her lower lip. Asha groaned in my mouth. "Now undress me," I growled.

I stood still as Asha unbuttoned my dress shirt and slid it off my shoulders. I heard her sigh as her fingers traced over my biceps and my tattoo. She then stood on the tips of her toes and she grazed her lips across my chest to one of my nipples and took a small bite. I hissed, loving the sensation her teeth were giving me. She licked her bottom lip as her fingers glazed down my chest to my slacks. She untied my belt and undid the button of my pants. My cock jerked as her fingers brushed against my zipper, begging to be released. Sliding the zipper down, she finally she reached her hand inside my pants and inside my boxer briefs to grip my dick firmly in her hands. I moaned loudly, loving the softness and warmth of her hands against my skin. She slowly began moving her hand up and down, using the pre-cum that leaked from my tip for easier lubrication. I gritted my teeth together to keep from shouting at the pure pleasure she was giving me. But I needed to halt her movements now; otherwise, this would be a really quick play session.

"Stop. Take my pants off." Asha slowly slid my pants and briefs over my hips, stopping to grab a handful of my ass along the way. I chuckled and let her continue to explore my body. She bent down as I lifted each leg to get free of the remaining clothes, of which Asha grabbed and tossed over into a corner. Still kneeling, I saw her eyes widen at the realization she was face to face with my dick.

"Suck me," I said.

Asha licked her lips once more and reached up to grab my cock. She gripped the stalk in a firm hold as her tongue ran along the vein pulsating under my cockhead. Slowly, she widened her mouth over the tip and took a slow suck, almost sending me to my knees. "More," I whispered. "Take more of me." My hand reached down to brush her hand out of the way, grabbing my cock to present to her. Asha smiled, and then lowered her mouth over me until I felt the back of her throat. Groaning, I began pumping into her mouth, relishing in the warm sensation. She took another strong suction before she released my cock with a sounding pop. I couldn't stop the groan that escaped me. She looked up at me and licked her lips.

"I love the way you taste," she murmured. I growled and grabbed the back of her head, unraveling the styled bun that lay there. I offered my cock to her lips once again. Instead, she rolled her tongue over the head before taking me on fully. I fucked her mouth with little restraint, ecstasy overtaking me as I felt my balls draw tightly against my body. At that moment, Asha gripped my hips with her delicate hands and swallowed. I lost it. Bursts of hot cum shot from my tip down her throat as I groaned out in ecstasy. Asha drank every drop, licking every inch of me in such a loving manner that caused my eyes to mist.

She drew her mouth slowly off me and I felt the loss of her touch immediately. "Thank you, *meu curacao*. Lie down on the bed and spread your legs." Asha followed my directive and spread herself across the sheets. I stood and watched her for a moment, basking in the feeling of peace and rightness I felt throughout my entire body. She was mine. Mine.

"Asha, my heart. You and I are getting married as soon as your tour is over," I informed her.

The smile that broke across her face was the loveliest thing I'd ever seen, and my heart melted. I vowed in that moment to make it my duty to ensure that smile stayed on her face for the rest of our lives. "Yes, we are," she simply replied.

"Grip your thighs and hold them open for me. I need to see my pussy again."

Asha obeyed and opened herself up to my scrutiny. My previously satisfied cock was already stirring back to life at the sight before me. Her pussy was perfection; something someone should be capturing in a piece of artwork somewhere. Of course, then I'd have to kill both that artist and whoever dared to admire the work, but still. It was a fucking masterpiece. I bent down to place my nose right against her labia and inhaled deeply. "You smell so good, baby," I said and she whimpered. I took my finger and slid it through the moist folds of her pussy, watching as it gushed at my touch.

"So fucking responsive. I love it..." I said to myself as I slid my finger inside. Curving it slightly, I bent down to softly suck at her clit. She bucked at my touch and lost her grip on her thighs.

"Keep them open, Asha, or I'll stop," I demanded. With shaky fingers, she gripped her thighs once more, holding them open for me. I bent back down, putting her clit in my mouth to suck at the straining muscle. I heard her whimpers above my head as I continued to savor her essence, each suck in a perfectly synchronized dance with every thrust of my finger. Suddenly I heard a loud gasp above my head and I knew I'd hit her G-spot. I added a second, then third finger to my invasion, curving upward on all three to stroke the top of her vaginal wall.

I continued stroking her with my fingers for a few minutes, her heavy panting and moaning inspiring every movement, before I decided to switch it up a little. Reaching up to grab her hips, I quickly flipped her on her stomach, hearing her gasp with surprise at the abrupt change. I reached under her stomach to pull her back up so that she was on her knees when I thrust my fingers back into her soaking hole. She began bucking into my hand as I plummeted into her, straining to get more of my hand inside of her. I leaned over and grabbed one of her ass cheeks with my free hand, squeezing the flesh around my fingers. Parting her ass to one side, I leaned over and drew my tongue across the outside of her anus and she finally flew. Moisture gushed across my fingers as I watched her back arch and legs shake with her orgasm. I heard her shouting my name over and over, 'SIR JAYMES, SIR JAYMES, YYYEESSS, oh SHIT!!"

I looked over at the toys I'd laid out and decided against them for tonight. If I didn't hurry up and get inside her I honesty thought I might pass out. *Next time*, I thought absently. Instead, I reached over and grabbed a condom, tearing the wrapper open with my teeth. After I sheathed myself, I gripped both sides of her curvy hips as her body was still absorbing the after shocks of her orgasm.

Leaning over, I whispered over to her. "I love you Asha, *meu curacao.* You are mine."

With that I pushed my pulsating dick inside her quivering pussy, going slow so I wouldn't hurt her. Her recent orgasm lubricated my way a lot, but her pussy was still really tight. "Damn," I groaned. "Your pussy feels like a vice grip on my dick. Push back into me, love." Asha wriggled her hips against me, pushing her pussy back against my cock slowly until I was fully embedded inside her. We both exhaled at the feeling of finally being united with each other, both body and soul. Finally, Asha wriggled the back of her thighs against mine. Chuckling, I took her queue and began slowly thrusting into her waiting heat. Her pussy felt like heaven, bathing me in light. My thrusts became faster and faster, losing any sort of rhythm or grace as the sensation rode in me higher to claim every inch of her. She pushed back into me with just as much vigor, crying out yeses and obscenities along the way. At one point she reached behind her to place her hand on my thigh, as if to tell me to slow down.

"You'll take what I give you," I growled, thrusting even faster into her channel and pushing her hand away. "If it's too much for you, you know what to say." I spit, my every thought filled with lust. Soon her hands began gripping my thighs instead of pushing against them, guiding and assisting with every stroke into her frame. I snapped my pelvis against hers over and over, causing a low moan to seep from her mouth. I released one of her hips to place one of my fingers between the folds of her pussy, wetting it thoroughly before I placed it against her ass. As I continued to plummet, I took that finger and grinded it against her anus, pressing firmly and methodically.

"This will be mine too," I growled, letting her know I fully intended to own every part of her. Asha screamed, shouting out her

194

orgasm in a beautiful display of release. Once again I felt my balls draw up as I cried out along with her, filling the condom I wore to the brink.

Finally I collapsed on top of her, completely spent and happy. Rolling over to my side, I pulled her back against my chest to breathe in her scent. My tongue snaked out to taste the outer shell of her ear as I felt her giggle. I smiled into her hair, reveling in her apparent happiness.

"Meu curacao..." I murmured. Asha rolled around so that she was facing me. She placed her palm on my beard and gently stroked my face.

"What does that mean?" she asked. Her hand felt like a soothing balm against my cheek.

"My heart. I learned a little Portuguese when my family took a summer trip to Brazil one year."

She smiled up at me. "Is that my unique endearment?" she said cockily.

"Only yours," I said, meaning every word as I grazed my lips lazily across her forehead.

She sighed and placed her head against my chest. "I'll have to find a way to let Austin and Alanna know you and I have gotten together. I'm sure they'll have a lot of questions."

It was my turn to respond smugly. "Actually, there won't be as many as you'd expect, especially Austin. He was quite happy when I let him know you and I would be getting married."

She leaned back from me with a surprised expression. "You've talked to him already? How?" After I explained the lengths of research I'd done to locate her whereabouts, she threw her head back and laughed.

"Never let it be said that you weren't tenacious."

"Not as much as I should have been," I said regretfully. "But I will make amends for that, too." It was hard to forget all of the wasted years we'd had simply because I didn't want to let Asha know what was going on.

Asha gave me a look I couldn't quite comprehend. "Sometimes the best way to move forward is to forgive yourself. No matter how bad the hurt and self-loathing might try to burrow its way inside of you, you have to eventually let it go. If not, you'll just end up suffering the most. Then who really wins? You end up not being truly happy, and because you're not happy, how can you give happiness to anyone else? Every day is a gift. Either you can appreciate that gift and savor each moment or spend years wallowing in regret."

I looked at her as I tried to understand the trigger behind her words. Finally, I asked, "What have you had to forgive yourself for, Asha?

She gave me one of the saddest and most heartbreaking expressions I'd ever seen. "A lot. And now, because I let go of the hurt, I feel freer than I've felt in my entire life."

"Tell me," I urged. Terri's earlier words of warning rang in my memory. *It was her story to tell.* I prayed she felt comfortable enough with me now to tell it.

And she did. She opened up to me about all the years of abuse and neglect Ramon had given her. She opened up about her parents and the circumstances surrounding her choice to come to NSU. She also opened up about her abortion, and the mishap that caused her to become hospitalized for a week afterwards.

As she told me her story, I held her, absorbing her tears and being the rock she needed to hold herself up with. My eyes clouded with tears at all the hurt she had been through. My rage overflowed at the vow that if I'd ever see Ramon again; he might not like how he ended up.

Never again, I vowed. Never again would she ever know that type of hurt. Not as long as I had breathe in my body.

Chapter Eighteen

Interview

Asha

"God, there are so many people here." I leaned over to whisper to Terri, looking out at the crowd.

Terri grinned. "People have been waiting for this forever, girl. They want to know who the Painted Lady is. Get ready to knock 'em dead."

I rolled my eyes at her comment. *I don't know about knocking them dead,* I thought sarcastically. Nervously, I wrung my hands together to stop the shaking that threatened to give away how anxious I really was. I'd hidden behind my persona for so long it was like a second layer of Teflon skin. Every critique and bad review could just slide off me since they really didn't know me. Now, everyone would know and be able to cast a big ass spotlight directly on me.

I took a deep breath. Reminding myself I'd been through so much worse than just taking off a damn mask in public, I smiled weakly at the sea of news reporters and paparazzi clicking away at me. *Just one more,* I thought. *One more concert until the end of my tour, then I can go back into hibernation for a little while until this sea storm blew over and the news of who I really was wouldn't be news anymore.*

As I thought about the end of my tour, I glanced out in the crowd until I spotted Jaymes sitting in the middle of the room. He seemed oblivious to all the commotion and excitement around him and seemed focused solely on me. He'd caught my look and sent the most heart-stopping grin my way. I bit my bottom lip to try and control the grin spilling uncontrollably from my mouth. My heart skipped a couple of beats as I remembered all that had transpired last night. It was one of the most important and momentous experiences of my life. Jaymes was here for me. For me.

God, it was still so hard to wrap my mind around it. I lowered my head as I felt my neck flush. It had been hard to wrap my mouth around his cock last night, too, but damn, it had been amazing. I shifted in my seat as I felt my folds moisten from last night's memories. I snuck a look back at him and he smirked back with a *cat that ate the canary* look splattered across his face. Ass. He knew what I'd been thinking. I bit my cheek to stop the laugh that threatened to break free.

"And I need for you to stop daydreaming about riding Delphi's dick long enough to focus on getting through this press conference," Terri muttered under her breath as she covered her hand over the microphones leaning my way. I grinned back at her and tried to straighten my face and prep my mind for the slew of upcoming questions.

"Thank you all for attending today," Terri started, drawing everyone's attention with her commanding voice. "It's been a long time coming and we are thrilled to share this moment with all of you." The buzz in the crowd lowered to better hear what she had to say.

"Four years and two albums ago, a legend emerged that would later ultimately define the next age in music revolution. Her music and lyrics have inspired, motivated, soothed the hearts and put voice to the voiceless of so many fans throughout the world. Ladies and gentlemen, I give you, The Painted Lady!!" Terri announced, applauding as she looked at me.

The room joined her in the applause as I stood up. I looked toward the middle of the room to find Jaymes again. Looking straight in his eyes, I removed my mask and smiled confidently; not for the benefit of the resounding applause, but for my love. His love gave me confidence.

Louder claps and calls for my attention broke my trance as I nodded to the first reporter who stood closest to me.

"Lady, why did you decide to reveal your true face at this stage in your career?"

I smiled at the reporter. "Because I felt it was time to stop hiding behind the mask. My music is about coming into your true self and letting go. I had to start living what I was preaching."

Another reporter got my attention. I nodded her way. "What did the mask represent to you? Why were you hiding behind it?" she asked.

I answered her confidently. "I've hid behind a lot of obstacles in my life, a lot of them not the most pleasant. But again, part of the healing in overcoming those hindrances is shedding the camouflage that everything is alright. It was time to reveal the woman behind the mask and behind the music."

A low roar sounded as people struggled to interpret the meaning behind what I'd just said. As I looked at Jaymes, I realized in that second that I really didn't care what anyone thought. These people didn't know me. They didn't know how far I'd come and what it took to get me here. Fuck anybody that thought negatively about it. At the end of the day I and I alone had to live with my decisions. And damnit, I felt pretty good about them right now.

I felt my stance grow more confident as I stood up straighter.

Terri leaned into the microphone. "We have time for one more question."

I looked around the room and nodded my head at a reporter I knew from E! News.

"Lady, your work has been an inspiration for so many young girls. What would you want them to know and take away from your actions today?"

I tilted my head as I thought about her question. I paused for a moment, making sure I articulated correctly exactly what I wanted to say.

"I would say this. No matter how bad you think a situation is, it's *your* perception that makes the difference. *Your* actions that can change your fate. Never stop believing in yourself, no matter how bad others may try to beat you down. Remember to keep singing, even when you don't feel like it." I smiled. "The song you end up creating just may lead to a Grammy."

The room erupted into a thunderous applause as I nodded and took my seat. I looked over at Jaymes and he mouthed the words, "I love you," to me, filling my heart with joy. I grinned at the affirmation and nodded his way.

"Thank you all for coming," Terri announced, turning off our microphones.

Joy filled my heart as I realized this was one of the happiest and most fulfilling moments I'd ever experienced. And I intended to savor each moment after this for the rest of my life.

A movement in the back of the room suddenly caught my attention. I strained to see the person quickly moving behind all the cameras and flashing lights. A man's outline finally revealed himself to me as he pushed his way past reporters and toward the exit doors. As he opened the door to leave, he turned and cast one final look of hatred my way. In that same moment, I'd also realized how immobilizing terror could quickly kill any level of joy and happiness.

"Ramon," I choked.

ᴧᴧᴧ

A few weeks later, Terri and I were finally back in Houston. Jaymes had flown back with us and had spent the time at my house, getting better acquainted with Alanna and me. It had been really great having him around. Not just for the wonderful steamy nights we'd spent together exploring each other in a way I never would have dreamed before, but for Alanna as well. She and Jaymes really seemed to have bonded quickly, especially when he didn't discount her love for the Jonas brothers and all things Johnny Depp.

She took the news of us getting married pretty well too, but she was initially surprised at the abruptness of it all. After sitting down with her to explain I'd actually known Jaymes for years, and that he, Terri and I all went to the same college together, she was able to relax her musing, and allowed Jaymes to really get to know her. Now it seemed like they were glued at the hip. During the Christmas break, Alanna tagged along with Jaymes to his office and grew extremely fascinated with his work.

She'd hung out with Evelyn and helped her with running errands and filing paperwork whenever Jaymes needed to go to court or had to meet with a client.

Austin came home for a few days during his winter break to spend some time with us as well. He confided in me one evening after Jaymes and Alanna left to go see the latest Pirates of the Caribbean movie that Jaymes had come down to NSU to actually meet with him. He told me how glad he was to see me so happy, something he'd wished for me for a long time.

Warmth curled in my belly as I thought about my wedding plans. Terri decided to help me by working a miracle to really pull out all the stops since I had such a laughing stock of a wedding before. She did it in an amazingly short amount of time. As my official maid of honor, she worked a lot with my wedding coordinator to make sure my small yet lavish affair was something I'd cherish for the rest of my life. The past weeks had been so surreal it was still hard to believe.

Now, as I sat in the studio dressing room applying my makeup for the Arena Theatre performance, I was surprisingly calm. Truth be told, this was the calmest I'd ever been before a show. Maybe for once in my life having everything I'd ever dreamed of helped to kill a lot of my anxiety.

After my makeup was done, I stood to ready myself for my warm-ups. I started to sing my normal tradition of *Superstar* when suddenly I had a change of heart. Jaymes told me he couldn't make tonight's performance because he had a brief to prepare in the morning, so I decided to sing something that would bring him to me in spirit.

Straightening my stance, I knew the exact song that would both stretch my vocals and express the emotion I felt. Whitney Houston's *"You Give Good Love"* poured out of me, every note and lyric a testament to everything I felt. I sang with such focus that I never heard the studio door open and close behind me. After the last chorus was sung, I arched my neck, stretching it from side to side. It was only as I reached toward the dresser for my bottle of water that I saw him.

He applauded slowly and purposely as he leaned against the dressing room door, blocking my exit.

"Excellent job, whore." Ramon sneered. "I always knew you would be a role model for young sluts everywhere. Congratulations."

I spun around to face him as anxiety tore through me. My eyes grew wide as my fear grew. I looked around the room for something to protect myself with as I tried to figure out what he wanted.

"How did you get in here?" I asked shakily, my eyes still wildly scanning the room.

"On my own two feet, idiot," he snapped sarcastically.

"I mean how did you get past security?"

"Easy. I told them I was your husband and showed them my driver's license. Top-flight security at its best. Good job of keeping my last name, by the way. It made my job so much easier."

I mentally kicked myself. "It was only because I wanted to hurry and get the divorce proceedings over with to make it easier for Alanna. It had absolutely nothing with wanting to keep some sort of tie with you."

"Whatever, bitch. You know you did it because you're hoping I'd take you back someday."

Was he crazy? His overconfident grin said apparently so. "Ramon, there is no way in hell we would ever get back together. I need you to leave my room right now."

"Hell no. I'm not going any fucking where. You owe me. I expect to get what's coming to me," he said in a monotone voice.

"What are you talking about?" My eyes landed on a large crystal lamp that sat on the table next to my dresser. I slowly inched closer to it. Judging by its size and apparent weight, it could work in case I needed to use it to defend myself.

"I'm talking about the fact that I lost almost everything when you humiliated me. That recording your friend made was part of the public records in our divorce and somehow got leaked to my CFO. I ended up getting fired and I haven't been able to find a job since," he snarled. "You caused all this and I expect some fucking payback."

"Is that the reason Alanna's support stopped?"

202

"You're damn right."

"Well, what did that have to do with you still trying to see her? Your daughter missed you during the early part of our divorce. There are years of bonding time that you've lost because you weren't around."

"Don't you question me, slut. You apparently made it really easy for my daughter to find a replacement father. I know she's been hanging out with Delphi. I've been following you two for a while. Looks like she's a love 'em and leave 'em type of whore just like her mother."

I gasped. "How can you say something like that about your own flesh and blood?"

"No daughter of mine would hang out with the very man that's fucking her father's wife."

"We are not married anymore, Ramon. And you have no right to judge anything that goes on between Jaymes and me."

He laughed but there was no humor in the act. "*Jaymes.*" He mimicked, venom dripping from every letter. "Oh, sweetheart, when you said 'I do,' that meant 'til death do us part. And since you aren't dead yet..." he said softy, almost too quietly. I'd been down this path before. I knew I had only a few moments before things got violent.

I quickly picked up the lamp and snatched the plug from the wall with a hard yank. I'd just about had it from this jackass and my tolerance for bullshit had reached its end.

"Listen here, you selfish son of a bitch. You can't intimidate me anymore. You aren't worth a pot to piss in nor the window to throw it out of, as my Momma would say. I've had it. GET THE FUCK OUT OF MY DRESSING ROOM or so help me, I'll not only try to knock the shit out of you with this lamp, you spineless excuse for a man, but I'll try my best to make you feel every bit of pain you've ever given to me. If you come any closer I'll also scream to high heaven so that Houston's finest will come barricading through this door and haul your ass to jail for a long fucking time after I hit you. Make a decision, jackass."

Ramon stood shocked for a moment at my outburst. We both realized I had never before spoken to him like that. He soon recovered and began walking purposely toward me. I swung the lamp toward my back to gain as much momentum for my upcoming swing as possible when suddenly the door flew open.

Jaymes stormed in; his fiery gaze going first to Ramon, then to me holding the lamp, and finally back to Ramon. A murderous growl escaped his lips as he charged straight for Ramon, lifting him by the shirt so that he was actually suspended a couple of feet from the ground. Since Jaymes stood almost half a foot taller than Ramon, it wasn't hard to do.

Jaymes slammed Ramon against the wall and wrapped his large hands around Ramon's neck. I quickly placed the lamp down and raced over to Jaymes. "It's ok, baby. It's ok..." I cried frantically, trying to calm his beast. "He didn't get a chance to hurt me. It's ok."

"He wanted to, that's enough for me damn it..," Jaymes spit, obviously unable to contain his rage. His hands gripped Ramon's neck a little tighter as he hit Ramon's head hard against the cinder block wall. Ramon's face began to pale as he struggled uselessly under Jaymes' hold.

Oh god, I thought. I couldn't have Ramon's pathetic blood on Jaymes' purified hands. I tugged uselessly at Levi's waist to pull him off Ramon--but it was like trying to move an impenetrable brick wall.

Suddenly, a couple of officers burst into the room, grabbing Jaymes and pulling him from Ramon. Ramon began choking for air as he slid to the floor while the officers struggled to restrain a still fully enraged Jaymes. When one of the officers began to read Jaymes his Miranda rights and pulled out a pair of handcuffs, I finally got over my shock and shook my head frantically at the police.

"No! Not him, officers. Not him. He was trying to save me from that man over there." I pointed toward Ramon. "That man broke into my dressing room and was going to assault me before this man came in to rescue me."

"Are you sure about that, Ms. Lady?" a portly officer asked.

"I'm positive. Please remove him. I'll be more than happy to press charges to the fact."

With that, the officers released Jaymes and gathered Ramon up from the ground. After reading him his rights, they placed Ramon into custody. Jaymes bent over at the waist, trying to catch his breath and calm his anger as we watched one of the officers place handcuffs on Ramon.

"It's not over, bitch!" Ramon spat in my direction as the officer who restrained him started to drag him away. "It's not over by a long shot, I promise you! You'll see me soon! I'll get what's coming to me— you just wait and see! Wait and see!"

"And I'll be waiting right here if you try, motherfucker," Jaymes growled.

One of the officers shook his head as he watched his partner lead Ramon out of the room. "And he is apparently not too bright either to threaten you in our presence." He turned to me with a concerned look on his face. "Are you sure you're ok, Ms. Lady?"

"I'm good, thank you," I said absently, focusing on Jaymes as he leaned over, his palms laid flat on his thighs. I placed my hand on his back, trying to offer comfort to my warrior protector.

"Ok. We'll haul him down to the station for booking. We'll need you to come directly after the concert and give your statement so the charges can be substantiated." He handed me a business card. "My name is Officer Jolston. Ask for me when you arrive. Our observations alone will not be enough and we'll need your statement in order for the charges to stick."

"I will, officer. Thank you again for your assistance."

"My pleasure ma'am. And by the way, I love your music. I hope you do an awesome job tonight. Knock 'em dead." He gave me a quick wink.

I smiled at him weakly as he walked out of the door.

"Now I feel like beating that officer's ass for winking at you. God woman, the men you attract." Jaymes finally spoke as he straightened up to stand next to me. He pulled me into his arms and I sighed at the connection.

"None of them matter, except the one that's holding me now." I said softly into his chest. "Thank you." I looked up at him. "How did you know he would come here?"

"I didn't. I wrapped up earlier than I thought and decided to surprise you tonight. But when I walked up to one of the security guys and he told me your husband had been here asking to see you, I knew some bullshit was about to jump off. I raced to your room as fast as I could after that."

"Well, my husband is here. He's here right now holding me in his arms," I said, rubbing my cheek into his chest.

He snorted. "And he would still feel so much better if the cops would have come a couple of seconds later after I'd squeezed the life out of the little pipsqueak."

I smiled at him. "Well, I'm not. I'd like to keep you out of jail, Mr. Attorney. It wouldn't look too good for potential clients."

His expression became serious as he bent down to kiss me softly on the lips. "If anything had happened to you..." he started, a catch in his breath stopping his next words.

I nodded my head. "I know, baby. But I'm ok. I'm ok." I repeated.

"Good, because I intend to cherish you for a few centuries more."

"You bet your ass you will," I replied cheekily.

"Little brat." He smiled down at me.

Chapter Nineteen

Told You So

Jaymes

I stood in the shadows offstage as I watched Asha perform. I could tell she'd once again captured the audience with her grace and pose by the sound of the applause penetrating my ears, but I was still too distracted to join in. Busting into that dressing room and seeing her attempting to defend herself against that jackass knocked me off balance. I was still reeling from the after effects.

My original intention this evening was to leave the office early, come to her concert to wish my little one a lovely performance, and make the announcement about our wedding gift two weeks early. I'd told Asha this morning I'd be working with Evelyn all day on a case brief; but I'd actually met with the closing agent of the banking lender who finalized the documents on our new Oak Estates home. I wanted her to start moving her things in as soon as possible so when we came back from our honeymoon, our family could begin its new life together.

But seeing Ramon so close to Asha rattled me more than I wanted her to know. Tension radiated from every pore. I clasped my shaking hands behind my back and widened my stance to control the adrenalin still pumping through me. If he could walk into her dressing room that easy and threaten to assault her, even with stationed policemen hanging around, what else could he be capable of? I shook my head as my resolve deepened. *Fuck that,* I thought. He would never get close like that again.

My eyes drifted back to Asha to watch as she strolled along the stage floor, singing and swinging those hips I loved so much. Gone was the barstool she usually sat on to face away from her fans. Now she tackled them dead on, singing boldly and freely the lyrics she held so close to her heart. As my attention finally fully focused back on her, I felt pride rise within my chest. This magnificent specimen of a woman would officially be mine soon. I huffed. Hell, she was mine now. I dared Ramon or anybody else to question my rights to her.

The spotlight shined brightly on Asha as she took her bow to thank the audience for their applause.

"Thank you all for coming," she spoke into her microphone. "I love each and every one of you. Thank you from the bottom of my heart for your continued support over the past few years. Now, as many of you know, my songs mostly center on lost love or a yearning for something greater than yourself. Well, I wanted to announce that in addition to my unveiling several weeks ago, I'll also be writing and promoting new material." Whistles and screams erupted as Asha continued to speak.

"My music will still focus on love, of course, but will also describe its wonderful ability to find its way back to you when you think it's lost forever. My last song tonight will be a track from my new album that's due to be released in the next couple of months. I hope you enjoy it. It's called *Letting Go to Find You*." Polite applause echoed throughout the concert hall.

"I'd also like to dedicate this song to my love, my hero, my warrior protector, Jaymes. I love you, baby." She turned to face me as I saw the spotlight split; one stayed focused on her while the other sought and found me standing on the side. More applause along with cheers sounded as she blew me a kiss. I felt my throat close at her public admission. I could only smile and nod my head to both encourage and acknowledge her. She winked my way, turned back to the audience, and began to sing:

I let you go
So long ago
Thinking I was doing right
Thinking I'd give up the fight
On a Mild Summer's eve
Among the Trace Magnolia trees

208

You walked away
Then my night turned into day
When you returned
You lit up my world
You vowed to stay
Couldn't push you away
My fear is gone
Our love has won
Thank you
For finding me again

I couldn't contain myself any longer. My restless energy needed an immediate outlet. I walked across the stage to Asha, startling her with my sudden appearance. Wrapping one hand around her waist while my other slid behind her neck, I pulled her to me to taste the lips whose flavor I'd never grow tired of.

A boom sounded through the concert hall as Asha dropped her microphone to wrap her arms around my waist, pulling me closer to her. I ravished her mouth, needing and finding comfort in her arms. Finally we broke for air, finally acknowledging the thunderstorm of sound around us. People were standing and cheering everywhere. The house lights had also risen, enabling us to see the audience and for them to get a good view of us together on stage. I brushed my lips across her forehead as she wound her arms tighter around my waist. She bowed slightly as I led her offstage, the whistles and screams a deafening roar.

"Wow," she said breathlessly as she looked up at me.

"Wow, yourself," I said, my hand resting possessively over her hip. Just touching her had such a calming affect over me. I took a deep, soothing breath. She was like my Balm of Gideon.

I looked up to see Terri directing a couple of stagehands around. She then turned and walked toward us. "Well, that turned out better than I'd expected," she said, placing her hand on her hips.

"What did?" I asked.

"Announcing Asha's new music. That kiss just put the acceptance of her new sound over the top." She playfully hit my shoulder. "Thanks, Delphi."

I rolled my eyes. "That was not for you, brat. But glad I could help. You know my goal in life is to fulfill your every wish and command."

She winked. "As it should be." She turned to Asha, a look of concern crossing her features. "Honey, are you sure you're alright?" Terri had been on her way to the concert when the situation with Ramon occurred. She'd been running late due to tying up some loose ends with her marketing firm.

Asha shook her head. "I'm fine. He's in custody, and that's all that matters."

"He shouldn't have gotten back here in the first place," I said, remembering my earlier concern. "Terri, I thought security was supposed to be tight back here. What the hell happened?"

"Chad hired this new private company who promised better surveillance at a cheaper price. Obviously that was a lie. I'm just glad I never cancelled the contract with the Houston Police Department and everything worked out."

"Me too," Asha sighed. "Can we talk about something else? Like how excited I am for this wedding? Happy thoughts, people. Happy thoughts."

Terri smiled and shook her head. "It's funny how some people act when they finally find the love of their life, isn't it Delphi? Then suddenly the world is a bright beacon of shining hope and we should all be saving kittens from trees or some mess like that."

I chuckled. "Actually, I'm quite fond of kittens." I bent and ran my tongue across the outer shell of Asha's ear, causing her to shiver in my arms.

Terri rolled her eyes to the ceiling. "I forgot who I was talking to." She looked back at Asha and smiled. "But seriously, I couldn't be happier for the two of you. I keep saying that, but I promise you I mean it from the bottom of my heart."

Asha stepped away from me toward Terri. "I know you do. And one day, you'll stop fighting what you're destined to claim for yourself and finally embrace what the future holds for you, too."

Terri looked at her wistfully for a moment before masking her face once again. She plastered a forced smile on her lips and waived her hand to dismiss Asha's words. "Yeah, well...are you two going to the after party tonight?"

I looked pointedly at Asha. "No. We have other plans after she goes down to the police station to file her report against Ramon."

She looked at me curiously. "We do?"

I raised a single eyebrow. She tilted her lips slightly and looked back at Terri and winked. "There's that look again." Terri grinned at her.

"Yeah, I guess we have plans." Asha looked back at me. "But I drove tonight. Can you follow me back home? I really don't want to leave my car here overnight. Besides, I like to leave the car at home if I'm not there while I travel just in case Momma needs to take Alanna somewhere."

I hesitated, but finally relented. "Sure. Let's go. We'll catch up with you later, Terri."

"Okay. See you guys at the rehearsal dinner next week."

"Definitely," I said as I walked with Asha past security toward the parking garage. As we rode the elevator to the eighth level where her car was parked, I grabbed her hand and entwined my fingers around hers, loving the soft texture of her hand in mine. We approached her parked Audi and I opened the door as she slid into the driver's seat. Leaning over the door, I bent down to give her a kiss.

"I love you, Asha *meu curacao.*"

"I love you, too, Sir Jaymes," she purred.

"Go ahead and pull out. I'll go get my truck and meet you down at the lower level, and then I'll follow you home so you can gather a few things before we head over to the police station."

"Okay."

I closed her door and started walking away as I heard her turn over her engine. Thoughts about her surprise filled my head until a glimpse of movement out of the corner of my eye caught my attention. I turned my head toward the exit doors and saw a sight I wasn't prepared to see.

"Tanya?" I said disbelievingly. "What are you doing here?"

But she didn't seem to hear me. Her entire focus was on Asha as she watched her pull her car from the stall and move rather quickly toward the exit turns. I was relieved Asha didn't notice Tanya standing in her rear view as I saw Asha's head jerk frantically from the window down toward her lap.

Looking back at Tanya, I saw her lips moving silently, as if she were having an intensely fierce conversation that only she was privy enough to hear.

"Tanya?" I called to her a bit more forcefully, really taking notice of her disheveled clothing and wild-eyed glaze. Her mouth was twisted in an ugly grimace as she tapped her hand to her thigh in a graceless manner. I stared at her for another moment before a chill of fear zipped through me as I recognized that look of pure crazy. I turned and started racing toward Asha.

"ASHA!" I screamed, running after the moving vehicle. "ASHA!!"

But it was too late. Asha's car now sped way too fast toward the downward slope of the parking level. My heart stopped as I realized the weak metal structure of the end railing would be no match against the 3,000-plus pounds of German-made muscle racing toward it.

I watched in horror as Asha's car hit the railing at full speed. I heard Asha scream as the railing buckled immediately upon impact, allowing her car to penetrate through its defenses. My stomach dropped as I helplessly watched her car ultimately dropped out of sight, plummeting to the hard cement surface below.

Chapter Twenty

Our Time

Asha

I hurt everywhere. My face and forehead burned and felt incredibly swollen. Every muscle in my body felt beat up and strained. It also felt like some sort of cloth covered the left side of my face. I tried to lift my head, but it was like trying to lift a cement block. Too tired to attempt again, I relaxed against the pillow I felt against my neck, opting instead to focus on what was going on around me. By the pungent smell of disinfectant, I'd guessed that I was in the hospital.

"It'll be alright, Delphi. She's gonna be fine." I heard Terri say.

"God, I couldn't live with myself if she doesn't come out of this ok." I heard Jaymes say in a strangled voice. My heart hurt at the sound of his obvious despair. I couldn't bear to hear his pain. Hell, I could hardly bear my own. *Why didn't they give me something stronger to knock me the hell out?* I thought with frustration. I tried to move my mouth to tell him I was ok, but moving my lips caused little stickpins of pain to stab every nerve in my face. God, it hurt to just try.

"The doctor will let us know in a minute what's going on. He said the concussion she suffered was a mild one, so we were lucky there." My heart fluttered. *Momma,* I thought. *Momma was here.* "He said it initially didn't look like there was any brain damage, just a lot of cuts on her face from the broken glass. However he still wants to keep her here overnight for observation. He had a couple more tests he needed to run and then he'll be in to discuss her progress."

"I knew I should have made her leave her car and ride with me," Jaymes said in a low voice. "I'll never forgive myself for letting her out of my sight, especially with what happened with Ramon earlier." I heard him sigh. "I feel so fucking helpless waiting around like this and not knowing what's going on."

"I know, but you gotta be strong for her. She'll need you to help her get through this." Terri spoke gently.

I heard some shuffling around and couldn't make out what was happening. Then I heard Jaymes take a deep, exaggerated breath.

"Thanks, Terri. Thanks for being the friend she needed all these years. And don't think I don't know what you've sacrificed for her, too. She'll need you as well."

"I know, especially knowing I'll have to really browbeat her ass to get her in decent enough shape to walk down the aisle." She paused. "Sorry, Ms. St. Claire."

I heard Momma chuckle. "No apologize necessary, sweetie. It's just so refreshing to see that Asha's opened herself up to having such good people in her life. For that, I am forever grateful."

"Where are the kids?" I heard Terri ask.

"Alanna is sitting with Levi and his father downstairs in the waiting room. I called Austin and he's boarding the next available flight from Jackson to get here. He should be here late this afternoon," Momma said.

"Good." I heard Jaymes say. "She'll want to see her kids as soon as she wakes up." I felt someone lean over me. "The small dose of medication they gave her should be wearing off pretty soon."

"Thank God you were with her in that garage. Who would have thought Tanya would do something so evil?" Terri asked incredulously.

"I just thank God there was an officer already waiting on the street to escort Asha to the station. Apparently they wanted to make sure she went to give her testimony about Ramon and were willing to escort her to make sure it got done. The officer saw her car going over the railing and ran over to help." Jaymes explained.

"I also saw him grab Tanya trying to escape from the side fire exit, too. HPD did their job today," Terri remarked.

"Yeah, well...they shouldn't have had to do it at all," Jaymes rumbled. "Officer Jolston called me once they brought Tanya down to the station and got a chance to question her. He wanted to let me know she'd confessed to the entire thing. She was saying some bullshit about the beauty of justice finally prevailing when Asha's car hit the street. Apparently she's had it out for Asha every since NSU. She confessed she was with Ramon when they saw her unveiling interview a few weeks ago. Ramon had suspected it was really Asha behind the mask, but wasn't quite sure, so he dragged Tanya with him to see for himself. In Tanya's eyes, Asha's success was just one more thing that should have been hers that was taken away," he added.

"She'd stood by as a lookout while Ramon cut Asha's brake line. She even admitted she was the one who told Ramon how to do it. She'd told him that if he did this, they could both benefit from any insurance money Asha might give to Alanna and cash in," Jaymes spat out.

"What a bitch!" Terri said disgustedly.

"Why would she confess to all of that?" I heard Momma ask.

"When the officer caught her at the scene, she started screaming that she'd *finally done it* over and over again, pointing at Asha's totaled car. It was cause enough for the officer on site to make an arrest for suspicion. When they took her down to the station and Ramon saw her being hauled in, he immediately started screaming it was all Tanya's idea like the spineless ass he truly is. Officer Jolston said Tanya actually took pride at being blamed and confessed she'd hoped Asha got what was coming to her. He told me the local public defender is going have to bring in a psych doctor," gritted Jaymes.

"No kidding," Terri said.

I couldn't take remaining silent any longer. I let out a low moan and attempted to open my eyes again. This time I was able to crack them open. Sunlight crept into the dark slits of my eyes, though my vision was still kind of blurry because of the puffiness I felt around them.

"Asha?" I felt a large calloused hand grab mine. "My heart, wake up. I need you to wake up, baby and let me know you're all right. Please," Jaymes pleaded. He moved over me and I was able to make out his face. Oh, how I loved that face. I whimpered. I bet my face looked a hot mess right about now.

I tried to squeeze his hand to reassure him I was ok but pain radiated through my arm from the movement. However Jaymes still noticed the weak attempt.

"It's okay, love. You don't have to speak. Just be still. The doctor will be here in a minute," Momma said. I felt a cool hand brush against my forehead.

"In other words, lay the hell still so you can recover like you're supposed to." I heard Terri command.

I tried to stop the smirk I felt trying to tip up the corner of my lip, almost assuring a promise of red-hot pain. My lip twitched despite my meek attempt to hold it in. *Yep, I was right*, I thought as white lightening pain streaked across my face.

At that moment, I heard the door open and some papers shuffling around as footsteps approached the end of my bed.

"Doctor!" I heard Momma say. "Please tell us she's going to be okay."

I heard a deep voice at the end of my bed speak. "Yes, Ms. St. Claire. She's going to be just fine." I felt the sighs of relief from everyone in the room. "As I told you before, she suffered a minor concussion and a lot of cuts. Overall, we had to give her 64 stitches across her face. She had cuts across her hairline, along her left eye, down the bridge of her nose, and right above her upper lip. The deepest cut above her eye was the most serious, but we were able to prevent any loss of vision. The stitches will eventual get smaller over time so they will hardly be noticeable at all. In addition, she suffered a broken arm, but thankfully there wasn't any internal bleeding or hemorrhaging. I usually see all sorts of nightmares when people don't wear their seatbelts during high-impact collisions. However, in this case, your daughter was very fortunate. The way her car impacted in the front actually caused her driver's seat to go back, tossing her into the back windshield. She was cradled in that space and it helped to shield her when the front end of her car completely caved in. Not having a seatbelt, in this instance, actually saved her life."

I listened as I heard Momma sob softly to the left side of my bed. Jaymes gripped my hand harder as if he wanted to assure himself I was still there. He pulled my hand to his lips and gently placed a kiss there.

"In any case, we'll set that cast for her arm in a couple of hours. I'd also like her to stay here one more night. After that, she should be fine to be released."

Hell, it didn't feel fine right now. I felt like shit. I forced my lips to cooperate. "Hurt..." I managed to choke out.

Jaymes immediately went into Dom mode. "Dr., you will give Asha medication to relieve her pain *right now*."

"I'm sorry, Mister...."

"Allen. Pain Medication. *Now*."

"I'm sorry Mr. Allen. But we can't administer anything stronger than some aspirin right now."

"And why the hell not?" I heard Terri demand.

"Because her pregnancy test results came back positive."

Everyone in the room grew silent.

"What?" Jaymes asked disbelievingly.

"Asha is pregnant. From the looks of the tests she's about five weeks along." I felt a hand pat me on my foot. "I'm sorry, ma'am. I know it must feel really sore and the pain from the stitches is probably really aching. I'll have the nurse come in and give you those aspirin."

With that, the doctor nodded his head and left the room.

Silence descended as the impact of the doctor's words penetrated everyone's thoughts.

"Pregnant," Momma said.

"Pregnant," Terri confirmed.

"Pregnant with my baby," Jaymes said, rounding out the declarations.

I laid there completely stunned, the pain in my body taking a backseat to the news I'd just been delivered. Panic started to creep in. God, I hoped Jaymes was ok with this. I didn't mean to get pregnant. I'd asked him to wear condoms because I still hadn't gotten on any type of birth control. We'd talked about making an appointment with a doctor soon to explore what other birth control methods I could try that wouldn't make me ill, but never got the chance with all of my rehearsals and Jaymes' court dates. Since I hadn't been intimate with anyone but Jaymes since my divorce, getting protected just wasn't on my immediate list of top priorities. Nervously, I tried to turn my head to look at his facial expression. I needed to see if he hated the idea.

What I saw completely threw me. Instead of the bile I was expecting, Jaymes stood over me with the widest, cheesiest grin I'd ever seen on his face. He stared down at me. "Asha *meu curacao,* you're pregnant with my baby," he said again, biting his bottom lip.

Tears formed as I saw the joy in his eyes. I nodded my head in agreement, too choked up to try and speak.

Jaymes threw his head back and let out the loudest yell I'd ever heard. "YEESSS! My baby is having my baby! Hot damn!" He let go of my hand and grabbed Terri, spinning her around the room. Terri laughed at his antics and swatted him across his head. "Put me down, crazy. Get yourself together. I guess now it's a good thing that wedding is coming up soon."

A soft kiss on my cheek prompted me to turn my head away from their antics. I turned to look at Momma, taking in the tears that flowed freely down her face. "Oh, my baby girl. I'm so happy for you." I saw her nod Jaymes' way. "I'm happy for you, too. You both bring me the greatest joy an old woman could ask for. To witness the birth formed from a union of absolute love. Thank you. Thank you both so much."

Jaymes walked over to Momma and picked her up in the sweetest of bear hugs. "No, Ms. St. Claire, thank *you.* Thank you for giving me my heart." He kissed her forehead and put her dangling feet back on the floor. "And you're not old." He frowned playfully.

She chuckled. "I most certainly am. But with age comes wisdom." She reached up and patted Jaymes' cheek; my heart melting at the sight. "And please, call me Momma as well. You are family now, my son."

Epilogue

Asha

"I now pronounce you Man and Wife. You may kiss your bride."
The words I'd long to hear finally sounded from the pastor's mouth as
Jaymes leaned over and pressed his lips firmly against mine. I felt his
tongue seek entrance to my mouth and I opened to accommodate his
request. His hands found their way to cup the sides of my face as his
tongue ran across my bottom lip. He dove back to taste me again and I
melted in his arms, feeling the heat all the way between my legs, my
folds moistening in anticipation of tonight.

"Geez, Mom. Leave something for the honeymoon. Good grief!
See what I've had to deal with Austin? Be glad you're at NSU." I heard
Alanna say loudly behind me.

The guests broke out in laughter as Jaymes and I broke apart. I
felt my cheeks flame with heat as Jaymes responded, "I can't help
myself, but by God I love this woman!"

More laughter and applause sounded as Jaymes released his hold
on my face to move behind me. He gave Alanna a quick hug, murmuring
so only she and I could hear. "And I love you as well, sweetheart.
You're my daughter now, my blood." I looked back and smiled at
Alanna, as she looked up at Jaymes with hero worship in her misty eyes.

The reception Terri helped to plan was breathtaking. She'd
managed to have the coordinator book the Chateau Crystale and the
venue was gorgeously decorated in rich purple and cream contrasts. The
walls were covered with deep purple and cream draperies with crystal
chandeliers hanging high in the ceiling, casting a dim, romantic light
across the room. The guest tables were covered in a creamy satin
material and each held crystal candelabra centerpieces filled with purple

gladiolus and white orchids, while the chairs were adorned with purple sashes slung across each back. The beautifully created four-tier wedding cake was covered in a delicious whipped cream vanilla frosting with strawberry filling. I didn't even want to think about how much the last-minute request had cost. Jaymes' parents insisted on springing for the entire thing, which pleased Terri to no end when she was given an unlimited budget to make our dreams come true.

Walking up to the reception hall while clinging to Jaymes' arm, I felt like the most beautiful woman on the planet. The beaded mermaid gown with its sweetheart neckline I wore showcased my frame in the most pleasant fashion. I was still in the early stages of my pregnancy, and the dress was loose enough so the baby bump I knew was coming wasn't visible just yet. The dress was a great last-minute find and didn't need any alternations, which was a blessing in itself. It slipped straight from the rack onto my body like it was made just for me. Although I wished I didn't have a casted arm to sport along with the dress, I told myself it was a badge of honor and a reminder of all the things I'd overcome to get to this point in my life.

The swelling on my face had gone down as well; and with Terri's genius skills in the makeup department, you could hardly notice the stitches that marked my face. I could tell Jaymes was pleased with my look too, by the way his hand never left my hip and his nose kept tracing the curve of my neck.

"And now, introducing Mr. and Mrs. Jaymes Allen." The intimidate gathering stood up in applause. I smiled widely as I held my head high, basking in the moment. Jaymes squeezed my waist and escorted me into the party.

Friends old and new had gathered to help us celebrate our union. Jackie and Kennedy, along with their handsome little boy, had flown in from Memphis the night before. Master B and Dr. Wilson drove from Mississippi a few days ago. They booked a suite of rooms and planned to celebrate the entire week. Master B also seemed to be extremely captivated by Evelyn's presence much to my amusement. It was nice to see the seemingly collected man get flustered every time she came near.

Nate had also driven to town to attend the ceremony, escorting a rather gun-shy young woman with beautifully wild, textured hair who he'd introduced to everyone as Paige. Even Kay, the friendly receptionist from Dove Studios was in attendance, along with her husband and teenage daughter. The only person who looked as if he wanted to be anywhere else but here was Levi. I tried to get my friend to loosen up, but his usually playful banter seemed to be lost. All throughout the evening as he stared a hole through Terri's frame while she danced and hung around with Chad; his face held a mixture of hurt, envy, and rage. Terri knew she was being watched, since she snuggled uncharacteristically closer to Chad, all the while casting longing looks at Levi from underneath her lashes. A feeling of sadness touched me as I wondered if both my good friends would ever realize the obvious connection they still shared.

I couldn't let myself dwell on it long, however. The overwhelming feeling of love by being surrounded with people who cared so much about me wouldn't allow me.

As Jaymes took me in his arms as we danced along to a slow rhythm, I felt his erection pressing firmly against my core as he hummed the melody in my ear. Grinning up at him, I placed my arms around his waist, holding him close. I reached up to run my palm along his groomed beard, loving the feel of masculinity that covered jaw gave me. The texture of it alone sent shockwaves straight to my core. He smiled down at me and leaned his face into my hand in the sweetest of gestures.

"Later," he promised, giving me a seductive wink. I bit my bottom lip at the promise and placed my cheek against his chest, loving the soothing sounds of his heartbeat. While we continued to dance, my eyes scanned the back wall and noticed Holley involved in a deep conversation with Austin.

"Come on," I grabbed Jaymes' hand and led him over to them. "There's somebody I want you to meet."

Austin grinned as he saw us approach. Taking in his appearance, I had to admit my son looked handsome in his black tux and shining loafers. Holley looked radiant in her custom-made ball gown. Her usually spiked flaming red and black hair was now just a flaming red, slicked down artfully in a soft wave against her back. Her sleeve of tattoos was showcased in her strapless gown, giving emphasis to her toned biceps and delicate shoulders. The piercings she usually wore were gone and in their place was a beautifully delicate pearl choker clinging to her neck. She looked absolutely gorgeous.

"Jaymes, I wanted to introduce you to the woman who saved my life, in more ways than one. Holley, this is my husband..."

"Mr. Allen. It's good to see you again," Holley said softly, looking down at the floor.

Shock and recognition crossed Jaymes' face and he stared at her. Jaymes grabbed her chin and lifted her face up so he could see her better. "Holley?" he cried out incredulously.

"Yes," she said shyly, smiling faintly.

I looked between the two of them, confusion settling in. "You two know each other already?"

Jaymes looked at me with the most incredulous smile. "Baby, this is the girl that Levi and I helped to get her case overturned when she was accused of murdering her father and brother some years back." He turned back to Holley. "Your hair is different. The red looks good on you. I wouldn't even recognize you. Hell, I didn't recognize you at first."

"Wait...WHAT?" I said, not comprehending at all. "What are you talking about?"

"Mr. Allen and Mr. Blackburn were my lawyers when I got arrested." She looked at Jaymes gratefully as tears misted in her eyes. She smiled at me and reached out to squeeze my hand.

"My father and brother had been molesting me for years. My mom died when I was just a baby and they never allowed relatives or friends to visit. I felt like I had no one to turn to for help." She gave my hand another small squeeze. "I know you know how that feels, that's why I wanted to be there for you." Tears I didn't realize had gathered fell silently down my cheeks as I nodded in understanding.

Holley continued on. "One night I couldn't take it anymore and demanded that they leave me alone or I'd call the police. Dad got angry and pulled out his knife, threatening that if I ever told anyone, he would gut me. He told me he would leave me somewhere to die and nobody would care. My brother held me down and played Russian roulette with his pistol, threatening to shoot me if I didn't give in to him, too." She took a breath to steady her voice.

"The next morning, I was in such a bad place. I felt dazed, numb. I just wanted to die. I snuck in my brother's room, found his pistol, and put the barrel of the gun to my forehead." I gasped and grabbed her to me, holding her as if she would somehow disappear as she continued telling me her story. "Instead, I found myself turning the gun toward him." I felt her take a deep breath. "I ended up shooting both him and my father."

"Oh, Holley, I'm so sorry," I whispered, holding her even closer to me. I knew what it felt like to have all hope completely lost and feeling like nobody would care if you just disappeared. I looked over at Austin. My saving grace was that young man standing next to her. I'd realized years ago that if anything happened to me, although I knew Ramon would take Alanna, Austin would have nobody there for him. I had to keep pushing for him and for Alanna. Poor Holley didn't have anyone in her time of need. I found myself squeezing her even harder.

"It's okay, Ash. It's far behind me now." Holley said soothingly as she hugged me once more. She then leaned back so she could look in my eyes as she continued to explain. "Somehow I'd ended up sitting outside of my dad's house covered in blood when Mr. Blackburn just happened to drive by the next morning. He stopped and took one look at me, then immediately called the police to help me out. It was a godsend."

She looked intently at me. "Apparently it was a godsend for both me and you." I gave a watery nod in her direction.

"After the case was over, I decided I needed a change of scenery. A change in everything. That's when I decided to move to Tyler, spiked and dyed my brown hair and decorated by arm with tats." She smiled. "That's when I ended up meeting you."

Jaymes bent over and picked Holley up, crushing her to his chest as her feet dangled in the air. He hugged her as she laughed, the lightness of the sound melting my heart.

"I will forever be grateful for you, Holley," Jaymes said, placing her back down. "If there is anything you ever need, please..."

"I know." She laughed. "Mr. Blackburn already gave me the same speech." She pointed toward Levi as he sulked in the corner still staring at Terri. "Although apparently today for some reason he needs a pick me up more than I do." She said observingly.

Jaymes waved off her comment. "He'll be all right. But we're serious, Holley. We consider you a part of this family now."

Austin nodded his head in agreement. "Same here. Although you're definitely too hot to consider *my* family. Maybe a long distant 17th cousin or something."

Holley laughed as she looked at all three of us, a genuine smile etched across her face. "Thank you." She said softly.

"Asha! Asha! Come here, sweetie. I need to introduce you to someone." I heard Momma call out to me. Jaymes leaned down to give me a quick peck on the lips. "Let's go," he whispered as he led me over to my mother.

Momma stood waiting for us with hopeful eyes. She looked stunning in her laced, off the shoulder A-line gown. "Hey Momma," I said as we approached. "What's going on?"

"I think it's time you finally met someone," Momma started, pointing her hand toward the table next to us. I turned and saw an attractive middle-aged woman with shockingly bright hazel slanted eyes staring at me. She smiled and stood up next to my mother.

"Asha, I want to you to meet your Aunt Sabrina. It's been long overdue."

Shock gripped me as I stared at the woman who had been my father's sister. I could immediately see the family resemblance in the shape and color of her eyes as well as the curve of her lips. She smiled at me as she opened her arms. "Asha, my goodness. You look absolutely beautiful."

I immediately walked into her embrace, accepting the hug she so graciously offered. A feeling of peace descended on me as I cherished her acceptance, tears falling freely down both our faces. She leaned away to wipe my tears with her hand before she accepted the napkin Jaymes offered to blot my face.

"My sweet, sweet niece. I am so proud to witness this day with you. Your father would be proud as well," Sabrina said.

"Do you really think so?" I whispered, still unable to believe I was looking at another piece of my family.

"Honey, hush. I know so." She looked at me, a melancholy look crossing her features. "You look so much like him," she acknowledged.

"Yes, she does," Momma said, gently touching Sabrina's arm. "Thank you so much for coming to see her."

"I wouldn't miss it for the world," she said. Sabrina turned to look at Jaymes. "And you, my dear, are one extraordinary young man."

Jaymes had the decency to look humbled. "On the contrary, ma'am. Your niece is the extraordinary one, and I am proud to call her my wife."

"Well, I brought a wedding present for your wife that I hope she'll enjoy," Sabrina said mysteriously.

"Oh?" I asked curiously. "What is it?"

She nodded toward the back of the banquet hall toward the entranceway and that's when I saw him. He stood about 6 feet, 3 inches, and looked to be about 200 pounds of pure muscle. The crisp, white Naval officer uniform he wore was a perfect contrast to his mocha-colored skin tone. His uniform fit his frame like a glove. His chiseled jaw and manly facial features would appear harsh to strangers, but right now his look softened as he stared back at me. Slowly he started moving in my direction as I tilted my head to the side, trying to place the feeling of familiarity assaulting me as I looked at him.

When he finally approached, he nodded his head first at Jaymes, then at Sabrina. He then turned to me as my eyes widened, taking in the slant in his hazel eyes.

"Asha," Sabrina whispered in my ear. "I want to introduce to you your brother, Killian."

A cry escaped my throat as all of the emotions of the day collided together. Killian rushed over to me before my legs could buckle and pulled me into his arms, holding me tightly in his embrace. We stayed that way for a long while, as uncontrollable sobs racked through me. After a moment, I broke away and patted his cheek.

"My brother," I whispered unbelievingly.

Killian smiled adoringly down at me. "Hello, my sister."

I beamed at his acknowledgement feeling every piece of my heart finally mending itself back together. I looked over at my mother, biting my lower lip to stop its quivering as I saw Jaymes comfort her while she sobbed.

Alanna and Austin walked up to us, looking at everyone's tears with confusion and wariness.

"What's going on?" Austin asked, immediately walking over to my side. He looked Killian up and down, taking in the fact he still held me. Alanna crossed her arms over her chest as she looked on.

I stepped back from Killian as I turned to Austin. "Son, I'd like you and your sister to meet your uncle, Killian." I looked up at his shocked face. "He's my brother."

"Well, hot damn!" Austin exclaimed, a huge grin spreading across his features. "I thought it was time to beat some ass around here. All the females are crying. I didn't expect to hear that."

I hit his arm. "Watch your mouth, boy," I said.

"Sorry, Mom," he said, not looking sorry in the least.

Alanna walked up to Killian, looking deep into his eyes. "So you're Momma's brother?" she asked skeptically.

"I am," Killian replied, smiling indulgently at his niece.

She looked first at me, then at Momma. "I have an uncle?" she still questioned.

"Yes, baby girl," Momma responded. "Your mother has a younger brother."

Alanna looked once again back at Killian, her eyes slowly taking in the way he leaned protectively around me. Her eyes seemed to make some sort of decision as she assessed this new person. She nodded her head.

"Cool. Look, I hope you'll treat Momma a whole lot better than Austin treats me. He won't even let me talk to my guy friends when he comes home from school because he thinks they aren't good enough. I'm like, who is he to judge? I mean really, he has no room to talk, especially with the line of skanky females I've heard he's been dating at college. And then to top it off, I heard him and some of his frat brothers actually visited some sort of kink club that's around campus. Honestly, my friend Josh is just that, a FRIEND. Absolutely nothing has happened between us. I mean, I'd like it to, but Josh seems like he's really shy. Well, he doesn't act shy around other girls, just with me. Well, just when Austin acts like a douche. I promise you..."

Austin quickly grabbed her and put his hand over her mouth while everyone burst out laughing. "Ok, little sis. He doesn't need to know everything right now, does he? Geez!"

Killian looked down at me as he wiped the tears from his eyes, his chest heaving with laughter. He looked over at Jaymes as Jaymes smiled and shrugged his shoulder.

"What can I say, man? This is family. Welcome to it, Killian. Welcome to it."

THE END

Don't miss Terri's story in the next chapter of *The Lady Chronicles*!

About the Author

Amanda (Mandy) has always had a love affair with the written word, especially when it's used to showcase love. Like many authors, her love sparked a desire to place her own imaginative thoughts into context.

Mandy currently resides in the south suburbs of Chicago, but considers Jackson, MS her second home. Her favorite pastimes are spending entirely too much money on shoes, traveling and meeting new people, and reading steamy novels from one of her favorite authors.

Coming Soon

The Swan Lady

Excerpt

"You wanted something?" she asked hesitantly. Her eyes drank in the sight of him as her insides tightened even further. God, he was so handsome. His thick wavy black hair, usually pulled back from his face, lay loose around his shoulders. Chiseled cheekbones sat high on his face that also accented his dark, intense eyes.

His eyes were now drilling a hole right through Terri. She shifted uncomfortably from one foot to another, lowering her eyes toward the floor in an attempt to avoid his gaze. She realized looking down was a big mistake. *Damn,* Terri thought as her eyes journeyed south, taking in a crisp white button up shirt hugging his broad shoulders. The top button was unfastened, hinting at the soft layer of hair she knew covered his massive chest. Dark jeans hugged his muscular thighs and designer loafers adorned his large manly and incredibly sexy feet. Terri shook her head slightly. She'd never before believed she had a foot fetish. But the sight of Levi's bare feet just did something for her. She sighed. Feet more than likely she'd never see again.

"You know you can't keep this up forever," Levi drawled.

Confused, Terri looked back up at him. "Keep what up?"

"Avoiding me. How long are we going to pretend there was never anything between us? And now with the new baby being born, it's going to get that much harder to dodge me."

Terri grimaced as she thought about her chat with Asha a few months prior. "I'm not trying to avoid you," she lied. "And I don't know why Delphi and Asha put it in their heads to make both of us the godparents of their baby. I mean, usually the godparents are together in a relationship, or at the very least, like each other."

Levi moved closer to her, so close that she could smell a hint of the minty toothpaste he'd used on his breath. One long finger reached up to gently stroke her cheek.

"On the contrary, little one. I like you. I like you very much."

Levi then cupped her cheek in the sweetest of gestures, compelling Terri to instinctively lean into his touch. His let his thumb graze across her lips, savoring the softness and fullness of their shape. On impulse, Terri's tongue darted out to moisten the skin his thumb had just touched. Immediately, Levi's eyes heated as he zeroed in on the movement of her tongue.

"Terri," Levi said darkly. "Talk to me baby. Tell me. I've been trying not to push you, but I can't take much more of this. Please love, open up to me. Tell me what happened."

Terri's eyes misted as she stared into Levi's eyes. She felt her heartbreak even further because she knew what he was asking was something she just couldn't give right now, if ever. "I can't," she whispered, stepping out of his touch. "I'm sorry, Levi. I just can't. I'm just not..."

Her words died in her mouth as she watched the coldness and distance once again appear on Levi's face.

"Fine. Let's go see how Asha's doing." With that, Levi turned and walked down the hall away from her.

Terri had to bite her tongue to keep from calling him back. Emotion gripped her as she rubbed her eyes.

Please just trust me, Levi. Terri thought miserably to herself. *It's just better this way. Please.*

Connect with Amanda Moncrefe

I really appreciate you reading my book! Want to tell others about the book you've just read? Feel free to leave a review or rating on my Author Page on Goodreads (www.Goodreads.com). You can also connect with me through my social media coordinates:

Visit my Webpage:
http://www.amandamoncrefe.com

Like me on Facebook:
http://www.facebook.com/amandamoncrefe

Follow me on Twitter:
http://www.twitter.com/amandamoncrefe

I'd love to hear from you!

Mandy